Troubling a Star

MADELEINE L'ENGLE

. . . .

Troubling
a Star

. . . .

**SQUARE
FISH**

Farrar Straus Giroux
New York

SQUARE
FISH
An imprint of Macmillan Publishing Group, LLC

Library of Congress Cataloging-in-Publication Data
L'Engle, Madeleine.
Troubling a star / Madeleine L'Engle.
[1. Mystery and detective stories. 2. Antarctica—Fiction.]
I. Title
PZ7.L5385Tr   1994   [Fic]—dc20   93-50956
ISBN 978-0-312-37934-6

Originally published in the United States by Farrar Straus Giroux
Square Fish logo designed by Filomena Tuosto
First Square Fish Edition: September 2008
17 19 20 18
mackids.com

AR: 5.1 / F&P: V / LEXILE: 850L

For Bion & Laurie
who were my companions in Antarctica

Troubling a Star

Introduction

"**W**ho are you in this book?" we would constantly ask our grandmother, Madeleine L'Engle, about every book that she wrote. Her books have protagonists that many people can identify with, generation after generation, whether it is the brave and clever, gawky and frustrated Meg Murry, or the vulnerable and awkward, but at the same time, sensitive and intuitive Vicky Austin. Madeleine also strongly identified with her characters, and said many times that she was both Meg and Vicky. There was so much that was recognizable as her and her life in her stories, and we wanted to be able to map her fiction to her biography, thereby fixing and understanding her place, and by extension, ours, in the family and the wider world.

Most children want to be told stories about themselves. We were no different, and so, reading the Austin books was always a special thrill, because the narrative is peppered with incidents and details that also featured in family lore, like the adorable malapropisms of Rob Austin and Vicky's bicycle accident. The Austin family house in the quiet New England village of Thornhill (as described in *Meet the Austins*) is ever-present as a touchstone of their domestic peace, and is modeled on Crosswicks, a pre-Revolutionary War farmhouse in northwestern Connecticut where our grandparents and their children lived in the 1950s. The cross-country road trip in *The Moon by Night* copies the Franklin family itinerary of 1959, during which Madeleine started writing *A Wrinkle in Time*. In *The Young Unicorns*, the Austin kids unravel a mystery at the Cathedral of St. John the Divine, where our grandmother was the librarian and writer-in-residence for more than forty years.

There is enough similarity of detail in the books to have caused us some confusion: If our grandmother is Vicky, how can she have the bicycle accident that left our own mother with a Y-shaped scar on her chin? If some of the details confounded our sense of reality, we never questioned the underlying truth of the characters and our grandmother's relationship to them. If Madeleine were Vicky, then we felt understood. Because we were Vicky, too.

People would joke that *Meet the Austins* could have been called *Meet the Franklins* (Madeleine's married name), and yet, we knew that Vicky and the Austins couldn't be a simple translation of our grandmother's life, because of the family tension and pain surrounding these books about this family. Madeleine's own children were often shocked at how their own lives were appropriated and rewritten for publication, and felt judged against this very happy and practically perfect family. The line between fact and fiction can sometimes be blurry for writers, and the temptation to inscribe a certain version of and authority on events is strong.

All of Madeleine's writing, fiction and nonfiction, was an example of how all narrative is fiction, and all fiction can be true. She wrote and lectured extensively on the difference between truth and fact, arguing that it is through story that we human beings approach the truth, not through facts, which can only get us so far. As her granddaughters, this was both liberating and confusing, but we happily suspended our disbelief, and some of our best-loved stories are ones that are culled from her real life, from her days in the theater, from her early years with our grandfather, and the mysterious decade of the fifties.

The five books that are now presented as The Austin Family Chronicles were written over a period of thirty years. A prolific writer of more than sixty books in a variety of genres, Madeleine created a web of characters that grew, changed, and surprised her. As we re-read these books over our lifetime, what strike us are the very different responses we have to this family. At eleven, we thrilled to the references to things that our mother or aunt or uncle would confirm were true. At seventeen, we were cynical about the blur between fact and fiction, and thought we could read our grandmother as if she were a book. In our mature adulthood, we recognize how rich and complicated our grandmother was, and that fact can be the springboard for fiction, and fiction can inform who we are and tell us about ourselves.

Charlotte Jones Voiklis and Léna Roy
March, 2008

One

The iceberg was not a large one, but it was big enough so that the seal and I were not crowded, and I was grateful for that. The seal was asleep after its night of hunting. It was a crab-eater seal, and crab eaters live on krill, not crab, and as far as I know do not eat people. I willed it to stay asleep and not even notice that Vicky Austin was sharing its iceberg, which was floating majestically in the dark and icy waters of the Antarctic Ocean, or that my heart was beating wildly with terror.

The sun was out and the sky was high and blue and cloudless. I was shivering uncontrollably despite my long winter underwear, turtle-neck, heavy sweater, bright red parka. I had on lined blue jeans with yellow waterproof pants over them. I wore three pairs of socks under green rubber boots. I was highly visible—if there had been anyone around to see me.

I tried to control my panic, to assess my situation. Several things could happen. I could be missed and someone would come for me. That *was my brightest hope. But I had to face the possibility that nobody would find me in this vast space, and that I would ultimately freeze to death. Or the iceberg might overturn, as they sometimes do, and I would be plunged into the water and die quickly from hypothermia.*

I looked around me in all directions. There were dozens more icebergs, many with seals on them. There was a hunched shadow of land on one horizon. No sign of human life. In the water I saw three penguins flashing by, heading for land. Penguins fly in the water, rather than in air. I watched them until I could not see them any longer.

They say that drowning people relive their entire lives in a flash. I'd been on the iceberg only a few minutes, long enough to be terrified, but not long enough to despair. That would come later.

How did I get to be on an iceberg in Antarctic waters in January, which is summer—but even summer is cold in that land of unremitting ice. It went back a few months to those last weeks of summer before school starts. I was still fifteen then, feeling lost and alien, though I had yet to learn what being truly alien feels like.

My family and I had come home to our little village of Thornhill, after a year away. My adored grandfather was dead. The only really good thing in my life was that I'd see Adam soon, Adam Eddington, who'd had a summer job in the marine biology lab with my older brother, John. Adam and I had become friends during the summer, and if the friendship meant more to me than it did to Adam, well, I would just have to live with that. I knew that some of the time I was only John's kid sister in Adam's eyes, but there were other times when it was a lot more than that.

In another week John would be going back to M.I.T., and Suzy and I would be in the regional high school, Suzy as an eighth-grader, and I'd be starting my junior year. Our little brother, Rob, would still be in the village school.

It all should have been normal and okay, but I'd been away for a year and I'd grown and changed, and even before school started I felt I no longer belonged. So when Adam called from New York to say he was spending a weekend with his Aunt Serena in nearby Clovenford before flying to California to college and would it be all right if he came for dinner on Friday, it was as though the sun had suddenly come out after a foggy day. He arrived around six-thirty, driving up in an old and beautiful Bentley, much to John's envy. I was sorting laundry, one of my least favorite chores, but I kept on folding clothes, rather than rushing out to join John and Rob, who were admiring the great old car.

The evening was warm, and I had on my best shorts and a clean blouse which I'd actually ironed. I'd have dressed up more than that, but I knew Suzy would be at me. My little sister and I do not always see eye to eye.

When Adam finally came in, he kissed me, or would have, if Mr. Rochester, our old Great Dane, hadn't been all over him, trying to jump up on him, wagging his tail, greeting Adam with all kinds of special affection. Adam managed to shove him down in a gentle sort of way, and kissed me again. But then he kissed my mother and Suzy, too. Then everybody talked at once, more or less, until my father came home from admitting a patient to the hospital. And finally we were all sitting around the dinner table, and that felt right and good.

When everybody had been served, Adam said, "Hey, I have terrific news."

We all looked at him.

"I've been given a grant to go to Antarctica next semester."

"You mean now?" Suzy asked.

"No, not this semester. Next semester, in December."

Our father raised his eyebrows questioningly. "Why Antarctica?"

Adam grinned at him. "Well, Dr. Austin, I *am* a marine-biology major, and it's a major opportunity. I'll be working at LeNoir, one of the small U.S. stations."

"I thought you were into starfish and dolphins," Suzy said.

"There'll probably be a few of those at Eddington Point, where the station is, but mostly I'll be working with penguins."

Mother asked, "Eddington Point?"

Adam grinned again. "Actually, it's named after my uncle. He's probably the reason I'm a marine biologist. He made a couple of expeditions to Antarctica, and he died in an accident while he was out there."

"Are you named after him?" Suzy asked.

"Yup. Actually, I'm Adam III. My great-uncle, the banker, was Adam I. Adam Eddington, the marine biologist, was Adam II. And I'm Adam III. Listen, Vicky, John's coming over in the morning, but how about if I pick you up in the afternoon, maybe a little before four, and take you to Clovenford to meet my Aunt Serena? I really think you two would like each other."

"Sure," I said. "I'd love to." I'd love to do anything with Adam.

My father smiled at him. "Your Aunt Serena is one of my patients, and one of my favorite ones. I agree with you, Vicky will enjoy her."

"And she'll enjoy Vicky."

"They'll be good for each other," my father said.

But if I'd never met Aunt Serena—if I'd never read Adam II's diary and found his letters—

Wait, Vicky. It's no good hindsighting.

After dinner Adam said he had to get on back to Clovenford to Aunt Serena, who was very old and retired early, and John and I went out to the garage to wave him off, with Mr. Rochester at our heels. Waving people off is a sort of tradition in our family.

Before he got into the Bentley, Adam put his arm about my waist. "I know you miss your grandfather, Vicky."

"Yeah. A lot."

"He was a special person. One reason I want you to meet Aunt Serena is that she reminds me of your grandfather. She's an amazing old lady."

"I look forward to it." I thought he might kiss me good-bye, but John was right there.

"Good night, you two," Adam said. "It's been a great evening."

"See you tomorrow," I said, trying to sound casual.

"Sure. See you."

I watched after his car as he drove down the road, and John went around the corner of the house to get Rochester. I started to go after them, but stopped and looked up at the sky, crisp and clear and full of stars. I was home, in the place where I had been born and grown up, and I responded to the beauty of the night sky and the great old maples and oaks, and I was lonely, a kind of loneliness that hurt like a toothache.

I shook myself and headed back to the house. I was going to see Adam the next day. Wasn't that enough?

He came for me a little before three-thirty, and I was ready and waiting. I'd put on a flowered cotton skirt and another clean cotton blouse, much as I hate ironing.

Mother asked Adam if he'd like to stay for dinner again when he brought me home, and he said he'd enjoy that. He and John had had lunch with Aunt Serena, and she was usually tired by evening and wanted to eat quietly and go to bed. He'd have to double-check with the chauffeur that it was all right to use the car.

I'd forgotten that a world with people who had chauffeurs still existed. But there's a section of Clovenford that's old and rich, with great nineteenth-century mansions and people who actually have servant problems. Thornhill is older than Clovenford. Our house was built in the middle of the eighteenth century, and it sags comfortably, all the boards slanting toward the big central chimney. One problem my mother's never had is a servant problem.

"See you later, then," Mother said, and Adam and I went out through the kitchen door and the garage.

"You'll like my Aunt Serena—great-aunt—" Adam said. "She's ninety and occasionally gets a little absentminded, but mostly she's terrific and interested in all kinds of things."

12

It was a gorgeous, pre-autumn day. Everything was still green, a bit dusty, because we needed rain. The roadsides were yellow with goldenrod, and occasionally a maple would be tipped with red or orange. We drove downhill, across the river, and then back up into the hills again. We passed the road to the hospital where my father's on the staff, and turned onto a wide street with houses set far back, and green lawns carefully manicured.

"Elm Street," Adam said. "No elms, of course."

"Lots of maples, though," I said. "These are beautiful ones. Suzy's passionate about the way we aren't taking care of the trees on our planet—you know Suzy."

"She's right," Adam said, "though we didn't exactly cause Dutch elm disease. Here we are."

Adam's Aunt Serena's house was large, white with black shutters, and a widow's walk. Adam stopped the car in front of a picket fence with a wrought-iron gate. The gateposts were topped with carved pineapples. "The sign of hospitality," Adam said, "though I'm not sure where that symbol comes from. You'll find Aunt Serena's very hospitable. You okay?"

"Sure." But I was a little nervous, a little self-conscious. I wasn't used to people who lived in enormous houses and had chauffeurs.

Adam opened the gate and we walked up a path of pale pink brick bordered with hydrangea and rhododendron bushes. The hydrangeas were in full bloom, a wonderful, deep purple.

A maid in a grey uniform and a white apron opened the door, and Adam flung his arms around her and gave her a big kiss on the cheek.

"Mr. Adam! Mr. Adam! You'll never——" She smoothed her hair, and straightened her small white cap, scolding and giggling all at the same time. I looked around the elegant front hall. There was an enormous mirror in an ornate gilt frame, and under it was a marble-topped table. On a silver tray were several letters. I glanced at myself in the mirror and thought I looked okay. I was nearly sixteen. I did not look like a child.

Adam introduced us. "Vicky, this is Stassy, who's known me since I was in diapers. Stassy, this is my friend, Vicky. John's sister."

At least he didn't say John's little sister.

Stassy welcomed me with a wonderful smile which lit up her whole face, and led us past a large living room to our right, a formal dining room to our left, on past a library full of what looked like thousands of books, and then to a sitting room where an old woman looked up from a wing chair by a bright fire.

"Mr. Adam has brought Miss Vicky, Madam," she announced with what sounded like real pleasure.

I stepped forward and took the old lady's hand. It was small and warm and dry. She had curly white hair cut as short as mine, and a finely wrinkled face and brown eyes that looked golden in the firelight. The room was a little warm, but I know very old people tend to feel chilly.

"You're good to come," she said. "And now we'll have tea, please, Stassy. Anastasia," she explained to me, "but Stassy is easier."

"Tea would be lovely," I said, sitting in the chair Adam had pulled out for me, across from his great-aunt, with a low table between us.

Stassy wheeled the tea in on a mahogany tea table, with a beautiful silver service, but also a big glass pitcher of iced tea. The sandwiches were little rounds, each with one slice of tomato. There was a big plate of cookies still warm from the oven.

Adam's great-aunt asked me to pour. "And will you be kind enough to call me Aunt Serena? That would please me."

"I'd love to." She made me feel completely comfortable, and glad to be calling her Aunt Serena instead of Mrs. Eddington. I poured tea, and Adam passed it to her, and then said he'd rather have iced tea.

I poured tall glasses for both of us. While I was sipping, she looked directly at me, saying, "So you spent last winter in New York."

"Yes. My dad had a research grant for a year."

She nodded. "I'm one of his many patients who are delighted to have him back. The doctor who took his practice was eminently qualified, but he didn't have your father's warmth or authority. He heals my spirit as well as my body. There's not much he can do about my arthritic knees, but he can keep my zest for life from flagging. So does my great-nephew, here. I'll miss him."

"So will I," I said.

"But he has given me the best gift he possibly could—his grant to go to Antarctica—and on his own merits, too. Despite the point which is named for him, Eddington Point, not many people remember my son, who spent many months in Antarctica and died there."

Her eyes were full of pain, so I just murmured that I was sorry, and I, too, was glad Adam had the grant. That was politeness on my part. I didn't want Adam that far away. On the other hand, Berkeley might just as well be as far as Antarctica, for all the chance I'd have of seeing Adam there.

She looked at me and smiled. "Coming back to little Thornhill can't be an easy transition. You're still in high school?"

"Yes. Next week I start eleventh grade. One more year after this, and then college."

"Are you going to miss New York?"

"Not the city. But I'll miss some of the people I met there. Talking about ideas, big things."

She held out her cup for a refill. "The art of conversation is becoming a lost one. I'm happy that my great-nephew still enjoys batting ideas back and forth. So does your brother. I can see that you come from a family that is not afraid of discussion."

I laughed. "Discussion. And sometimes dissension." I was amazed at how totally at ease I was with this great-aunt of Adam's, in this elegant, gracious room. There was just enough furniture to be comfortable, but no clutter. Over the mantelpiece was a portrait of a young woman. I knew it was Aunt Serena from the eyes, which were the same firelit gold.

"You have beautiful eyes, Aunt Serena," I said.

She laughed and clapped her hands. "Miracles of modern technology! In the old days I'd have had the blind white eyes of cataracts or, at best, those Coke-bottle glasses. I still wake up every morning and rejoice at seeing through my lens implants.

Now, pour yourself and Adam another glass of tea, my dear, and"—she looked at Adam—"Owain will drive Vicky home. He's Stassy's husband, and I don't know what I'd do without them and Cook."

Adam said, "If it's all right with you, Aunt Serena, I'll drive Vicky home. Mrs. Austin was nice enough to ask me to stay for dinner again, and she's a fabulous cook—good enough to make Cook sit up and take notice."

If I'd forgotten there was still a world where people had chauffeurs, I'd equally forgotten a world where people had cooks.

"Of course it's all right with me," Aunt Serena said, and then, as though she'd read my mind, "I suspect your mother most graciously does all kinds of things I didn't have to do. Life was gentler."

"Things change," Adam said. "Entropy."

To my surprise, Aunt Serena frowned. "I really don't approve of the Second Law of Thermodynamics. I refuse to believe that the entire universe is on a downhill skid. The theory may be more sophisticated than that of the nineteenth-century positivists who believed that as knowledge increased, each civilization would rise higher than the one before, but it's equally nearsighted. I'll have half a cup of tea, if you'll be so kind."

Well! Aunt Serena was certainly not boring! This was the kind of conversation Adam and John throve on, the kind of conversation I'd told Aunt Serena I'd miss in Thornhill. But maybe I was being unfair.

She finished her tea quickly, and rang a tiny silver bell which was on the tea tray. In a moment Stassy appeared.

"Adam and Vicky are leaving now, Stassy dear. And Vicky might like to take the cookies home."

"I have a younger brother and sister who'd love them." I rose.

Stassy said, "Owain drove the car around to the back."

"Splendid. They can leave through the kitchen and Vicky can meet Owain and Cook. You will come again, my dear? Adam must leave tomorrow, and though he's promised me another weekend before he goes to Antarctica, I will be lonely without him, so it would be most kind if you would come to tea."

"I'd love to," I said. "School starts next week for me, too, and I'll have to see what my schedule is."

"Perhaps you could get off your school bus in Clovenford?"

"Well, yes—"

"And Owain will drive you home."

Adam said, "Take Aunt Serena for a walk when you come, Vic. She's supposed to exercise more than she does."

She looked up at me. "Your father would appreciate that. My legs do not do well once autumn and winter damp set in."

Stassy led Adam and me farther back into the house, through a large sun porch that was part greenhouse full of flowers and plants, then through a beautiful kitchen with a restaurant stove, the kind Mother's always wanted. Copper pots hung from the ceiling. A tall, thin man who had a fringe of brown hair around his head and who looked like a monk was standing at the stove. He turned and smiled as we came in.

Adam said, "Vicky, this is Cook, and he keeps me out of

18

trouble. If I'm about to do something and think Cook wouldn't approve, I usually don't do it."

"My name is Adam Cook." The tall man shook my hand with a firm, friendly grip. "There are already more than enough Adams around here, so everyone uses my last name, and I hope you will, too. Quite appropriate, isn't it?" He moved from the stove and handed me a large red tin of cookies. "I kept a few out for Madam. It's not easy to whet her appetite. Do come again, Miss Vicky." He had a crisp British accent.

"Oh, I will," I promised.

Stassy opened a door that led through a small pantry and to a covered drive between house and garage, where the car was waiting. Stassy introduced me to Owain, who looked as Welsh as his name, with black hair, blue eyes, fair skin. Like Stassy and Cook, he seemed delighted to see me and urged me to come back. "Madam's outlived her family and friends," he told me, "and none of the relatives think they live near enough to come by, saving Mr. Adam and his family. They come when they can. And your father—he drops in more often than he's needed as a doctor. It's done her a world of good, having Mr. Adam here for a few days. I'll look forward to seeing you again, Miss Vicky."

Miss Vicky. Aunt Serena lived in a world I didn't know much about, a world of formality and privilege. I felt clumsy, but Adam seemed to take it all for granted.

Owain said, "The key's in the car, Mr. Adam."

"Thanks, Owain. I'll be careful."

We backed onto the drive that curved around the house. "Mr. Adam. Miss Vicky," I said.

Adam shrugged. "I was Master Adam until a few years ago, and I really had to do some major insisting before they were willing to let me grow up."

The trees were a dark green against a sky that was already turning pink. The days were growing shorter. I glanced at Adam. "Thanks for taking me to meet Aunt Serena."

"I knew you'd like each other," Adam said. "She's very special, and I don't introduce just anybody to her."

I felt my cheeks go warm. "She does remind me of Grandfather."

"Same quality," Adam said. "I'd think it was a generational thing, except that I've known other old people who've closed down and are cranky and do nothing but tell the same old stories and are totally boring."

"Boring she's not. Adam, what happened to her son, Adam?"

"Adam II, my uncle? I told you. An accident in Antarctica."

"What kind of an accident?"

"He was out in his Zodiac—"

"His what?"

"Zodiac. They're inflatable, motorized rubber boats, like the ones you see in nature programs on TV. The assumption about Adam II was that the motor must have given out and he had no way to get back to land. There are heavy tides and undertows and he may have been swept out to sea."

The way he told me made me want to ask further questions, but it also made me know I shouldn't. So I didn't say anything.

I looked at him questioningly, but he was staring ahead at the road.

We were silent for a mile or so, and then he asked, "What did you think of Cook?"

"I liked him. He looks kind of like a monk."

Adam burst into laughter. "Vicky, you're amazing!"

"Hunh?" I asked inelegantly.

"Cook *was* a monk for about ten years."

"Oh, my! Why did he stop?"

"He had to leave the monastery to take care of his brother, who was at the point of death. Cook and his brother are twins, born in the Falklands. Seth, Cook's brother, is a naturalist—he's still in Port Stanley."

The Falklands. I knew they were British islands, which explained Cook's accent, and that they were somewhere near the bottom of South America, and that there'd been some kind of war about them, but that's about all I knew.

Adam went on, "Seth accidentally antagonized a fur seal, and they can be quite vicious when they're angry. It nearly killed him, and Cook went out to nurse him. He told me that when he came back to the U.S. he felt he no longer had a vocation to the monastic life. He's a great guy. Listen, I really feel good knowing you'll go over to Clovenford. I worry about Aunt Serena. I'll miss you when I go back to Berkeley. I'm a lousy letter writer, but I'll try to keep in touch. Getting this grant for the internship in Antarctica was beyond my wildest hopes, but it means I'll be away over Christmas."

"Thanksgiving?" I asked.

"I'll try to come home. I did promise Aunt Serena another

weekend, and my parents are going to want to see something of me."

"Aunt Serena seems excited—about Antarctica."

"I think she sees it as a kind of completion, that I'm going to finish Adam II's journey." He pulled up by the garage, but didn't block Daddy's way. That was thoughtful of him. "Aunt Serena'll probably talk to you about Adam II as she gets to know you better. And what she doesn't tell you, you can ask Cook—that is, if you're interested."

Of course I was interested. Fascinated.

Two

I *wasn't sure how long I'd been on the iceberg. Time had no meaning. The white of the ice was so dazzling it made everything look shimmery. I was afraid of whiteout, sort of the opposite of blackout, and just as lethal.*

I looked at the dark bulk that was the seal, and it raised its head, made a low, sort of grunting noise, and appeared to go back to sleep. For a moment I had a crazy desire to lie down beside it, to get some warmth from its sleek body. But I knew it was crazy and I still had enough sense not to do it.

As my body got colder, so did my mind.

Help!

But there was no one to help.

We tend to eat dinner later than most people in Thornhill because of Daddy's hours. The wind was blowing from the northwest, and I thought of the cheeriness of Aunt Serena's

23

fire, so even though it wasn't really cold enough, we built up
the fire and sat around and talked while we were waiting for
Dad. Mr. Rochester came and sat at our feet, and so did Rob,
curling up sleepily beside the big dog and snoring slightly, as
he usually does in the autumn when he has allergies. Mother
had made pollo verde and it was simmering in a big pot on the
stove, and it smelled wonderful.

Suzy asked Adam, "So why'd you choose Antarctica?"

"I didn't choose it. It chose me."

"How?" Suzy demanded. "Why not the Arctic? Isn't it
easier to get to?"

"There isn't any continent there. Antarctica is the fifth-
largest continent on the earth."

"Oh."

"Live and learn," John said lazily. "One of Adam's profs is
an Antarctic buff."

Suzy continued, "You'll get to see all kinds of animals,
won't you?" Suzy adores all animals.

"Not that many," Adam replied, "because it's a hostile climate and not conducive to much life. Glaciers and rocks and a
little lichen and moss. There'll be penguins, seals, seabirds
like albatrosses and skuas, and that's about it."

Daddy came home then, and after he and Mother'd had a
few minutes together, we all went to the table.

"So when you get to Antarctica," Suzy pursued, "what exactly will you be doing?" When Suzy gets hold of a topic in
which she's interested, she doesn't let go.

Adam answered her patiently. "I don't know exactly what

24

I'll be doing. I'll be the low man on the totem pole, that's for sure. I'll probably be measuring wind flow and glacier drift and counting penguin eggs and doing anything anybody else doesn't want to do."

"What about the hole in the ozone layer?" Suzy asked. "Isn't that where it is?"

"You're right. But actually we don't know a great deal about it because we've only recently, in geological terms, discovered the hole. It may have been there for a very long time."

"But it's getting bigger, isn't it?"

"Yes," Adam answered, "but it would seem that even without the hole the creatures who live at that latitude are less protected from the dangerous rays of the sun than you are here, for instance."

"Ironic, isn't it?" Daddy asked. "We couldn't exist without the sun, and yet what gives us life is also a danger to us."

Mother smiled. "It's the happy-medium principle again. Too little sun, and we'd die of cold. Too much, and it's equally killing."

Suzy said, "My science teacher—he's terrific—says Americans tend to think if something is good, more is better. A couple of aspirin can help a headache, but you shouldn't take a whole bottle. So, won't you have to use a strong sunscreen?"

I semi-tuned out. I was more interested in Adam than in Antarctica, though he'd got me intrigued about Adam II. I thought there was something mysterious about his death, but that may have been because, as my family constantly reminds me, I have an overfertile imagination.

I half heard Adam saying, "People who live at the southern tip of South America, or in the Falklands, for instance, have to be careful to wear sunglasses. If you're outdoors without being well covered, you can get a terrible sunburn."

Well, I'd done my traveling. A school year in New York, summer on the Island, and now I was back in Thornhill.

Adam turned to my father. "Aunt Serena's really in great shape for her age, isn't she?"

"She is, indeed," my father agreed. "I just wish her legs were better. She needs more exercise."

"Vicky's promised to take her for a walk when she goes back to see her."

"Excellent," my father said. "Serena Eddington is a fascinating old lady, and I'm glad you're getting a chance to know her, Vicky."

John said, "I envy you, Vic. Adam and I had lunch and spent a few hours with her, and she knows more about a lot of things than some of my professors."

"The Second Law of Thermodynamics, for instance," I said.

"You never know what she'll come up with." Adam had another big helping of green chicken and yellow rice, and then we talked for a while about Thornhill, and how the hundred-acre dairy farmer can't make it anymore, and how many of the farms are being sold.

Suzy looked at Adam and asked, "How do you *get* to Antarctica?" and couldn't understand why the rest of us laughed.

Adam answered, "It's a long trip. I'll fly to San Sebastián in Vespugia, then on to Santiago in Chile. Then I'm going to spend a couple of days in the Falklands, and finally I'll get to the Antarctic peninsula."

It was a nice evening. Sad, because both Adam and John were leaving for their respective colleges the next day, but I tried not to think about that.

School started for the rest of us, too. I'm not sure exactly what I expected. Sort of to pick up where I'd left off, I guess, but I learned quickly that Thomas Wolfe is right and you can't go home again. I'm not sure whether I'd outgrown the other kids or whether they'd outgrown me. Even Nanny Jenkins, who used to be my best friend, was more interested in boys than in anything else. It wasn't that I wasn't interested in boys, but the boys at Regional weren't interested in me. And it was at least moderately mutual. Some of them were good-looking, but we didn't have anything to say to each other.

Nanny still sat by me on the school bus, and we ate together at lunch, but we had become almost strangers. We were friends because we'd always been friends, and we both like to sing, so we were in choir together.

I liked my English teacher, who was so excited about Shakespeare and his plays that she got us excited, too. She read some of the love sonnets to us, and suggested that it would be fun, later on, to work on scenes from some of the plays. I signed up for a class in medieval history, because I thought it would be romantic, but I was wrong. The teacher was a sourpuss interested in nothing but dates. The science teacher was young and dark-haired and I realized the first day that he was going to be totally over my head. Suzy had a crush on him, but then, Suzy's always been good at science.

School was not a total waste, at least academically. Those of us on the college-preparatory track would do all right. Otherwise, it was a barren desert, an opinion I tried to keep to myself. Suzy fit right back in without any trouble, and if she burbled on and on about the science teacher, she also sat in the back of the bus between a couple of boys, and they weren't always the same boys. No matter how little attention she seemed to pay to her work, she'd bring home a good report card, because she always did. She was taking Spanish, because there was a Spanish teacher at Regional for the first time. Everybody was in the beginners' class together, and I didn't want to be in the same class with my sister. I'd taken Latin and French in New York and would have liked to continue, but they weren't being offered.

Rob was young enough to adjust. He picked up with his old friends and they were into making rockets, which fizzled when they tried to shoot them off, but they had fun, anyhow.

A couple of times Nanny Jenkins asked me, "What's wrong with you, Vicky?" And I'd say everything was fine.

The second Monday of school it was rainy, a heavy rain that my father said was the fringe of what had been a hurricane farther south. The fringe was nasty enough.

Mother had left oatmeal in a double boiler on the back of the stove. It was full of raisins and was the right food for a miserable day. Suzy and I were alone in the kitchen. Mother and Daddy were upstairs, and Rob was out with Rochester: I could see him through the kitchen windows, wearing his yellow slicker and walking across the field with the big dog.

I fixed myself a bowl of oatmeal, muttering, "Now is the winter of our discontent."

Suzy was buttering toast. "What are you talking about?"

"I'm quoting. Shakespeare."

She snapped, "No wonder you never get invited to anything. You're a politically illiterate literary snob."

"I don't see anything particularly snobbish about Shakespeare. We're reading some of the sonnets in English."

"So leave them at school." Suzy plunked herself down at the table.

"I like them. They say a lot of what I feel."

"They're lovesick drivel," Suzy said, "and you're a lovesick idiot, always dreaming about Adam Eddington."

"What about you and Mr. What's-his-name?"

"Neddocks. We call him Ned. He likes it. He's a super teacher and he says I'm one of the best students he's ever had."

Mother and Daddy came in then, and Daddy helped himself to oatmeal. Mother asked, "Ladies, do you have plans for after school today?"

Suzy said, "I'm having a special science lab. Ned's offering it to ten of us."

"Vicky?"

"I thought I'd call Aunt Serena and see if I could have tea with her."

"Good," Daddy said. "She needs company." He sat down and picked up last night's paper and began reading it.

29

——So do I, I thought, and headed for the phone.

Cook answered and said Aunt Serena was still upstairs but he knew she'd be delighted to see me, and to come along after school. "Owain can meet you at the school-bus stop."

"No, thanks," I said quickly. That was all I needed, having the kids see me picked up in a Bentley driven by a chauffeur in uniform.

Perhaps Cook understood, because he said only, "The rain's supposed to stop this afternoon. Stassy'll have some good hot tea waiting for you."

When I got back to the kitchen, Mother said, "I'm glad you're going to Clovenford. I met Mrs. Eddington a couple of times when she was still going to hospital benefits, and she was charming."

My father added, "We should all age with that kind of wisdom, but not everybody does." He folded the paper and pushed back his chair. "I'm off. I shouldn't be late this evening. I hope."

Almost always when my father said that, there was some kind of emergency and he was late. If he wasn't home by eight, Mother fed us and waited for him.

I got off the school bus in Clovenford and walked the mile to Aunt Serena's. Cook was right; the rain had stopped, but it was still dripping off the trees. It wasn't cold and the occasional drops of rain plopping on my head felt good. Walking along Aunt Serena's street was like being in another world where I could forget Thornhill and school and everything else that made up the winter of my discontent.

The pink bricks that led to Aunt Serena's house were shiny from the rain. There were big copper buckets of golden chrysanthemums on either side of the front door, and Stassy was there to open it and greet me. "Come along, Miss Vicky, dear."

I followed her to the sitting room, where, again, the fire was bright. I kissed Aunt Serena hello. It felt quite natural to do so.

Then I told her I'd promised Adam I'd take her on a walk before tea, and we'd just walk around the house, indoors, so she creaked reluctantly to her feet. She walked with one hand on my arm, a little wobbly at first, but steadying. We walked all over the house. There was a little elevator, just big enough for the two of us, that took us upstairs. There were plenty of bedrooms and bathrooms, so nobody would have to share.

Aunt Serena's bedroom was a large front room over the living room, with a big sleigh bed. There was a fireplace with a wood fire burning. A chaise longue was by it, and a couple of comfortable chairs. On the floor was a great gorgeous rug with the same soft silvery-green background as in her sitting room downstairs. She saw my admiring look. "Adam brought it from China."

"Adam?"

"Adam I, as your friend Adam III would call him. Adam III was named after my husband and my son."

"A goodly heritage." I quoted one of my grandfather's favorite phrases from the Psalms.

She smiled at me radiantly. "Oh, my dear, yes."

We rode the elevator downstairs and Aunt Serena took me through the kitchen to the greenhouse room, where it smelled warm and springlike, and where there were the largest geraniums I had ever seen. Then we went back into the dining room and she showed me a portrait of her husband which hung over the sideboard. Adam I was a kindly-looking man with a big nose and a slightly crooked mouth which gave him a smiling look. On the opposite wall was what I thought at first was a portrait of Adam, but then I realized the clothes and the haircut were different.

"The resemblance is remarkable, isn't it?" Aunt Serena was smiling, but there was a sadness in the smile. "My son, Adam."

Adam II.

"My great-nephew's father is the son of my much younger brother. However, Adam III is very similar to my son in nature, sweet but determined. We are very close, young Adam and I."

"I'm glad," I said as we moved back to the sitting room. Somehow this was bringing me even closer to Adam. Adam III.

She asked, "Would you like tomato sandwiches again?"

"I'd love them. Do you grow tomatoes in your greenhouse?"

She nodded. "Owain has a green thumb. Both he and Cook enjoy gardening, and the way vegetables are grown today, bred to be picked by machines, with a concomitant loss of taste, I am grateful for their talent."

Stassy wheeled in the tea tray. I poured again. Aunt Serena's hands looked too thin and frail for the heavy silver teapot. Today the slices of lemon had cloves in them, and I think it was a different kind of tea. Cook had made cucumber-and-watercress sandwiches as well as tomato, equally tiny and delicious and totally unlike the sandwich I'd eaten for lunch in the school cafeteria.

Aunt Serena again bathed me with the radiance of her smile. "I gather that you and my great-nephew are—an item? Is that what it's called today?"

"We aren't exactly an item." How I wished we were. I looked into my empty cup, at the lemon with the clove.

"Because you're both too young? I could see that Adam is truly fond of you."

I put my cup down. "I'm truly fond of him. He makes me feel real."

She nodded. "My son, Adam, had that quality, too. He was a fine scientist, and it does please me that Adam III is following in his footsteps. Not that I would wish young Adam or anybody to try to fulfill someone else's destiny. In this day and age, it's all anyone can do to fulfill his own. Or, in your case, her own. Do you know where you're aiming, Vicky?"

I shook my head. "I wish I did. My brother John is a scientist. You've met John."

"Yes. A good friend for Adam."

"Suzy, my younger sister, has always wanted to be a doctor or a vet. My little brother, Rob, is too young to have to worry about what he's going to do."

"What do you most like to do?"

"I like to read and to write. Sometimes I write poetry. But not many poets earn their living with poetry. I don't think I'd make a very good teacher. I get too impatient. Suzy says I'm snobby, and I hope I'm not."

"You have high expectations," Aunt Serena said. "That's not a bad thing."

"Thanks. Adam is lucky to know what he wants to do."

She smiled again. "He, too, will have to decide how he wants to use his experiences. Antarctica should teach him a few things. It is one of the most beautiful places in the world, but not hospitable. It took me several years to give up hope that my Adam would be found—not alive—but that there would be some trace. Cook and his brother went to see if they could find any—any evidence."

Evidence of what? I wanted to ask. But just looked at her, and listened.

"Cook went with Adam—my Adam—on his first expedition, so he knew the terrain reasonably well. I've been there, on pilgrimage, as it were, and the beauty is awesome, but I hope heaven will be a little gentler. At least Adam, my son Adam, Adam II, died doing the work he loved, and while he was in the midst of life. My husband lived up into his eighties, but he never enjoyed his work as Adam did his. I have a pricking in my thumbs that Antarctica may be important to you."

What? That didn't make sense. The only reason Antarctica meant anything to me at all was that Adam was going to be there. My Adam. Adam III.

She went on, "Cook's got a package of cookies for you to take home. He loves to bake, so you're giving him a marvelous excuse. He's a fine cook, much too good for me now that I seldom entertain."

It was time for me to go, not to ask questions. "Thank you, Aunt Serena. I'll come again if I may."

"Of course you may. When?"

"Tomorrow I have to study for a heavy test, and Wednesday I have choir practice, but I could come Thursday, if that would—"

"Thursday would be splendid. And perhaps another time you could stay for dinner. Cook would like that. And so would I."

I went out through the kitchen, where Cook was polishing a big copper pot. He looked up at me. "Owain has your cookies in the car."

"Thank you. Cook, Adam said I could ask you something."

"Go on."

"I think Aunt Serena thinks I know more than I do know about—were you with Adam II in Antarctica?"

Cook rinsed the pot and applied more polish. "On his first expedition. Yes."

"Is that how you met him?"

Cook shook his head. "We met in graduate school. He was taking courses in economics to please his father, and I was reading classics, not a very fiscally helpful area."

"So you were friends."

"Very good friends. A group of us lived together in a big old house in Cambridge—the one in Massachusetts. Five of us went with Adam on his first excursion. By the time he was ready to go again, I was in the monastery." He dried the pot with a big towel.

I shifted my weight back and forth, from one foot to the other, trying to sort things out. "And on the second expedition something happened to Adam II?"

Cook hung the pot on a big rack near the stove. "He went out in his Zodiac and never came back."

"Adam—Adam III—said maybe his engine failed."

Cook's face was expressionless. "That is one assumption."

"Do you think that's what happened?"

"We will never know."

"Could the air maybe have leaked out, or something like that?"

"Not likely. The air for the Zodiacs is in separate compartments, and if one should spring a leak, the others would keep it afloat."

Owain came in then, wearing a black slicker over his uniform, and said he was ready. So I didn't get the chance to ask Cook if Adam II's death was not an accident. I'm not sure I'd have asked even if I'd had the chance.

When I got home, Suzy and Rob were waiting for the cookies, and I was glad Cook had made a big batch. Rob took a handful and went out to the tree house.

Suzy spoke through a mouthful: "About the school dance."

"What school dance?"

"Come on, Vicky. The Halloween dance."

"What about it?"

"Do you want to go?"

"Not particularly." There'd been no bunch of guys swarming around me asking me to go. I knew Suzy'd had several invitations. That morning she'd sat in the back of the bus between two seniors, both of them basketball stars.

36

For once she sounded tentative. "Well, Vic, listen, if you want to, I could, you know, fix you up with someone."

"That's nice of you, Suze, really, but no thanks."

"Why not?" she demanded. "Don't be such a snob."

Was I? If nobody asked me to the dance on his own, I didn't want to go out of Suzy's charity.

"It's an important dance," she pressed.

"I know, and I'm sorry."

We were both trying to be nice. I didn't want Suzy to be sorry for me because nobody'd asked me to the dance. But I didn't want to snap at her, so I kept my mouth closed.

"Suit yourself," she said.

I missed John. When John was home I used to get invited to the dances, and he never made me feel he was arranging things, either.

That evening I was studying for my English test, *Hamlet*, which I really thought was a wonderful play, and a lot funnier in some of the scenes than most of us had realized, when Mother came in to say good night. She had those two little frown lines between her eyes that meant she was worried. "About that dance—"

Just as I'd expected. Suzy'd been talking to her. "I don't want to go."

"Suzy—"

"No!" I was louder than I meant to be. "I know Suzy means it kindly, but I'm really not looking for a date to go to the dance with. If I wanted one, I'd—"

"Find one?"

"At least I'd try. I just don't want to spend a whole evening with some guy who's caught up in the changes that have pushed kids out of perfectly good roles. When you and Dad moved to Thornhill, it was a dairy-farm community. But now—how many working farms are left in Thornhill? And half the factories in Clovenford have shut down. It's a depressed area. People are out of work and kids no longer know who they are or what they're supposed to be—" I broke off because Mother was laughing, gently, but definitely laughing at me.

"Thanks for the instant course in Sociology 101." She smiled at me.

"Sorry," I mumbled.

"*I'm* sorry, Vic. I know coming back to Thornhill has been hard for you."

"What about you?" I wanted to shift the focus.

She hesitated. "It hasn't been easy for me, either, but I'll readjust. I love our house; I love the countryside. John has one foot out of the nest and you'll follow soon, but Suzy and Rob will be around for a while."

"Still—"

"Don't worry about me, Vicky, love. I've made my own choices and I'm happy with them. It's your choices I'm thinking about."

I opened my paperback *Hamlet,* closed it again with my finger holding the place. "Maybe I've chosen just to mark time. Another year and I'll be off to college." I looked down at the orange cover of the book. I didn't know where I wanted to go to college. I'd thought about Berkeley, but even if I got a good scholarship, did I want to chase after Adam that way?

When I got home from choir practice on Wednesday, Suzy looked up from her homework. "Adam called."

"When?"

"About half an hour ago."

"Did he leave a message?"

"He said it wasn't important, he was just calling to check in. He did leave his number. Here." She handed me a slip of paper.

I called back. Nine-thirty at home, six-thirty in California. I was relieved when Adam, rather than some other guy in his dorm, answered the phone. "Just wanted to tell you I'll definitely be coming to New York for Thanksgiving, since I'll be going to Antarctica in December and won't be home for Christmas. I'm taking about ten days off, so I'll be up to see Aunt Serena for a few days."

"Oh, good. I had tea with her on Monday."

"I'm glad. I like my favorite people to get to know each other."

That made me feel good. "She's wonderful."

"Hey, Vic, don't you have a birthday coming up?"

"The week before Thanksgiving. I'll be able to get my driver's license."

"Sixteen's pretty special. Got any plans?"

"Not really. We decided to wait till Thanksgiving to celebrate, because John will be home."

"Maybe you and I can do something while I'm in Clovenford."

"I'd love that." I wanted us to go on talking, but I heard somebody yelling at him to get off the phone.

"We'll talk again in a week or so," he said. "Give everybody my love."

On Thursday I went to Aunt Serena's, as planned. We had a lovely time. We drank tea and ate sandwiches and she talked to me about her girlhood, and what Clovenford was like then. We talked about Adam, and his internship.

"It's very unusual for an undergraduate to get that kind of grant," she said. "I'm extremely proud of him. And at the same time I'll miss him. Cook will be gone, too, in January, for a month. He goes to the Falklands every other year to see Seth, his brother. I encourage these trips, much as I'll miss him. Not just the cooking—Stassy's a more than adequate cook—but his presence. He's like a son to me."

"Adam said he was going to the Falklands—will he and Cook see each other?"

"Alas, no. The timing doesn't work out. Adam goes in December and Cook's not leaving till January. Adam will stop off at the Falklands for a few days at Government House with Rusty and Lucy Leeds, the governor and his wife. Wise and warm people. They're very fond of Cook and Seth. You should see Rusty when he's dressed up for government functions—" She looked up, saying, "There are some old photograph albums up in the attic, with snapshots of the Falklands, and of Antarctica. You might enjoy looking at them."

I like looking at old pictures. "I would."

"Just take the elevator upstairs, and you'll find the attic stairs at the end of the hall. Go on up and feel free to poke around. Don't expect tidiness. Neither desks nor attics should be tidy."

"Our attic certainly isn't. Shall I bring the albums down?"

"Please. I'll tell Owain you'll be a little late."

I found my way to the attic stairs without difficulty, and fumbled around on the wall till I found a light switch. The stairs were as steep as ours, and I climbed on up, smelling the fusty odor that always seems to be in old attics. It wasn't quite as untidy and cluttered as ours, but Aunt Serena was right; it wasn't neat. There was an old clothes dummy, or whatever those things are called that look like female human torsos and were used when people made all their own clothes. There was a straw hat perched on top, full of faded silk flowers. There was a wonderful old rocking horse, a big one, which must have belonged to Adam II, but probably Adam III had ridden it, too. There was a big wooden box full of books, and I knelt down beside it, pulling them out, and finding some of my old favorites, *The Jungle Books,* and *Charlotte's Web* and *The Enchanted Castle,* books Mother had read aloud to us, and which had been hers when she was a child. There were others I didn't recognize, all about explorers, and then there were some textbooks on marine biology, and a big one on economics. I could have stayed there for hours, looking at the books, but Aunt Serena expected me back with the photograph albums, which I found on some shelves under one of the windows. At least, I found two big white albums which had pictures of penguins and icebergs, so I dusted them off with an old towel that was hanging over a wooden rack, and took them downstairs.

Aunt Serena was delighted. I put the albums on the table between us, and she opened one and laughed and pointed to a picture of a man in a uniform right out of Gilbert and Sullivan, wearing a sort of cocked hat with a great white plume. "That's the governor of the Falklands, not Rusty Leeds, but an earlier one, who was governor when Adam went on his expeditions. He does look like a character out of a musical comedy, but Rusty wears the same dress uniform for special occasions."

"Honestly? Today?"

"Honestly." She turned the page to a picture of a group of men in fur-lined parkas, with what looked like a glacier behind them. I recognized Aunt Serena's Adam because, although he was older, he still looked so like Adam, Adam III, that it was staggering. And there was Cook, looking just like himself, though his parka hood was pushed back, showing a full head of hair.

"Even there," I said, "he looks like a monk."

"Doesn't he, though! He's always had a monkish quality. There's something about him that makes him easy to talk to, easy to confide in. He has a strange, slightly unworldly quality, as though he can see around corners that are hidden to the rest of us. I have sometimes wondered, if he hadn't gone into the monastery, if he had gone with Adam on his second expedition, if then perhaps my son might have come home safely. But that is foolish speculation. There are many things we will never know. Not in this lifetime."

We sat in silence for a while, and finally, to break it, and her look of sadness, I asked, "How did Cook get to—to cook?"

She smiled. "When he and Adam were at Harvard, living in a big old house—did you know about that?"

"A little. Cook told me."

"When they distributed the jobs, he decided that he would prefer cooking to any other part of housework, and discovered he had a flair for it. After he left the monastery, and he did much of the cooking there, he was at loose ends, and Seth told him to go get a job as a chef, so he went to one of the good cooking schools and ended up in one of New York's most prestigious restaurants. When Cook suggested coming to me, I was flabbergasted. He had a hard time making me believe he was serious. But I have to believe him, that his monastic vocation is basically that of a hermit. He likes the peace of the country, and the lack of stress. He has a few friends he listens to music with, or plays chess with. I will miss him in January when he goes to see Seth, but it is right that he should go. The brothers should not be apart for too long. Now, my dear, I have talked overmuch, and I am suddenly very tired, and when I am tired, my old brain does not work well. Will you come again soon?"

"Of course."

"Do you have plans for Saturday? Could you perhaps come for dinner?"

"I don't have plans, and I'd love to come for dinner."

Going to Aunt Serena's became my reality in an autumn that was otherwise a drag. Not the countryside, not the glorious

43

flaming of the trees, but my daily life. I knew most of my discontent was my own fault, but the only thing that seemed to get me out of it was getting off the school bus in Clovenford and having tea and talk with Aunt Serena. As long as I did my assigned chores at home, my parents didn't mind what I did after school. Suzy was involved in various activities, and we were apt to get home at about the same time. Daddy said I was doing Aunt Serena a world of good, so nobody bugged me about it.

I began doing most of my homework there in the peace and quiet of the attic. Under one of the windows was an old green velvet sofa, where I curled up with my books. Probably in summer the attic would be too hot, but it was just right in the autumn weather. When I finished my homework, if Aunt Serena was resting I'd go through the boxes of books, most of which seemed to have belonged to Adam II.

The Halloween dance came and went. I didn't go. I helped Suzy get dressed, and then I watched an old movie with Rob. I tried not to feel left out. Nanny Jenkins had offered to get me a date, too. I could have gone to the dance. But I didn't want to. Not that way.

The next day, while we were having tea, Aunt Serena handed me a big book wrapped in heavy, oiled paper. "One of my Adam's journals," she said. "The only one that hasn't been lost. It gives some of his impressions of Antarctica, and since our present-day Adam is going there so soon, I thought you might enjoy glancing through it."

"Oh, yes! Thank you."

I took Adam II's journal to the attic and curled up on the green velvet sofa. Adam II may have been a marine biologist, but he was also a poet. His description of the wind gave me prickles. Our house in Thornhill is on a hill, and I've always thought of it as the windiest place in the world, especially in winter, when the wind is unremitting. I'd even written a poem about it. "The wind is blowing fiercely from the poles / Swirling from north to south / Then south to north . . ." I'd sent it, and a couple of other poems, off to a contest suggested by my English teacher.

Adam II wrote, "Wind is the milieu of the albatross, not water or earth or fire, but air, and in the sky they spend most of their lives. They are creatures of the wind, and their enormous wingspan would be crippling anywhere but in the eddies of wind which direct their course. They are the largest of all seabirds, but incredibly light in weight; their bones are hollow and air-filled. Their energy is the wind's energy. Cookie says my bones must be hollow, too, because I, like the great birds, pick up energy when the wind is at its most fierce. I wish I could join them as they circumnavigate the globe, but I and my companions are bound to the earth, held down by our weight on this land of ancient ice."

Another day he wrote, "The six of us here are good friends. We each have our different areas of work. Cookie goes off in the early morning to meditate, or whatever it is he does when he is by himself. God is his milieu, as wind is that of the albatross. He comes to earth to do the cooking for us, and he is incredibly inventive with lentils and other dried beans, and makes heavenly messes out of them." Adam II described the other four members of the team, and how the strange environment drew them together. "Cookie is enraptured that fire accompanies ice, that there are still active volcanoes in this place of glaciers and bone-chilling cold. Bill is studying the evolutionary process that produced volcanism, and is very matter-of-fact about it. Cookie sees God's fingerprints, but he is such a marvelous cook that nobody bothers him when he disappears for hours at a time. Disappears is not right, since we must at all times be within sight of each other. But if his body is visible, we cannot follow wherever it is that his spirit goes."

For the next few days he wrote about politics and economics and Argentina and Vespugia and Chile not caring about the Antarctic continent as much as they cared about power and having their share of the continent. "El Zarco of Vespugia is the only visionary among them, understanding that we cannot abuse the Antarctic continent without grave danger to the rest of the planet. Guedder, the old Vespugian general, wants power, and sees it under the ice cap. His vision is of oil or even diamonds. His son, the younger Guedder, is even more frightening. I hope El Zarco will be able to continue to control them. If they think Argentina or Chile will get in ahead of them, I'm not sure."

This stuff did not interest me, so I put the journal on a small table. Most of it was too beautiful just to gobble up. I wanted to savor it over several afternoons.

That night at dinner I told the family about Adam II's

journal, and how fascinating it was, except for the political stuff about Argentina and Vespugia and Chile.

"Hey," Suzy said, "get your head out of the clouds. That's important. Ask Adam."

"Okay, I will." I did not sound gracious.

Daddy asked, "What about it, Suzy? What's important?"

"Ned was talking about it today."

—Here we go, I thought. —Ned again.

Suzy continued, "Our Spanish teacher is from Vespugia and he showed Ned a clipping from *The New York Times* about Argentina giving missile parts to the U.S. for disposal. They have this ballistic-missile project called the Condor II, and Ned said Vespugia and Chile were upset because Argentina had more missiles than they did. At least I think that's what it was. Anyhow, Ned said he was telling us this because he was interested, but what we were meant to be studying was elements, and we'd better get back to plutonium and uranium."

Rob asked, "Are they named after Pluto and Uranus?" I didn't realize Rob was old enough to ask that kind of question, but when we were in New York he loved the Planetarium, and he did know the names of all the planets.

"I'm not sure," Daddy said. "It's an interesting suggestion. Maybe Suzy could ask her teacher."

"Why are politics always bad?" I asked.

Suzy said, "Because they're about power."

"Ugh."

Mother said, "You can't ignore politics entirely, Vicky."

"I suppose not."

"Even the dreamiest poets have to know something about the world they're writing about."

"I know." I did, but it was something I hoped to put off at least until I got into college.

The next day after school I went up to Aunt Serena's attic and checked one of the boxes of Adam II's books, looking for Shakespeare. I'd done well on my *Hamlet* paper, and now I was doing some work on the sonnets for extra credit. Lots more interesting than politics. Sure enough, I came to a leather-bound copy of the sonnets inscribed to Adam II by the other five members of his first Antarctic expedition. I began leafing through it, looking for some of my favorites, when out fell an air letter. It had never been opened. It was addressed to Adam Cook, Holy Trinity Monastery, and it was in Adam II's writing.

I took it downstairs and went out to the kitchen, where Cook was washing wild greens he'd picked that afternoon. I said, "I've been reading Adam II's journal. Aunt Serena gave it to me."

He nodded; kept on with what he was doing.

"He calls you Cookie."

"Um."

"Would it be all right if I do, too? It sounds—well, less stark than plain Cook."

"Cookie's fine."

"And I found this—" I held out the letter.

He dried his hands carefully before taking it. Then he took a sharp knife and opened it, reading rapidly.

Then he turned white. All the blood drained from his face. I thought he was going to faint. He turned to me, his eyes suddenly enormous and almost black. He opened his mouth. Closed it. Walked out of the kitchen and out of doors, starting to run.

Three

The seal slid off the ice and into the water, barely making a splash. He did it so unexpectedly and so quietly that I hardly realized what was happening until he had disappeared.

I watched the small ripples in the dark water where he had vanished. The sky was still high and blue, but there would be no night, as I thought of night, until well after midnight. The seal's leaving probably meant that he was going fishing, because seals fish at night. What is night to a seal? Six o'clock? Ten o'clock? Or just whenever he's hungry?

I wrapped my arms about myself, not so much because I was cold, though I was, as because I was so alone.

And frightened.

I suddenly realized that, like Adam II, I might never get home.

I had my sixteenth birthday. Adam called. That was nice. He was taking a Shakespeare course, too. "We've just read *Measure* for *Measure*," he said, "so I'll quote to you from it. '*The hand that hath made you fair hath made you good.*' Don't change because you're sixteen, Vicky. I like you the way you are."

"I'm still the same me," I assured him, "even with a driver's license. And I don't think I've ever been very good."

"All depends on how you define it. This is just a happy-birthday call. I'll see you after Thanksgiving when I come to Aunt Serena's."

John called, too, and said he'd give me my present when he got home Thanksgiving weekend. I managed to keep Suzy and Nanny quiet at school about my birthday. And afterwards I went to Aunt Serena's for tea.

Her eyes were bright. "I had a letter from Adam III today. He tells me this is your birthday."

"Yes." I looked down, feeling both pleased and slightly embarrassed.

"Your sixteenth."

I nodded.

"He says you're going to have your celebration on Thanksgiving."

"John will be home then."

"And Adam is coming to Clovenford on Sunday. Can you come for a post-birthday dinner that evening?"

"I'd love to. John will have to leave sometime in the afternoon to get back to Boston, so I'm sure it will be fine. Aunt Serena, where are you going to be on Thanksgiving?"

"Right here, my dear. Stassy, Owain, and Cook will have the day off to visit family and friends, and I will enjoy my solitude. Do you have homework?"

"Some."

"Get it done, then, and we'll have another cup of tea before you go."

I went out to the kitchen. Cook had never referred to the letter I had given him, or to his extraordinary reaction, and I did not feel I could ask him about it.

"Cookie," I said, "can Aunt Serena go out?"

He turned to me questioningly. "She does go out, and fairly frequently, to the hairdresser, her lawyer, and so forth."

"What about the evening?"

"She no longer enjoys evening functions."

"What about Thanksgiving? Do you think she could come to us for Thanksgiving? We don't eat dinner till evening, because Mother usually has a solo in church, and she doesn't like to be rushed about cooking. This year we're celebrating my birthday, and I'd love it if Aunt Serena could be there. Would it be too much for her?"

Cook thought for a moment, rubbing his hand slowly over the bald top of his head. "I think it might be a good thing. Ask your father, and let him make the decision. He's the one who could convince her."

He did, to my joy.

Aunt Serena seemed really pleased at the idea, and she said that, like John, she would save her birthday present for me till then.

I went out to the kitchen. Cook, Stassy, and Owain were sitting at the kitchen table, drinking tea and talking, but greeted me smilingly.

"It was a good day when Master——when Mr. Adam brought you here," Owain said. "Madam was losing interest, and now it's back."

Stassy said, "She can't read as much as she used to, despite what she calls her new eyes. She's had time on her hands."

Cook nodded. "We were worried about her loss of *joie de vivre*. She used to do a great deal of entertaining, and the house was always full. But she's at an age when many of her contemporaries are dead."

"I'm glad she's coming for my birthday party," I said. "It won't really be a party, just my family and Aunt Serena, but John will be home. I guess my best birthday present is my driver's license."

Owain asked, "You won't be needing me to drive you home anymore?" He did not look pleased.

"Oh, yes. I mean, I'll still be getting off the school bus in Clovenford, and we don't have an extra car, anyhow. But I'll be able to run errands for Mother and do things like that."

"Good, then," Owain said.

"I'm going up to the attic. Aunt Serena said to tell you we'd have tea a little later, when I come down, if that's okay."

I left the sweet-smelling warmth of the kitchen and went up to the attic and sat on the green sofa and wrote Aunt Serena a poem. Poetry had not been flowing that early winter, but finally words came. I looked out the attic window at the great maples. Their last leaves were slowly drifting down, and their bare branches darkened the sky. I didn't do any homework that afternoon, just spent time on the poem, and then copied it in my best italic writing.

53

In winter structure is revealed.
Water and rock, root and tree
In summer are by green concealed.
Now bare branches reach out free
To lean against the snowy sky.
Your structure, too, shows through the skin,
And wisdom is uncovered in your face.
When I am with you, then I can begin
To learn from all your years of grace.
You touch me even when I'm bruised
And bathe me with your quiet gaze.
And somehow, too, I am transfused
By love's accepting, warming ways.

It was getting dark; the days in November were shorter and the nights longer. Cook had plugged in an old bridge lamp for me, but the shadows in the attic seemed to draw in closer, and I knew it was time to go downstairs, have a cup of tea with Aunt Serena, and tell Owain I was ready to go home.

But I wasn't ready. Not quite.

I picked up Adam II's journal.

We are all awed by the proliferation of diatoms in these frigid waters, which is, Tim remarked, to the rest of plankton like the Milky Way to the other visible stars in the sky. This particularly intrigued Cookie, the non-scientist in our party. Dirk pointed out that there are, in the sea, somewhere around ten billion billion diatoms, little particles of energy invisible to the naked eye, and each as individual as a maple

leaf or a snowflake. Ten billion billion is about the same or-
der of magnitude as all of the stars in the universe. Cookie
took this information and went off to meditate on it, his
own face as luminous as a star.

I liked the glimpses Adam II was giving me of a Cook who
was far more complex than the quiet man I saw in Aunt Serena's kitchen. Cook's kitchen.

When I got home, bearing the usual package of cookies, there
was a letter from Adam waiting for me. I took it off to read in
what Rob calls *privatecy.*

> *Dear Vicky,*
>
>   *I need to take a break from preparing for my next Span-*
> *ish literature lesson. I'm pretty fluent in Spanish—my best*
> *friend in high school was Puerto Rican. But my street vocab-*
> *ulary is very different from that of the great writers, and it's*
> *not as easy as I thought it was going to be. I comfort myself*
> *by thinking that brushing up on Spanish before my trip is a*
> *good idea, though I'm not sure why. I'll be in Vespugia only*
> *a night or so, and everybody at the station will be English-*
> *speaking and most of them will be American. Aunt Serena*
> *says the Puerto Rican accent and the Vespugian accent are*
> *very different, but she thinks I could get along if I was*
> *dumped alone in the middle of Vespugia. It's an interesting*
> *country, but right now politically troubled.*
>
>   *Hope all goes well with you. Did you say Suzy was tak-*
> *ing Spanish? My favorite non-science course is Shakespeare.*

I think my parents are right, and that I need to keep my horizons as wide as possible. I guess these are our "salad days, when we are green in judgment." That's from Antony and Cleopatra. *One of the men on my hall has a good Shakespeare book of quotations and I enjoy leafing through it.*

I'll see you Thanksgiving weekend, and I look forward to that.

Love,
Adam

That was a really nice letter. I put it carefully in my school copy of *Hamlet*. I'd look up some quotations to send to Adam when I answered his letter.

Suzy came home then, and I was glad I'd read the letter from Adam in privatecy and put it away before she could see it. She began talking about the next school dance, the Christmas dance, in mid-December. I had Adam's friendship. That was more important than any school dance.

John came home on Wednesday before Thanksgiving, and I was amazed at how glad I was to see him. I no longer felt put down or overshadowed by my big brother. It was snowing lightly, but he suggested, "Want to go for a walk with Rochester and me?"

"Sure. Love to. Let me get my boots."

We struck off across the field and then went into the woods, where it was protected enough from the snow that we could sit on the stone wall, with Mr. Rochester lying beside us, lowering himself a little arthritically so he could put his head down on John's feet. John bent down and scratched between the big dog's ears.

I asked, "What do you know about South America?" Adam was going to expect me to be a lot more literate than I was about Vespugia and all the places he was going. Adam II's journal had helped fill me in, but I still needed to know more.

"Not much. Lots of unrest. Lots of problems. Why?"

"Adam's going to be there."

"Antarctica isn't South America. It's another continent, and a big one."

"Aren't a lot of the South American countries interested in Antarctica?"

"The whole world's interested in Antarctica. We're running low on fossil fuels. We're going to need another source of energy. Messing around with Antarctica would be a bad idea. Just because it's nearly empty is no reason to think of it either as an untapped mine or as a potential dumping ground. Adam's written me about it. Have you heard from him?"

"I had a letter. And he's phoned a couple of times."

"Don't let him be too important to you, Vic. You're too young."

Too young. How I hated the way everybody rubbed that in. "I'm sixteen."

"You're still too young. You don't want to be like the girls who get pregnant and married and drop out, do you?"

"It takes two to get pregnant or married."

"Good. I'm glad you realize that."

I asked, "John, have you seen Izzy?"

Izzy Jenkins is my friend Nanny's older sister, and she and John used to see a lot of each other. She goes to the local branch of the university in Clovenford. John moved his foot from under Rochester's head, then bent down to scratch the grizzled muzzle. "Yes."

"And?"

"Not that it's any of your business, but she's dating some guy from Clovenford, and we didn't have much to say to each other. It happens."

"Sorry. I didn't mean to pry. Nanny used to be my best friend in Thornhill, and now she's pretty much my only friend, but it isn't the way it used to be."

"Things change. Going to M.I.T. has changed me. The year in New York changed you."

"But everything around Nanny just seems to be going on and on, the way it always has."

A small shower of snow fell through the branches onto Rochester's nose. He jumped. His ears went down and he growled, then sighed, and went back to sleep. But John stood and stretched. "How about some hot cocoa?" he suggested.

Adam II's unmailed letter that had upset Cook stayed stuck in the corner of my mind. I almost told John about it, but it was Cook's private letter. I couldn't just out and out ask Cook what was in the letter that shook him so I thought he was going to pass out right there in the kitchen. I was sure it had something to do with Antarctica, and maybe at least a hint of why Adam II had gone out in his Zodiac and never come back. But that might well have been my usual imagination exaggerating

58

everything. Whatever it was, it was important enough to upset Cook in a way I'd never seen before.

I made hot cocoa for John and me, and then Suzy and Rob came in and wanted some, so I made more, and John got the fire going and we relaxed, and I stopped thinking about the Adams and Antarctica.

When we were all sitting together in the living room before dinner, Mother handed me a letter. "This came for you this morning, Vicky, and I thought it appropriate to save it till this evening."

I opened it. I had won second prize in that poetry contest. I sputtered, "But—but—"

Everybody laughed. "Your teacher had a letter, too," Mother said, "and she called me in great excitement."

"Congratulations!" John applauded.

I knew I was blushing. "I'm totally surprised."

After the excitement had died down, we talked about school. The best I could say was how much I liked my English teacher. Suzy raved on and on about Mr. Neddocks. The Spanish classes were boring. "Our teacher comes from Vespugia and he has oily black hair. But he and Ned are good friends and talk a lot."

I wanted to know more about Vespugia, and that gave me an opening. "Who's the president of Vespugia?"

"It doesn't have a president," Suzy said. "There's a Generalissimo Guedder, who's going to take Vespugia into the twentieth century—that's what Señor Tuarte says."

Daddy remarked, "Generalissimo Guedder took over the country in a bloody coup."

"Señor Tuarte says that doesn't mean he isn't interested in progress."

I wanted to get from Vespugia to Antarctica, so I said, "Adam's going to go through Vespugia on his way to Antarctica. Isn't there a lot of interest in developing Antarctica?"

Daddy looked up. "I don't think 'developing' is the right word. A lot of countries want their share, and more."

Suzy said, "Ned says it should be made into a global park. He says it would be a real disaster if people started dumping their waste there."

"What kind of waste?" John asked.

"Anything. Ned says that it's terrific that so many countries are dismantling nuclear weapons, but then all the stuff they're made of is still dangerous and has to go somewhere."

Ned says. Ned says. We were all getting a little tired of hearing Suzy quote Ned. But at least I'd managed to get some information. Suzy was a lot less politically illiterate than I, and so was John.

Daddy went for Aunt Serena about five o'clock on Thanksgiving afternoon, when dark had come. We had an applewood fire blazing in the big fireplace, and the house smelled marvelous, applewood and turkey and spices.

John handed me a package. "Here's my present. I think it's pretty apt." It was a Thesaurus, a really nice one. Suzy gave me a paperback dictionary of quotations, which would be good for looking up Shakespeare to send Adam. I was truly pleased, and that pleased Suzy. My parents gave me a fountain

60

pen, the kind that's all the rage at school, and a new backpack that was lightweight but would hold a lot of books.

Daddy said, "And we've added a bit to your college fund."

I flung out my arms as though to embrace the entire room. "Thanks a million, everybody!" Then I put my poem into Aunt Serena's lap, and she looked down, and I could see her reading it quickly.

"I'll read it properly at bedtime, and treasure it. It's been a long time since anybody's written me a poem. Thank you." She had brought a large reticule—I think that's what it would be called—and she pulled out a brown manila envelope.

"Here, Vicky, happy birthday." She handed the envelope to me.

Inside were airline tickets. I looked at them curiously: to Miami, Florida. To San Sebastián, Vespugia. To Santiago, Chile. To Punta Arenas, Chile. There were some other, larger tickets. "Wh—what—?" I gasped.

"Antarctica." Aunt Serena smiled at me. "I'm sending you to Antarctica."

"But, Aunt Serena—" I looked at my parents, and I could see that they were as startled as I was. Even Suzy was struck dumb.

Aunt Serena smiled at us all. "No, I'm not out of my mind. I knew that if I tried to plan it with you, I'd meet with all kinds of resistance." She turned to my parents. "Cook is going to the Falklands in January to visit his twin brother, and he will be an ideal chaperone for Vicky. He will be with her until they reach Port Stanley. Then, while Cook and Seth have

61

some time together, Vicky can continue on to the Antarctic peninsula on the *Argosy*. It's a pleasant small ship, and Cook knows several of the lecturers, so she'll be properly cared for. She'll see Adam, of course, when the ship anchors off Eddington Point, where LeNoir Station is. Then when it comes back to South America, Cook will meet Vicky when she disembarks, and they can fly home together." She paused, quite breathless.

I was breathless, too. Speechless.

John had been studying Aunt Serena. Now he looked at me. "It's a great opportunity, Sis."

"Oh, wow!" Suzy's tongue was loosened. "If you don't want to go, Vicky, I'll go."

Rob said, "And she'll be okay, won't she?"

"Of course." Aunt Serena smiled at him. "The *Argosy* has an ice-hardened double hull, especially prepared for moving through ice."

My parents seemed to have been struck as speechless as I was, but now Daddy said, "It is a generous and beautiful gift, Miss Serena, but much too large for us to think about tonight. Let's just relax and enjoy our Thanksgiving dinner. We have much to be thankful for."

Aunt Serena said, "I won't enjoy Thanksgiving dinner if you're going to deny me this pleasure."

Daddy said quietly, "If it's at all possible, we won't deny you the pleasure, but it's a major trip, and we'll need to discuss it."

I still felt as though I'd been kicked in the stomach. Me? Antarctica? I looked around the room, at the familiar comfortableness of home. Mother had chamber music playing softly in the background, something of Dvořák's, I think, music she played a lot. I looked at the table set with a white damask tablecloth and our best china and silver, and I knew I wanted to leave it all and go to Antarctica more than I'd ever wanted anything.

John said, "My vote is for Vicky to go."

Suzy said, "I s'pose. Mine, too."

Rob, always anxious about separation, asked, "Is Antarctica safe?"

Aunt Serena said, "As safe as any place in the world, Rob." She looked at my father, and I thought of Adam II going out in his Zodiac and never coming back.

John said reassuringly to Rob, "Just think of all the postcards of penguins Vicky can send you."

"Polar bears?"

"That's the Arctic. No bears in Antarctica. But there are penguins."

"And seals," Suzy said.

Aunt Serena changed the subject. "My! What wonderful smells coming from the kitchen. And how lovely the table looks."

Mother said, "I use the linen cloths for Thanksgiving and Christmas. They take forever to iron."

At dinner Aunt Serena was seated at my father's right, and I was next to her. I whispered, "Aunt Serena, I'm so stunned, I—I can't quite take it in."

"That's all right, my dear. I know your parents need to discuss it before they're willing to let you go off on such a long trip. However, I think they will. I'd go myself if I could. But since I can't, the next best thing is to send you."

My parents did discuss it with Aunt Serena, at length, and with Cook. Cook, as usual, was calm, but positive. "Madam's heart is set. The trip will be an education for Miss Vicky, and she'll make the most of it."

By Sunday of Thanksgiving weekend no decisions had been made, but I had the feeling that my parents were going to give in to Aunt Serena's determination.

John left to go back to M.I.T., and Adam came to take me to Clovenford. He gave me a big hug and swung me around. "So you're going to Antarctica! Terrific!"

Mother said quickly, "It's not decided yet."

Adam sounded wheedling. "You'll really make Aunt Serena unhappy if you don't let Vicky go. And hey, congratulations on winning that poetry prize, Vicky!"

Mother beamed, and I blushed and said, "Thanks."

"Aunt Serena showed me the paper with the winning poems. I thought yours was much better than the one that won first prize, and so did Aunt Serena."

Actually, the first-prize poem was pretty bad, and that made me wonder about the caliber of the judges, and if maybe my poem wasn't very good, either. I'd mentioned my suspicions to my English teacher, who'd told me that my poem was excellent, and it was recognized as such, and not to worry about anything else.

Adam said, "We'll be off, Mrs. Austin, and I'll have Vicky home by ten o'clock."

"At the latest," Mother said. "The school bus will come tomorrow morning as usual."

When we drove down the road, Adam said, "If I had to bet on it, I'd bet they're going to let you go."

"You could have knocked us over with a feather. All of us."

"When Aunt Serena makes up her mind to anything, she doesn't budge. You do want to go?"

"Of course."

"I'll write you and let you know what it's like, give you a preview."

"Thanks. Geography's never been my major interest." Now that there was the possibility that I'd be heading down to Antarctica, too, my interest level had risen radically.

Aunt Serena had the photograph albums open to pictures of a city. "You'll like San Sebastián," she assured us, "although there's not a great deal of the colonial city left and the pollution is appalling. I do think you'll enjoy the side trip to the pyramids."

"It's not exactly on the required list for marine biologists." Adam grinned. "But I've read about the lost cities in South America, and I don't want to miss my chance to see one."

"San Sebastián's the capital of Vespugia, and it's an interesting country, though I gather life is far more difficult there than it used to be, now that they've lost their democracy and are under a dictator."

"Medex Guedder," Adam said. "I've gone to the library

and looked up some stuff. The last president, El Zarco, was evidently a really good guy, progressive and innovative, but after his death there was a coup. The old General Guedder was assassinated by his son, Medex Guedder, who took over."

I said, "Suzy's Spanish teacher says he's going to bring Vespugia into the twentieth century."

Aunt Serena looked sharply at me. "I suppose that depends on how one defines the twentieth century. I hope he's not teaching Suzy Spanish with a Vespugian accent." Then she looked back at the album, turning the pages until she came to some pictures of rather weird-looking pyramids, not smooth like the Egyptian ones, but going up in rough steps. "You'll be in Vespugia just long enough to get to the pyramids. They're more like the ones in Tikal, in the jungle of Guatemala, than those in Egypt."

Adam said, "Too bad Cook's not leaving till January. It would be fun if Vicky and I could do the first part of the trip together."

"I think Vicky's parents would take a dim view of her being away over Christmas," Aunt Serena said. "This gives them a little more chance to get used to the idea."

"True," Adam said. "This time next week, I'll be seeing icebergs."

"You'll pave the way for Vicky." Aunt Serena and Adam were taking it for granted that I was going to go. "And if your path and Cook's don't converge, at least you'll have a chance to meet Seth while you're in Port Stanley. He and Cook still look very much alike, though Seth has scars from the time the seal went after him."

She turned the page to pictures of what looked like a

small, old-fashioned village. "Port Stanley, the capital. The Falklands get an unduly bad press," she said. "Granted, it's usually raw and rainy, but the landscape has the wild beauty of the Scottish wilderness."

Adam grinned. "I wouldn't bad-mouth the Falklands in front of Cook."

Aunt Serena agreed. "Not even the weather, which is rather like March here. Cook never seems to feel the cold. The people of the Falklands are still reacting to that attempted takeover by the Argentineans, and they want the world to know they are British, not Argentinean."

I didn't want to seem stupid, but I asked anyhow, "Why did the Argentineans want the Falklands if the weather's so bad and everything?"

"They didn't really want the Falklands," Aunt Serena said. "Whoever has the Falklands has a sizable slice of the Antarctic pie."

I undoubtedly looked as dumb as I felt. Aunt Serena turned to the back of the album and pulled out a small black-and-white map. In the center was the South Pole, and raying out from it to a large circle were lines forming triangular wedges.

"It really does look like slices of pie," Adam said. "Very valuable pie. And the Falklands do give Great Britain a hunk that the Argentineans would like to have."

"And so would the Vespugians," Aunt Serena said, "though they've had the sense not to go to war for it. I feel a lot less secure about Vespugia than I did when El Zarco was president." She turned back to the pictures. "That's Government House." She pointed to a rambling white building.

"You'll like Rusty and Lucy Leeds, both of you. Rusty's mother was an old school friend of mine, and we've kept in touch, partly because of Cook and Seth."

The snapshots meant a lot more to me, now that I'd actually be visiting the places pictured.

We had tea, and then Adam and I walked out to the car. He said, "What I'd really like to do is just go straight to LeNoir Station and get going on my research, but this is a once-in-a-lifetime trip, so I shouldn't be impatient. It means a lot to Aunt Serena, and Port Stanley is one of the ports of call. I'm glad we'll be going to the same places. It will be fun to compare notes."

It wasn't nearly as hard to say goodbye to him as it would have been if I hadn't had the very real hope that I'd see him at LeNoir Station.

Finally, one night the next week, when I was reading in bed, Mother and Daddy came in to me.

"Vicky," my father said, "you really do want to go on this trip to Antarctica?"

"I do." I put my book down. I knew my parents weren't wildly enthusiastic about my going that far away, and right in the middle of the school year, too.

Daddy touched my shoulder gently. "It is enormously generous of Aunt Serena."

Mother added, "We want you to go, Vicky. I'm managing to squash all my protective mother-hen instincts."

"I'm sixteen."

"Yes, and a responsible sixteen. But Antarctica is a very long way away."

My father sat in my desk chair. "Your mother and I agree that a chance like this is not likely to come again, but remember, there'll be nobody your age on the *Argosy*. You'll be by far the youngest, probably the only young person—"

"I know that, Dad. It's okay. I don't underestimate the older generation. I've talked more with Grandfather and Aunt Serena than I ever have with anyone my own age." —Except Adam, I thought, but did not add.

My father smiled. "It's a wonderful opportunity. Make the most of every minute of it."

"Thanks," I said. "I mean, really, thanks a million."

"Thank Aunt Serena," Mother said.

Preparing to go to Antarctica was far more on my mind than Christmas. I had to get a passport, and that was exciting in itself. Then there were shots, most of which I wouldn't get till early January: tetanus, and finally, just a couple of days before leaving, a gamma globulin shot because of hepatitis. Aunt Serena told me I had to be very careful not to drink the water in San Sebastián, not even use it to brush my teeth, and I shouldn't eat any fruit or salad or anything that wasn't cooked. Once I was on the *Argosy*, the food would be safe.

I got a wonderful long letter from Adam. The postmark was San Sebastián, and the envelope was dirty and looked as though it had been through one of our post-office machines that tend to rip mail. But the letter itself was not torn.

Dear Vicky:

It's so hot here in San Sebastián that I'm dropping beads of sweat onto the page—not tears. December is mid-summer here. I'm enjoying poking around this city and real-izing how much more I would be enjoying it if you were with me. I'm having fun listening in on conversations people don't realize I can understand. This is a strange place. It's quite obvious that it's no longer the democracy it was under El Zarco. There are too many soldiers with automatic weapons for my liking. They seem ready to shoot, and one of them for no reason that I could see simply stopped me from walking down what looked like an ordinary street.

Tomorrow I'm going to the pyramids, and I've been as-signed a soldier to accompany me. I don't know why. I can go by myself perfectly well. Maybe I'm being paranoid, but it's as though they don't want people to see everything. I remem-ber my dad talking about feeling the same way during a trip to Russia when the KGB was in power in the Soviet Union. I'm not sure it's that bad here, and I guess soldiers and guns are common in any country where there's a dictator. I'm very glad Cook will be with you. Despite his monastic otherworld-liness, he's also a very with-it guy, and you'll be fine with him. His Spanish is good—a little more classical than mine.

I paused, letting the pages drop in my lap, wishing momentar-ily that I was taking Spanish at school. Then I read on.

You'll be here in another month. Yay! Seeing everything I'm seeing. I'm looking forward to getting to the Falklands, not just to see Seth and the Leedses, but to get my first glimpse of penguins.

I hope everything is okay with you, and I feel really terrific that you're coming to LeNoir Station. I look forward to showing you around. Not that there's much to see, but maybe we can ride an iceberg together.

Love,
Adam

My heart soared. And then, probably because I didn't need it, I got asked to the Christmas dance, and by a reasonable guy who played soccer and was in my Shakespeare class. But, on the whole, school seemed pretty peripheral. I did my homework, but most of my mind was on Antarctica. Nanny promised to keep notes for me, and she'd also let me know all the gossip. But I was in a hurry each day for school to be over so I could get on the bus and go to Clovenford to Aunt Serena's. Usually I stopped off in the kitchen to see Cook.

"I'm glad you're having this trip, Miss Vicky." He was stirring something on the stove that wafted a delicious odor into the room.

"I'm too excited to tell you how excited I am. And I'm very glad I'm traveling with you. Can't you just call me Vicky?"

Cook gave me his most monkish look. "In this day and age of instant intimacy, it isn't bad for you to be treated with a little formal courtesy. If I am old-fashioned, you will have to humor me."

"Shouldn't I call you Mr. Cook, then?"

The crown of his head, where it was bald, caught the

light. He flashed me a smile. "Cookie is fine. Perhaps when we're traveling I'll be less formal."

"Okay."

"After I leave the ship at Port Stanley, Benjy Stone will take charge of you. Benjy is the penguin expert, and a good friend of Seth's and mine. And then, at the end of your trip, I'll meet you at Puerto Williams—that will be the *Argosy*'s last port of call for this voyage."

"How will you get to Puerto Williams from Port Stanley?" I asked.

"Seth has a fifty-foot stinkpot he bought from an old friend in the Pacific Northwest. He sailed it from Seattle all the way to the Falklands, so I can promise you she's a seaworthy ark. The *Portia*, Seth's boat, has been in very rough waters and weathered many a storm."

"I'll get to meet Seth!"

"Of course, Miss Vicky, in Port Stanley. I say 'of course' and I hope it will be of course, but Seth is more reclusive than I ever was, and since his accident with the seal he's been more so, and sometimes he does not see anybody, and that can even include me. I've written him about you, so I'm hoping we'll find him in one of his more gregarious moods." He smiled at me, turning from the stove. "I'm considered an odd character hereabouts. Seth is considerably odder." He turned back to the stove. "Your Aunt Serena's waiting for you."

"Just a sec. I had a letter from Adam, and he didn't seem to like Vespugia. At least, not San Sebastián."

"It's changed since the coup. As a Falklander, I'm always uneasy when freedoms are taken away. But the Vespugian

72

pyramids are extraordinary, and we'll be in San Sebastián only a couple of days. It will, at the least, be an interesting experience for you."

Stassy had the tea cart all ready for us. I sat in my usual chair and noticed that Aunt Serena had the album on the table between us open to a snapshot of a woman standing near a group of penguins, black and white and smaller than I'd expected.

"Is that you?" I asked. The woman was wearing what seemed to be the uniform in that part of the world, a hooded parka, the hood thrown back to show beautiful dark hair; and pants and high rubber boots. She looked not at all fragile, but still recognizable.

"It is, indeed, with rock-hopper penguins on New Island in the Falklands."

"It's amazing to see penguins and sheep wandering about together."

Stassy came in with a plate of warm cinnamon toast. "Madam can tell you a great deal about penguins, Miss Vicky."

"Probably more than she wants to know at the moment." Aunt Serena bit delicately into a piece of toast. "But she *is* going to Antarctica, and I am merely preparing her for what she's going to see. Cook does not always offer adequate explanations." She pointed to a picture of what looked like hundreds of penguins. "Too bad the photographs are so small you can't see their feathers."

"Do penguins have feathers?" I asked. "From the pictures I've seen, I've always thought of them as sort of leathery."

"Not at all. They have beautiful, dense feathers. They are birds, after all."

73

"But they can't fly."

"No, they can't fly. But they are birds. If it has feathers, it is a bird."

As Stassy left us, Aunt Serena said, "This is very much an in-between sort of year for you, isn't it, Vicky? Are you being patient with yourself?"

"Patience has never been one of my virtues. Ask my parents."

"I'll make up my own mind, thank you. This is a growing time for you. Learning what and where your place is. Learning patience while you finish your education."

"Then what?" I demanded.

"That is what you need patience for."

"I guess so."

"It's worth it, Vicky, because I believe you do have the poet's ability to see through the clouds to the light beyond."

Nobody'd ever said anything that nice to me before, nobody I trusted like Aunt Serena.

"Antarctica should be a good place for poetry," she said. "Do you know whether or not you get seasick?"

"I don't think so. I don't get carsick. And sometimes the ferry from the mainland to the Island can be pretty rough. But I guess I've never been tested." There was one half piece of toast left on the plate. The kids at school have a superstition that if you eat the last piece of something you'll be an old maid——even in a day when the words "old maid" are pretty much obsolete. I ate it anyhow.

She said, "The Drake Passage, between South America and Antarctica, is known as the roughest water in the world, and having taken the passage, I believe it. But I think you'll be fine. Do you have a lot of homework today?"

"Some. If it's okay, I'll go up to the attic and get it done."

"I enjoy thinking of you sitting on that old green sofa. Say goodbye to me before you leave."

"Of course."

The homework took less time than I'd expected. I memorized a few of those dates my history teacher insisted on, then went to one of the boxes of Adam II's books and pulled out *The Jungle Book*. I started to read "Rikki-tikki-tavi," an old favorite, which I thought Rob would enjoy. I turned the page and there was a sheet of paper, the thin kind you used to have to use for airmail. I looked at it, and was compelled to read on.

Dear Cookie,

Oh, how I wish you weren't off at the monastery being a monkey! Plans are nearly complete for this new excursion to Antarctica, and I am being beautifully politic, planning to spend two weeks at the Brazilian station, two weeks at the Vespugian, on to the Argentinean, and so forth. If the Guedders know that I suspect them, I am in deep trouble. El Zarco wants me to see if he is correct in his assumptions of what they are up to, and get word to the U.S., to the UN, so they can be stopped before irreparable damage is done. When that first atomic bomb was exploded at Alamogordo, no one knew quite what a tiger had been unleashed. But we know more now. And we know more about the part the Antarctic ice cap plays in the world's weather. No matter what riches are underneath it, if another ice age is started no one will be able to enjoy the riches. But greed is always nearsighted.

You will be desperately missed. Have you thought that, without you, we might have to eat penguins? Penguins are wonderful creatures, and it is probably one of their safeguards that they are so unpalatable. Thinking about penguin stew is a digression from my real concerns. I haven't told the others just how far I think things have gone at the Vespugian station, things that have to be stopped. The camouflage is beautiful. They have collected every kind of starfish found in Antarctic or sub-Antarctic waters, and they have two fine marine biologists at the station. Cookie, I wish you were here to advise me, because—

There the letter broke off.

I felt cold.

I shouldn't have read it. It was private. But it gave me an idea of what might have been in the letter that caused Cookie to behave so strangely.

I shut the unfinished letter in the book. I needed to think. If Adam II had neither completed it nor mailed it, perhaps he didn't want anybody to know what he had written. Perhaps I had blundered into a secret that had better stay a secret. On the other hand . . .

I went downstairs and out to the kitchen, grateful to find Cook alone. "Cookie, why did Adam II go back to Antarctica on the second expedition?"

"It's an addictive place. Very few people go only once."

"But about his death—*was* it an accident?"

Cook turned from the sink, leaving the water running. "What makes you ask that?"

"I don't know. I just wondered." My words sounded lame, and my voice drifted off.

Cook turned the water off. "The exploitation of Antarctica has been a concern for a long time. After his first expedition, Adam managed to prevent drilling for oil on the peninsula, and he was not loved for that by those who were ruled by greed."

"Who?"

"At that time the Communists were the enemy, but they were by no means the only enemy."

"You mean, 'We have met the enemy and it is us'?"

"That's always part of it. Did Madam say anything to upset you?"

"No, oh, no."

"Suspicions are ugly things, Miss Vicky. Accidents do happen in that wild and nearly empty space."

"But do you think Adam II's death was an accident?"

He did not answer me. The silence grew between us. Finally he said, "Go say goodbye to Madam, and I'll call Owain and tell him you're ready to go home."

When I got home, there was another letter from Adam waiting for me, and that pushed my anxiety about Cook and Adam II out of my mind. The envelope had the Falklands address, but inside he had written "San Sebastián, Vespugia."

Suzy was helping Rob with his arithmetic homework, sounding bossy. But she's good at arithmetic and Rob's lucky to have her help. Anyhow, she wasn't paying any attention to me, and Mother was studying the open page of a cookbook, so I slipped quietly into my room and shut the door.

Dear Vicky,

I'm mailing this from the Falklands. I'm told mail service is more reliable there. San Sebastián is certainly another world, though you can tell it's the end of the twentieth century by the pollution. However, they're handling it well. Trees are being planted, and people are allowed to drive six days a week. Then they have to take a day off, buses as well as cars. New York would do well to do the same.

The soldier who was my guide to the pyramids is named Esteban and he's an oboe player and will be playing in the San Sebastián Symphony when he's out of the army. Everybody has to serve two years. He thinks Vespugia is the most wonderful country in the world. He's a cousin of the present dictator, Medex Guedder, and believes he's an enlightened despot who will bring Vespugia out of the dark ages.

I paused. From what I'd learned of the history of Vespugia, it did not seem to have been in the dark ages under El Zarco.

Esteban was an excellent guide at the pyramids, which looked just the way they did in Aunt Serena's pictures, but bigger and more mysterious. I climbed to the top of the tallest one and there was a magnificent view of the entire complex, at least the part that's been excavated. Some of it is still covered by jungle. It was worth seeing, despite the

78

heat and the bugs, just for the architecture. The stones aren't huge, like the ones in the Egyptian pyramids. These are small enough so they could be carried by one or two people, and you can see how these enormous edifices could have been built by a civilization that didn't have any machinery.

That evening Esteban took me to a coffeehouse where some of the younger soldiers hang out. Several played guitars, neat stuff, and then Esteban played his oboe. He's really terrific, classical things mostly. He's eager to get out of the army and back to his music, full-time.

This is a really tiring trip, I just want to warn you. Be prepared. "But break, my heart, for I must hold my tongue."
Hamlet.

All the best,
Adam

There was something wrong with this letter, and not just the warning words at the end, or that he'd signed off with "All the best," instead of "Love." It was chatty and informative, like the other letter, but there wasn't anything in it especially for me, except maybe the warning, and I wasn't at all sure what he was warning me about. I might not have paid it any attention if it hadn't been for the letter I'd just read of Adam II's.

This second letter from Adam III, which I carefully put in my Shakespeare book with the earlier letter, was somehow more careful, as though he thought somebody else might read it.

Adam hadn't said he missed me, or that he was looking forward to my coming.

I went to the kitchen to make the salad, which was my

79

job for the week. Suzy was on pot duty, and I'd wash the dishes, and Rob would help me put them away.

At dinner Suzy said, "So you had another letter from Adam."

"Um-hm."

"Any news?"

"It's evidently hot in Vespugia at this time of year." Outside, a cold wind was dashing at the house, and I had on a turtleneck and a sweatshirt. When the wind blows from the north in the winter, our house is never quite warm enough.

Suzy said, "He's quite the letter writer."

"Well, he knows I'm going next month, so he's preparing me."

Warning me. About what?

Suzy looked at Daddy. "I'm really surprised at your letting Vicky go all the way to the bottom of the world with someone you hardly know."

Daddy looked back at her and smiled. "I know Adam Cook pretty well, Suzy."

"I suppose. It's still far away. And Aunt Serena's son got killed there in an accident."

Without stopping to think, I said, "I'm not sure it was an accident."

"Vicky!" Mother exclaimed.

Daddy asked, "What makes you say that?"

I wished I'd kept my mouth shut. "Oh, just a feeling."

Suzy's eyes were eager. "What kind of a feeling?"

"Just a feeling," I repeated lamely.

Daddy said, "Unless you have something to substantiate such feelings, they're best not talked about."

"Sure. Sorry." I changed the subject. "Adam seemed to indicate that Vespugia's sort of a police state."

Daddy said, "It's ironic, but police states are usually the safest for the ordinary traveler."

"Strange, isn't it," Mother suggested, "that democracy seems to bring out crime."

"Ned says——" Suzy could not get through a meal without mentioning Ned. "Ned says that Vespugia has some really fine physicists at their station on the Antarctic peninsula. Señor Tuarte told him. Señor Tuarte never tells our class anything interesting. Just verbs and idioms and grammar and dull stuff."

"But are you learning any Spanish?" Mother asked.

"Some, I suppose. Not enough to speak."

"Not yet," Mother said. "Give it time."

So the conversation got safely onto Spanish and what a dull teacher Señor Tuarte was, versus the brilliant Ned.

I went to town to get my passport. It gave me more of an understanding that I was really going to Antarctica.

A couple of days later I had a postcard from Adam. It was a little battered-looking, and the postmark was San Sebastián, Vespugia. I had a feeling it had been written before the second letter mailed from the Falklands. All it said was, "*There's something rotten in the state of Denmark, but I don't know what. Love, Adam.*"

"Something rotten in the state of Denmark" is from *Hamlet*. I was glad I'd studied *Hamlet* thoroughly enough to recognize it. I put the card in my backpack with the two letters and scowled. I had no idea what was going on.

The Monday before Christmas, when I went to school, there was something stuck in my locker. I pulled it out, an ordinary white index card, the kind we're encouraged to keep notes on. Someone had written in careful capital letters: THOSE CONSIDERING FOREIGN TRAVEL HAD BETTER WATCH THEIR TONGUES.

What?

Suzy was with me, and I handed her the card.

She read it. "What's this about?"

"I have no idea. Do you?"

"Nope. Sounds like someone doesn't want you to take your trip. Crazy."

"Do you recognize the writing?"

"It's all capital letters. Forget it."

I tried to, but I didn't like it. Suzy didn't seem to think it was important, but who wouldn't want me to go to Antarctica?

After school I went over to Clovenford. Aunt Serena had asked my family, except for John, of course, to come for dinner. Stassy let me in and told me Aunt Serena was resting so she'd be fresh for the evening. Cook was in the kitchen, she said, or I could go on up to the attic and do my homework.

I went first to see Cook. The kitchen, as always, smelled marvelous, a mixture of ginger and cinnamon and garlic and onion—at least, that's what my nose told me. Cook handed me a big mug of steaming cocoa, with whipped cream on top, and I sat in the rocker by the window, adding the smell of the geraniums in their pots to the cooking smells.

"No cookies today," he said. "I don't want you spoiling your appetite."

I sipped and rocked and watched Cook cutting up leeks and carrots. After a while he turned and asked me, "Have you heard from Adam?"

"A couple of letters and a postcard."

Cook said, "I had a rather odd postcard, too, in this morning's mail."

"What did it say?"

Cook closed his eyes and quoted, *"There are a kind of men so loose of soul that in their sleeps will mutter their affairs."*

"Shakespeare?" I asked.

"Othello, I think."

"Mine was Shakespeare, too. *Something rotten in the state of Denmark."*

"Hmm. Not like Adam to be cryptic."

We were silent, and finally I spoke. "Cookie, you never tell me anything about yourself unless I ask."

He turned from the sink. "My monastic training, probably. During my time in the monastery we were taught never to talk about ourselves unless directly confronted, and that was discouraged."

"Even with your friends?"

"My close friends already knew me pretty well."

"Like Adam II?"

"Yes."

"Did you see each other when you were in the monastery?"

"He visited us quite often. He was popular with the brethren."

83

"And after you left?"

Cook placed leeks and carrots in a large, flat pan. "Friends are forever, Miss Vicky. When I knew Seth was going to recover and I came back to the States, I was restless. I had a job in a good restaurant, but I was not happy. Nothing seemed very real."

"Well, then—why are you with Aunt Serena now?"

"Miss Vicky, did no one tell you it is not polite to ask direct questions?"

"Sometimes it's the only way to find anything out."

"After Adam died, I called Clovenford occasionally, just to keep in touch. One time, when I was working in New York, Madam's voice sounded terrible. So I came up on my day off and she was ill with pneumonia. Her cook and maid had picked that day to vanish. Your father had nurses for her, but they weren't interested in cooking and cleaning, so he had to put her in the hospital. The first thing I did was find Stassy and Owain. They'd been working for an elderly lady who'd died not long before, so they knew how to take care of older people. Then I wandered around in the acreage behind the house and discovered a cabin which Mr. Eddington had built for himself as a getaway from the world of business. He'd done it well, with electricity and running water, and I fell in love with it. I realized that I was bored out of my mind in New York, tired of the rich and famous I cooked for, tired of the stresses of the city. I knew Adam would have been horrified at his mother's condition, so I moved into the cabin. I loved Madam then, and I love her now. We're a happy household, and if we have griefs, as who does not, we share them without words. There, Miss Vicky. That is the longest autobiographical speech I have ever given."

"Thank you." My voice was small. "I didn't mean to pry."

"I don't think you were prying, Miss Vicky. You and I will be taking a long journey together, and you wanted to know something about me, and that is quite understandable and not necessarily prying."

"Thank you," I murmured again. I rocked back and forth and pondered Cook's story. There was no sign of disquiet in him now. His spirit pervaded the kitchen in a gentle way. I wondered if he might not have gone back to the monastery if it hadn't been for Aunt Serena.

I went up to the attic and finished my homework. Then I took Adam II's letter out of *The Jungle Book* and put it with Adam III's letters and card. And the weird card from my locker.

Then I wrote Adam. I'd mail the letter to LeNoir Station, because that's where he'd be by the time my letter reached him. I knew mail was delivered there only sporadically, whenever a ship stopped by, but it still seemed the best address. I told him about Adam II's journal, his unfinished letter, and the unmailed letter I'd given Cook. I told him I'd had his letters, and both Cook and I had received strange postcards. Then I told him about the card stuck in my locker at school, and that I had no idea who it had come from or why anybody would want to warn me off.

I went downstairs as I heard Daddy's car drive up. He was coming directly from the office. I met him in the sitting room, and the photograph album was open and on the table, waiting. Stassy said she'd bring Aunt Serena right down, and

85

for us to make ourselves at home. We bent over the album and looked at snapshots of penguins, the babies huddled together in what Aunt Serena had told me were called crèches. They were balls of fluff, and very cute.

I turned to my father. "I'm actually going to see them!"

Aunt Serena, leaning slightly on Stassy, came in and joined us. "You will find that penguins are totally communal creatures. If one penguin heads for the sea, two or three others will follow. If they stray from each other, they become easy prey for their predators."

"Who are their predators?" I asked.

"Skuas, which are large, brown, carnivorous birds. Raptors. And seals. But while penguins are communal, living in community, they have no intimacy. They are dutiful with their babies, but they do not love."

"Why?" I looked at a snapshot of a line of penguins which seemed to be hurrying down to the water.

"Life is too treacherous. If you become intimate with spouse or child who may be eaten in the next hour, you are too vulnerable. You cannot afford affection."

Something in her voice made me shiver. "Penguins," I said. "But human beings can't live that way."

"Sometimes they have to," Aunt Serena said. "When parents knew that they were going to lose their babies and young children to scarlet fever, diphtheria, measles, they could not afford the kind of secure love that exists between parents and children today."

My father said, "It's only in the past few generations that

86

parents have been able to count on raising their children to adulthood. Modern medicine has changed a lot of things."

"But people still loved each other, I mean, they always have!" I cried.

"True," Daddy said. "But we allow ourselves to love more easily now that we have a greater hope for a reasonable life expectancy."

I looked at a fluffy grey ball cuddling up to a grown penguin. "But mothers nursed the babies! How could they help being intimate?" I'd watched Mother nursing Rob. I'd watched Daddy watching Mother nursing Rob.

"They couldn't help it," Aunt Serena agreed, "but you already know, Vicky, that the more people you love, the more vulnerable you are."

Yes, that was true. If I hadn't loved my grandfather in a most deep and wonderful way, I wouldn't miss him so much. If I didn't love Adam, I wouldn't be hurt because he'd signed his second letter "All the best," instead of "Love."

I said, "Maybe our intimacies are more precious if we know they may be taken away."

Daddy looked at me and smiled and nodded slightly.

Aunt Serena said, "You are wise, my child. I do not regret my intimacies, no matter how expensive, not with any of the people I have loved: my husband, Adam. I loved him with great utterness, and when he died my life was split in two as though by lightning. And then my son——" She caught her breath. "I have known people who have drawn back after one devastating hurt, but that is a kind of suicide, at least to my mind. I am very fond of you, my dear, and I think you are fond of me."

"I am! I love you!"

"But you know quite well that I will die long before you do."

I whispered, "I know it's a—a statistic."

"It's what being mortal is all about. I believe that Antarctica will awe and delight you, but you will be glad that you are a human being."

"I *am* glad." Then I added, "But I don't think I like statistics."

Aunt Serena nodded. "Statistics help free us from the compassion that is part of intimacy. Statistics do not understand that until we accept our mortality we cannot even glimpse the wonder of our immortality."

Before I had time to digest that, Stassy came in to announce that Mother had arrived with Suzy and Rob. They had come in the back way, so they could chat with Cook, and would join us in a moment.

We could hear voices and laughter from the direction of the kitchen. Then Mother and Suzy and Rob came in, and Rob hugged Aunt Serena, and Suzy turned right to the photograph album and the pictures of the penguins.

"I'm green with envy," she said to me. "Promise me you'll keep a list of everything you see."

"Sure. There isn't that much wildlife, but I'll do my best."

"There are lots of different kinds of penguins," she said. "What's this?" And she pointed to a picture of a church outside which was a very large double arch.

"The jawbones of two whales," Aunt Serena said. "It gives

you an idea what enormous creatures they are, the largest in the world."

We moved into the dining room. Stassy helped Aunt Serena into her chair. "Meanwhile, my dear Vicky"——Aunt Serena reached for a crystal glass and took a sip of water——"we need to double-check that you have all the right clothes for Antarctica."

We'd checked and rechecked my wardrobe several times. "Two pair of lined jeans. Long johns. Thick socks."

Mother said, "And I think we'll get Vicky a new pair of boots, because the treads on her old ones are worn down."

Stassy came back in with a cheese soufflé, high and puffy and golden.

"Aunt Serena," Suzy asked, "why did Adam——your Adam—— want to go to Antarctica?"

Aunt Serena smiled. "He had an inquiring mind, like you." Suzy smiled with pleasure. Aunt Serena continued, "He loved marine biology. And he'd traveled to the Falklands with Adam Cook to visit Seth, Cook's brother. Seth had been to Antarctica several times and waxed lyrical about it, and the two Adams were always ready for adventure."

"Two Adams?"

"Adam Eddington and Adam Cook."

I could tell that Suzy had a lot more questions, but she let Aunt Serena talk about some work Adam II had done with ice-fish, fish which adapt to the low temperature of the water by becoming transparent. The conversation was mostly about marine life, which kept Suzy happy, and it was an okay evening, though I realized that I was used to having Aunt Serena to myself.

The next day was the last day of school before Christmas vacation. There was another card stuck in my locker. Capital letters. TOO MANY ADAMS. TOO MANY QUESTIONS. KEEP OUT OF IT.

Suzy was hovering, so I showed it to her. "Wow, not nice," she said. "Who on earth do you think it could be?"

"I don't know. I don't like it."

"Are you going to tell anybody?"

I thought for a moment. "Yes. But I'm not sure who. Don't worry Mother and Dad. Okay?"

"Okay."

John came home for Christmas. He hadn't been in the house more than an hour when I got him alone in his room. "John, I need to talk to you."

"Sure."

I spread Adam's letters, his postcard, Adam II's unfinished letter, and the two cards which had been stuck in my locker out on my bed. "Read these, please. They're in chronological order."

I stood anxiously looking out the window at the bare branches of a willow tree, still holding a touch of golden color, as my brother read.

He looked up from Adam II's letter. "What about this?"

"I found it up in Aunt Serena's attic."

"Have you shown it to anyone?"

"Not yet."

He finished with the two cards from school. "Vicky, what is all this about?"

"That's what I'm asking you."

"Who knows about all this?"

"Nobody. Well, I wrote Adam, and Suzy saw the cards that were stuck in my locker, but that's all."

"Adam seems to be warning you about something."

"Yes."

"And these two cards——"

"Suzy thinks someone doesn't want me to go to Antarctica."

"Who? And why not?"

I shrugged.

"You haven't shown Adam II's letter to anybody?"

"No."

"You obviously think it's important. Why?"

"Oh, John——Adam II's death strikes me as——as——"

"Ambiguous?"

"Yes. Something's wrong. I'm not sure Cook thinks it was an accident."

"How well do you know Cook?"

"Enough to think he's wonderful. I'll show you Adam II's journal. It's made me know Cookie a lot better than I would otherwise."

"Do you trust him?"

"Completely."

"I think you ought to show all this to Mother and Dad."

"No. Please no."

"Do you think if they saw it they wouldn't let you go to Antarctica?"

91

"I don't know. I don't want to show them until I can make a little more sense of it all."

"Vicky, who would know all of this well enough to want to stop you?"

"I haven't the faintest idea."

"What about Cook?"

"Cookie! No. No!"

"There's nobody else who has all this information."

"But why would he want to stop me?"

"I don't know. But I'm asking the question."

"John, Cookie has—he has *integrity*."

"Somebody's threatening you."

"Do you think it could be a joke?"

"Who'd want to play that kind of joke on you?"

"Suzy?"

"Come on, Vicky. I know you and Suzy spat a lot, but this isn't the kind of joke Suzy plays."

"I know."

"You said you wrote Adam?"

"Yes."

"That's good. But you need to find out more about Adam Cook."

It was a terrible thought to put into my mind, though I could see why John had it. But he didn't know Cook. He hadn't read Adam II's journal.

I was glad all the Christmas preparations at home and at church were keeping everybody busy. Rob was in the kids' pageant, and Suzy was doing the reading. I was singing in the senior choir, with Nanny, and Mother was doing two solos.

I kept my fears and suspicions to myself.

Everybody gave me things for Antarctica for Christmas—lined mittens, ragg socks, a new journal, a pad from Suzy where I was supposed to write down every bird or seal I saw. Mother and Daddy gave me a check.

We went to see Aunt Serena after church Christmas morning, and she had presents for all of us. She and Cook and Stassy and Owain were going to have Christmas dinner together, according to their tradition, and the big house smelled as marvelous as ours.

When we got home, Mother said, "Aunt Serena's really getting a lot of vicarious pleasure helping you plan for your trip, Vic."

Yes. And I didn't want to do or say anything to spoil that pleasure. Or that might make Mother and Daddy stop me from going to Antarctica. The warnings, rather than frightening me off, made me all the more determined to go.

At bedtime I looked at the collection of letters and cards I had in my copy of *Hamlet*. I wasn't sorry I'd talked to John, but I didn't want to show any of this to my parents.

The night before John left for college, he asked me.

I shook my head. "Not yet."

"I think you should."

"I know. I will, if anything else happens."

"This isn't enough?"

"Nothing goes together. It's like a picture puzzle with not

93

enough pieces. I need more pieces before—before I know anything. Don't say anything, John, please."

"It's against my better judgment."

"But please don't."

"Okay. But let me know if anything else happens, if you get any more cards. Or anything. Anything."

"Sure."

"Promise?"

"Promise."

The first day of school after the Christmas holidays, Cook was waiting for me when I got off the school bus. He had a string bag full of vegetables and another with a couple of long loaves of bread. He greeted me, saying, "It's such a pleasant day I thought I'd walk home from marketing, and my route takes me right past your stop."

There'd been nothing more in my locker at school. I wanted to forget those cards. I wanted to forget John's suspicions of Cook. Nothing I knew about Cook made it seem possible to me that he would write threatening cards and stick them in my locker. How could he do it without someone seeing him, anyhow? Regional's a big school, but not so big that someone strange could come to the locker room without being noticed.

Cook said, "Something on your mind?"

"I've got a lot of homework," I said, "but it seems silly to do it when we'll be leaving so soon."

"It's not a bad discipline to get it done."

He was walking along calmly, swinging his string bags.

The thought came to me that he was the one I should have shown Adam II's letter to, rather than John, but maybe that was because I didn't want to face John's suspicions.

I went to the attic and opened Adam II's journal.

I know that some explorers have had to eat penguins. The seals, particularly the leopard seals, grab them and slam them against the water with such force that they skin them, and the empty skins wash up on shore, where it is so dry that the flattened corpses last indefinitely. Cookie is not a vege-tarian, but I think we'd have to be starving before he'd cook a penguin. He is one of the most gentle people I have ever known, and his quiet presence keeps the rest of us from bick-ering or even quarreling, which we might well do, shut up day after day in this small, cramped space. I believe that it is entirely thanks to his presence that we are so amiable, and that we have so much fun. Laughter in this pervading cold helps keep us warm.

This was the Cook Adam II showed me in everything he wrote, not the person John had suggested might have put those threatening cards in my locker.

I had one last meal with Aunt Serena and it was probably the most elegant meal I'd ever had. We started off with caviar, and I wasn't at all sure I was going to like it, but I did. We spread it on Melba toast with finely chopped onion and egg and it was odd and delicious. It was followed by a very light French sorrel soup, and then chicken breasts stuffed with arugula and Jarlsberg cheese—Cook was really providing a farewell banquet.

We had a split of champagne. "I checked with your father," Aunt Serena said, "and he assured me that you were quite capable of managing one glass of champagne. A toast, my dear, to you and to Cook and to Adam and to the Antarctic." She raised her glass.

One thing I couldn't do was say anything that would make Aunt Serena anxious about the trip. I raised my glass. "And to you, Aunt Serena. Thank you."

"Angels watch over you," she said softly.

When I went to the kitchen, both Owain and Cook were there.

"Thanks for the marvelous dinner," I told Cook.

He handed me something. "To protect you from the sun." It was a canvas hat with a big brim, and could be folded and put in my suitcase.

"Terrific! Thank you!"

Owain said, "We'll miss you, Miss Vicky."

"I'll miss you, too. But I'll send you lots of postcards."

"Angels watch over you," Owain said, just as Aunt Serena had said.

"Do you believe in angels?" I asked. I hoped he did. I had my copy of *Hamlet* in my suitcase, and folded in it were Adam's letters and cards, and the two strange cards which had been stuck in my locker at school. Angels watching over me sounded good. John had called to say goodbye, and urged me again to speak to our parents. I said I'd think about it. He knew then that I wasn't going to.

"Oh, yes, Miss Vicky," Owain answered my question. "We need our angels."

"With wings?"

He smiled. "Beautiful wings."

"With feathers?"

"Most artists depict them with feathers."

I said, "Most artists paint angels with wings that wouldn't be able to fly."

Cook smiled. "It's simply one way of representing them so that the human being can get an idea of the loveliness of angels. They are pure energy, you know."

"So they aren't birds," I said.

Cook laughed heartily. "Madam has mentioned about penguins and their feathers."

"Yes. If it has feathers, it's a bird."

Owain said, "Feathers or not, Miss Vicky, Stassy and I shall ask angels to watch over you."

Cook said, "Stassy and Owain have an in with angels. I find it very comforting."

"Ready to go home?" Owain asked.

"Yes. Say good night to Stassy for me."

Stassy, I knew, was helping Aunt Serena get ready for bed.

Owain and I went out to the car, and Cook stood looking after us.

Four

*M*y eyes began to droop with weariness, and I didn't know if this was one effect of the continuing, penetrating cold, or if it was, according to the clock, nighttime and my body was ready for sleep. It was impossible to look at the sun, as I could do at home, and say, It's moving to the west, it will be dark soon. It was impossible to "tell" time in this land of perpetual day—or nearly perpetual day. For the past several nights, if there had been any darkness, I hadn't seen it, because I was already asleep.

One thing I knew was that, no matter what was causing the sleepiness, I must not give in to it. If I slid off the iceberg, that would be the end of me. I leaned against the ice tower that rose up behind me, though my body wanted, more than anything, to lie down, to curl up, to let go. I knew about travelers being lost in a blizzard and knowing that they could not lie down and go to sleep, or they'd freeze to death. I would certainly freeze if I could not make myself stay awake.

∙ ∙ ∙

Owain drove Cook and me to New York to the airport. My parents had planned to come see us off, but there was a flu epidemic in Thornhill and Clovenford, and Daddy had a lot of patients in the hospital, and Rob was sick and Mother didn't want to leave him. In a way, it was almost easier to say goodbye at home than it would have been to have my parents at the airport. I knew Mother was having second thoughts about my going. I was having second thoughts about not showing them Adam II's unfinished letter and those funny warnings stuck in my locker.

Cook and I didn't talk much on the drive down to New York. That was okay. Cook and I didn't talk unless we had something to say.

At the airport, Owain shook hands formally with me, then gave me a quick hug. Cook and I had our tickets checked, then went through security and on to the boarding area. I was excited, excited by the bustle at the airport, excited at the idea of flying to two continents, South America and Antarctica. If I'd been younger, I'd have reached out and held Cook's hand. But there was something aloof about him as he sat beside me on one of the plastic chairs, and I couldn't push John's warning suggestion out of my mind. There wasn't anybody except Cook who could have known all that I knew. But Cook hadn't seen Adam II's unfinished letter I'd found in *The Jungle Book*. John was the only other person besides me who'd seen that.

Then Cook turned to me and smiled. "I'm glad we're sharing this adventure, Vicky."

"You called me plain Vicky!" I said.

He grinned. "I told you I'd be more informal once we started our travels."

When we boarded the plane, Cookie gave me the window seat, so I could look out as we taxied along the runway, gathering speed, and then the plane nosed up and we were flying above buildings, above water. I looked at the land dropping below us and finally disappearing as we flew through a layer of clouds and then burst out into the sunlight, blue sky above, white cloud below. The flight attendant came around with lunch, and after lunch Cook suggested that we both snooze, because we were going to have a long wait in Miami before the overnight flight to San Sebastián. I was sure I was too excited to sleep, but I surprised myself by drifting off, and when the pilot announced that we were going to be landing in a few minutes, I lifted my head from where it had drooped onto Cook's shoulder.

In Miami, retrieving our bags from the luggage carousel took forever, largely because half a dozen flights came in at the same time and they were all being unloaded onto the same carousel.

Cook said, "I gather these delays happen more and more frequently nowadays. It's a good thing we don't have a close connection."

Our bags finally arrived, and as we headed to the boarding areas we saw two people in blue uniforms holding up a sign: ANTARCTIC ARGOSY. We had tags for our bags which said ARGOSY, and blue-and-white plastic name pins, which Cook had suggested that we wear. The people with the sign saw us and waved, and we hurried over to them. They were friendly and greeted us by name, checking their clipboards. They took our bags with the ARGOSY tags and told us we needn't worry about them till we arrived in San Sebastián. Then they directed us to a lounge where we could wait till time to board. Some of the other *Argosy* passengers, who'd flown in from California and other points west, were already there, and probably would be stretched out on couches, trying to sleep.

As we walked toward the lounge, Cook commented, "One thing that helps protect the Antarctic is that it's so hard to get to." He found us a couple of chairs and brought Cokes from the bar. "We'll get dinner on the plane, but it probably won't be before midnight. Do you want to scavenge around for something to eat? That lunch on the plane was pretty plastic."

I shook my head. "I think I'll be okay."

"The fare tonight will be good. The Vespugian airline is really trying to please its North American customers. I'm off to find a newspaper. You'll be all right?"

"Sure. I'll catch up on my journal." I settled into my seat and started to write. "Here I am in a large waiting room in the airport in Miami. Even though I'm with Cook, I'm suddenly feeling displaced. I wish John hadn't——" I stopped, holding my pen over the page. Started to scratch out what I'd written when I noticed a tall, elderly man standing in front of me, looking at me questioningly. He had a cigar in his mouth, but it wasn't lit.

He chewed on it, and looked at my name pin. "Hello. You're going on the *Argosy*?"

"Yes, sir."

"Vicky Austin?"

101

"Yes." I tried to read his name, but his jacket covered half of his pin.

"Sam White," he said. "My suspicion is that I'll be the oldest passenger on the *Argosy* and you'll be the youngest. I'm eighty-three. How old are you?"

"Sixteen."

"How does it happen that you're footloose and fancy free?"

"A trip to Antarctica is considered educational by my high-school principal—and my family."

"You're traveling alone?"

"No, sir, with Cookie—Mr. Adam Cook. He's going to visit his brother in Port Stanley, and I'm looking forward to seeing a friend of mine who has an internship at LeNoir Station." I closed my mouth, remembering someone saying that the Austins always told everybody everything, because we're so naïve. Maybe so, but I liked this man. Maybe I tend to like older people because of Grandfather and Aunt Serena.

"So you're a student." He looked at me benignly and I nodded. He continued, "I'm a retired explorer and lawyer, the old-fashioned kind, more like Atticus, I hope, than like some of the vultures around today." Atticus is the lawyer father in *To Kill a Mockingbird*, which is one of my favorite books. I liked Sam White more all the time. He went on, "I bunged up my knees skiing last winter and had to have surgery. My doctor said I needed therapy, and that's what this trip is for me. Getting in and out of Zodiacs ought to use all the right muscles and strengthen my quadriceps."

Skiing in his eighties—that sounded pretty good. He was big-boned as well as tall; what hair he had was shaggy and

102

yellow-white; he walked a little creakily, but his eyes were alert and friendly.

"Forty years ago," he continued, "I climbed Mount Everest, but I fear my mountain-climbing days are over. Do you do any climbing?"

I grinned. "I've climbed Mount Everett, which is in Massachusetts. Mostly I just hike in and around the woods where we live."

Cook came back then and introduced himself. Mr. White said, "Call me Sam. And did I hear Vicky call you Cookie?"

"You did. Quite a few of my friends call me that."

"I may, too?"

"Certainly."

Sam said, "We're all on a first-name basis here, that is, those of us going on the Antarctic trip."

Cook smiled at me. "I told you everything would be informal, Vicky."

I nodded. "Good."

Cook sat down with his paper, and Sam took his unlit cigar out of his mouth and waved it at two women sleeping on one of the couches. "They've flown in from California. That's too much flying in one day for me. I came in from San Francisco yesterday and spent the night at one of the Miami Beach hotels, and had a chance to walk by the ocean."

Then he pointed out a man in a dark suit and tie, with black hair and an olive complexion. "Jorge Maldonado. He's a Vespugian and has a ranch near the pyramids. Interesting bloke. And you should see his camera—it's the largest Hassel-blad I've ever seen, plus everything to go with it——three huge carrying cases of state-of-the-art photographic equipment, so he's had to do some urgent arguing about his carry-on bags."

Mr. Maldonado was sitting on a couch, talking with a couple of middle-aged women. They were laughing and enjoying each other, and drinking coffee out of little white cups.

It was a long wait before our flight was called, but interesting, because we met some more people who'd be on the *Argosy* with us, including the ship's doctor, Dick Hawkins, and his wife, Angelique. Dick had a cane and walked with a limp. In private life he was a pediatric orthopedic surgeon. He had a nice smile, the kind that would put kids at ease even if they were scared. He reminded me of my father, and I was glad he was going to be on the *Argosy*. Angelique did not remind me of my mother in the least! She was, she told us smilingly, a librarian, and she was one of the most stunningly beautiful women I'd ever seen, with skin dark and lustrous as mahogany. She spoke with an Islander's slight lilt, something I wouldn't have recognized before my year in New York. Thornhill doesn't have much ethnic variety.

As the time for our flight approached, the lounge got more and more crowded, and the air began to get stale. Half the room had NO SMOKING signs, but not the other half. Quite a few people were smoking. Sam White wandered around with his cigar in his mouth, but he never lit it.

Mr. Maldonado, a newspaper tucked under his arm, approached us and bowed. "Jorge Maldonado—please pronounce it 'George,' the American way. Mr. White tells me you are Vicky Austin and—"

"Adam Cook. Cookie," Cook said. He indicated an empty

seat on the couch nearest us, and Mr. Maldonado took it. He told us that his business was forest preservation, and he was just returning from Finland, where he had been studying their methods.

Cook asked, with interest, "Vespugia is concerned about forestation?"

"We have a well-established program," Jorge Maldonado said, "started many years ago by El Zarco. General Guedder is keeping it up and constantly looking into new and improved methods." His English was very good, with only a trace of accent.

Cook said, "Sam White tells us that you are also a rancher."

"In a modest way. I used to breed cattle, but with the world grown smaller and hungrier, I am trying to shift to crops that are kinder to the land." He added, wryly, "And, of course, that make a reasonable profit. But now—I am on vacation. I will see my wife and children tomorrow; the children are away at school for much of the year, but they are still on their long break. You, Miss Vicky Austin, are not in school?"

"Yes, but this trip is a sort of educational vacation."

"Educational, indeed. It will be delightful for all of us to have you aboard the *Argosy*. But there will probably be no other young people for you."

"Well, I am hoping to see a friend when we get to LeNoir Station; he's working there."

"LeNoir. One of our most interesting stops, on Eddington Point. It is a long, fascinating trip," Jorge Maldonado said pleasantly. "But before we get to Antarctica, I hope you will

105

enjoy my small country, which is very dear to me." He rose and bowed slightly toward us. "Time to stretch the legs. I will be staying with you overnight in San Sebastián. My ranch is not far from the pyramids."

Our flight was called then and along with everybody else we gathered up our hand luggage, got out our boarding passes, and headed for the plane.

The flight was late, and it was after eleven before we took off. Cook gave me the window seat again, though there was nothing to see except our reflections in the glass. The Vespugian flight attendants had long, black braids down their backs, and didn't speak fluent English, but Cook spoke to them in Spanish and they beamed at him gratefully.

We were given a really good meal, much better than the lunch we'd had on the way to Miami. The flight attendants served from large, rolling trays full of dishes of vegetables and platters of fillets of beef, nicely rare, which they carved for us. It was past midnight, but I was hungry, and I enjoyed the meal and the solicitous service. After we'd eaten, we were given blankets, and we leaned our seats back, put up our leg rests, and tried to sleep. It was certainly not like sleeping in a bed, but I did sleep, and even dreamed a little, and I was still dozing when breakfast was brought around and people began opening their shades. We saw some cone-shaped mountains, so I figured they were the volcanoes Adam II had written about. Jorge Maldonado paused at our seats on the way back from the lavatory, and told us that some of them were still active, and that there was one on the Antarctic peninsula that was sending up

106

smoke and occasional spurts of flame, so we weren't going to land anywhere near, in case it decided to erupt.

When we reached San Sebastián, the airport was steamily hot. I'd brought a cotton top and skirt, and was ready to get out of my winter clothes. Sweat trickled down my back as I stood in the passport line.

A man from the *Argosy* was waiting for our group, and he told us to get into the two buses which were outside, and our bags would be collected and delivered to our rooms in the hotel.

Cook and I got on the second bus. The last person to climb in carried a big something wrapped in a canvas case, and she was very careful with it, trying not to bump it.

"Say, Siri, what's that?" Sam asked. He seemed to be on a first-name basis with everybody.

"My harp." She found a seat across the aisle from me and held the harp carefully, as though it were a baby.

"You're taking a harp to Antarctica?" someone asked.

She laughed, a nice, bubbling kind of laugh. "I'm hoping to play it for the penguins and seals."

"You're kidding!"

"Not at all."

"How about playing for us?" Jorge Maldonado asked.

"Be glad to."

Someone else asked, "Is it a Venezuelan harp?"

"No, a Celtic lap harp. They're not dissimilar."

Suddenly we realized that the guide was trying to get our attention, introducing himself and the driver, and telling us a little about where we were going. San Sebastián was a mixture of old and new, and had been founded by someone with the unlikely name of Modesto Pugh. Jorge Maldonado, whose English was lots better than the guide's, told us that many people from the British Isles had helped free the South American continent from the domination of Spain.

The guide, who obviously didn't want anyone else to take over his job, announced loudly that the water in San Sebastián came from the Andes and was very pure, but had minerals we weren't used to, so we'd better drink bottled water.

When we got to the hotel, we were herded into a room where we were offered orange juice and a delicious kind of *empanada* filled with seasoned meat or cheese. Then our passports were collected and we were given room assignments and keys. Several people were handed letters; there was an envelope and a couple of postcards for me. The first postcard was from Adam. No salutation. No signature. But it was his writing. *This is miching mallecho; it means mischief.*

Cook saw me reading it, and asked, "What's that?"

I handed it to him, and he read it, laughed, then sobered. "*Hamlet*, I think."

"Yes," I said. "I was kind of intrigued by that 'miching mallecho' when we did *Hamlet* in school. Sneaky evil, our teacher said. So what is Adam . . ." My voice trailed off.

"I don't know."

"Did you get a postcard or anything?"

"A note from Seth, saying he's looking forward to seeing me, and to meeting you."

"So what's Adam talking about?" If he'd received my letter, this postcard gave no indication.

108

With his typical gesture, Cook smoothed his bald pate. "Vicky, I wish I knew. Here, have another of these." And he handed me one of the *empanadas*, which I popped into my mouth.

The second postcard was from my brother John, in his dark, scrunched-up writing: *Hope all goes well. Write details. Wish you'd told parents about school locker, otherwise least said. Hope Suzy doesn't blab. January thaw here. No snow no skiing. Have two papers to write. Take care.*

The letter was from my mother, written a week before I left, so it would be waiting for me, with P.S.s from Suzy and Rob. Mother wrote how much they'd miss me and wished me a wonderful time. She'd try to have a letter for me at Port Stanley. Otherwise, she wouldn't try to reach me, but hoped I'd write them when I could. Suzy wrote that the weather was terrible and Ned was wonderful and her Spanish teacher was interested in my trip because he was from Vespugia and had always wanted to go to Antarctica. Four boys had asked her to a dance and she didn't know which one to choose. In his careful printing, Rob wrote that there was no snow and come home soon.

Somehow I felt very far away from them all.

It turned out that I was sharing a room with Siri and her harp. Siri Evensen, her whole name was, from Minnesota. She was a biochemist, she told me, and her harp was her relaxation. "I'm taking a long-overdue vacation," she said, and yawned. "All I want to do at this moment is go to bed and sleep."

I was pretty sleepy, too, though I did want to go on the

bus tour of the city at four. Siri yawned again, like a kitten, and said she'd been to San Sebastián before, so she was going to sleep until time for dinner. "Is Cookie going on the bus tour with you?"

"Yes. We're going to meet in the lobby."

She lay down and put eyeshades on. I looked at my suitcase and thought of the spy novels John loves, which I sometimes read. I had Adam's "miching mallecho" postcard in my hand. I opened my backpack, heavy from my Shakespeare book and my journal, and added it to his other cards and letters, plus Adam II's letter, plus the warning cards from my locker. I had a weirdly sinister feeling. I should have shown everything to my parents. But then they'd never have let me go.

As though looking for inspiration, I dug around in the pocket of my backpack where I keep paper clips, fillers for my pen, an old Swiss Army knife of John's which has a small pair of scissors, and an ancient bottle opener from the days when Coke or ginger-ale bottles had metal caps; Rob had found it and given it to me for Christmas as an artifact, as proud of it as he was of his Indian arrowheads. There was a small bottle of whiteout, which is almost becoming an artifact itself, and then my fingers touched a small roll of Scotch tape, and a crazy idea came to me. I tore off as small a piece of tape as I could and put it over the zipper on my suitcase, feeling both stupid and scared, living in a world of imagination as usual.

I flopped down on the other twin bed, listening to Siri breathing. I slept for an hour, woke up feeling hot and sweaty, and put on my bathing suit and went for a quick swim in the hotel pool, which was out back in a gracious courtyard full of flowers. The water was cool and eased the cricks left over from all the flying.

The bus trip was interesting. San Sebastián was my first foreign city, Vespugia my first foreign country, South America my first foreign continent. Sam, who sat behind me on the bus, said that some people took the Antarctic trip not so much because they were interested as because they wanted to go to their seventh continent. Seven continents: North America, South America, Europe, Asia, Africa, Australia, Antarctica. I still had a lot of traveling to do.

We went to a museum with a collection of pre-Columbian artifacts, and a room which was a sort of Madame Tussaud reenactment of the Spanish Inquisition. I hadn't realized before that the Spanish Inquisition had reached South America. There were life-sized figures in brown habits, their cowls pulled completely over their heads and faces, so the people being tortured couldn't see their torturers. And there were some of the original instruments of torture, thumb-screws, racks, and other horrors.

Cook stood by me. I looked at one of the cowled monks. "How could monks do this kind of thing?"

Sam, standing near us, said, "Not only monks."

"Who?"

Cook said, "Remember Salem, and witch-hunting. The Spanish Inquisition wasn't the only evidence that religion can become fanaticism."

Sam said, "It seems to be a taint in human nature, this need to torture and kill those whose belief in God differs from yours."

111

I looked at a wax Indian who was being squashed by some kind of machine, and turned away, feeling sick. One man was taking pictures with a camera which Sam said was almost as complex as Jorge Maldonado's.

"Why does he want pictures of this stuff?" I demanded.

Sam replied, mildly, "It's historically interesting, Vicky."

I was very glad to get back on the bus and have a drive up and down the streets of San Sebastián. The city was a mixture of beautiful nineteenth-century architecture and modern drabness. Very little from the colonial period a century before; there was one interesting old church, but we saw it only from the outside. At many intersections there were soldiers with rifles slung over their shoulders, just as Adam had written. Our guide, whose English was hardly a second language, managed to make us understand that the Vespugian border was always in danger.

Sam, leaning over the back of my seat, said that when he'd been in San Sebastián before, during the presidency of El Zarco, there hadn't been this kind of military presence. "There's no velvet glove around this iron hand."

It was amazing to see green trees and grass and all kinds of flowers when at home it was midwinter and when, in a few days, we'd see icebergs. We went to an elegant horse-racing club; races were held every Sunday and were a big attraction in San Sebastián. The last thing we did was drive up a horrendous winding narrow road to the top of a mountain from which we had smoggy views of the city.

Going down the mountain with all the hairpin bends was even more scary than going up. Our mountains at home are old mountains, worn by time and wind and rain. There was a raw newness to the mountains around San Sebastián, a feeling that here the planet was young, that the mountains had recently been formed.

Several people on the bus fell asleep; it was hot and humid, way up in the eighties. Even in my summer skirt and top, I was sticky and hot. I tried to listen to our guide, who was really interesting when I could understand what he was saying. He told us what Adam had told me about efforts to combat pollution.

When we got back to the hotel, our passports were returned. I stuck mine in my backpack and went up to the room. Siri was in the shower. I checked my suitcase, and there was no small piece of tape across the zipper. Something flip-flopped in my stomach. I opened the suitcase and it looked to me as though my things had been gone over and then put back in place, but not exactly. I couldn't be sure. I looked on the floor and didn't see the tiny piece of tape. Certainly Siri wouldn't have gone through my things. And who would have come in while she was sleeping? Anything worth taking was in my backpack, which I'd had with me on the bus tour. I shook myself for feeling like a character in a fourth-rate international-intrigue novel.

Siri came out of the shower and said the water was only a trickle, so I put on my damp bathing suit and went back to the pool. Jorge Maldonado and Dick Hawkins were there, swimming tidy laps back and forth. Jorge Maldonado saw me, swam to the edge of the pool, and waved.

"Hello, Mr. Maldonado," I greeted him.

"Jorge, Vicky, please, Jorge, the American way. Did you enjoy the bus trip?"

"I did, but now I'm ready for a swim."

"The water is a great deal cooler than the air." He pulled himself up onto the side of the pool. "Enjoy it." Dick Hawkins kept on swimming, but paused in his stroke to smile and wave at me. Swimming must have been good for his lame leg.

Cook was sharing a room with Sam, and Siri and I joined them for dinner in the hotel dining room, along with Dick and Angelique. It was a beautiful meal, with interesting combinations. I had chicken with avocado and artichoke hearts.

We learned that Dick and Angelique usually took their vacations aboard a ship where Dick was ship's doctor, and had seen a lot of the world that way, but this was their first trip to Antarctica. After dinner we strolled around the gardens, enjoying the evening breeze and the summer smell of flowers. Dick leaned on his cane, limping heavily, and shortly he and Angelique excused themselves and went in. It wasn't long before the rest of us headed for our rooms.

San Sebastián was my first foreign experience, and I wasn't going to see very much of it, because it was simply a stop on the way to our real destination. I wrote about the afternoon—though not the Scotch tape on my suitcase zipper—in my long letter to Aunt Serena, which was going to be shown to my teachers when I got home. It was more fun writing to Aunt Serena than it would have been to keep a school-type journal. While I was writing, Siri took her harp out of its case and began to play it, softly. I looked at her, enjoying the music and her grace in playing it. Her ash-blond hair swung across her cheek; she wore it shoulder-length, parted on the side, and held out of her face with a tortoiseshell barrette, sort of the way I used to wear my hair when I was ten, only it didn't look childish on her, or as though she were trying to be younger than she was. It was simple and right.

"After having been bounced around in all our travels"—she plucked the strings gently—"she needs to make a little music."

I finished writing and got into bed. Siri played for a few more minutes—one of my favorite songs that we sang in choir, "Come, My Way, My Truth, My Life." Then she turned out the light. The air conditioner in our room was noisy and ineffective. I shoved down the blanket and slept under the sheet.

The next morning we boarded two buses again and were taken back to the airport and divided into groups. Jorge Maldonado was there and explained that the trip to the jungle would be in small prop planes. He was standing near two men in army uniforms, one young, not much older than I, and one considerably older. Jorge told us that all Vespugians must serve two years in the army, and these two soldiers would be with us as our guides on the trip to the pyramids. He introduced them, Captain Nausinio, the older one, and Second Lieutenant Esteban Manuel, the younger one.

Esteban! That was the name of Adam's guide to the pyramids. He was nice-looking, with soft, curly black hair, bright blue eyes, and fair skin.

"Esteban's forebears came to Vespugia from Wales." Jorge smiled. "Which accounts for the dark hair and blue eyes. He is a musician and will be playing the oboe in the San Sebastián Symphony once his term in the army is over. He is very talented."

While we were waiting to board the planes, I went up to Esteban. "Hi. I'm Vicky Austin. I think you know my friend Adam Eddington."

Esteban frowned and held out his hands helplessly, and I realized he didn't speak any English, and, unlike Adam, I didn't speak Spanish. Jorge, carrying his camera cases, came over and I explained, so Jorge told Esteban what I was trying to say, and Esteban beamed and shook my hand and poured a torrent of enthusiastic words over me, and I couldn't understand him any more than he'd understood me. Jorge laughed and said that Esteban was delighted to meet his friend Adam's friend. Then Jorge asked me, "Your friend's name is Adam Eddington?"

"Yes."

"Is he perhaps related to the well-known explorer?"

I hadn't realized Adam II was well known. "His nephew."

"Tragic, his uncle's death. You knew him?" I shook my head. "Ah, true, his death was a good many years ago. He was a remarkable man, remarkable."

We were called to board then, and Cook and I were on the third plane. As it left the runway on takeoff, it bumped into the air so wildly that I reached out and grabbed Cook's hand, and he held mine, firmly, for the entire flight, which took about half an hour.

When we got out of the plane, climbing down some portable steps, we saw the battered bodies of two dead-looking planes.

"Oh, my word," somebody expostulated. "Look at these planes that didn't make it. I wish we could walk back to San Sebastián."

116

I looked around. The landing strip was not very big, and jungle was pressing in on all sides. A jeep-type car bounced to a stop near one of the planes, and Jorge ran to meet two children who jumped all over him, hugging and shouting. He put his arms around them, asking Captain Nausinio to help him with his camera equipment. It was stowed carefully in the back of the car by Captain Nausinio and Jorge's wife, who had black hair hanging down her back in a thick braid, which I was beginning to think of as the Vespugian way of wearing hair.

Siri had walked over and was standing near me. "Beautiful, isn't she?"

"Gorgeous." Mrs. Maldonado got in the jeep and they bounced off, and Captain Nausinio and the rest of us followed along a narrow path that cut through thick bushes, with overhanging trees.

Captain Nausinio talked as we walked, pointing as he spoke, and I couldn't understand a word he said. Finally Cook told him to speak Spanish, and he'd translate.

"Yay, thanks, Cookie!" Sam exclaimed.

Someone else said, "I thought I could understand Spanish reasonably well, but the Vespugian accent is beyond me. Thank goodness for you, Cookie."

It was a ten-minute walk to a clearing in the jungle where suddenly, as we left the trees behind us, we saw the pyramids. Here, in the middle of nowhere, were great stone edifices even larger than the pictures in Aunt Serena's photo album had indicated. The largest one was a massive series of steps rising up at least ten stories. The photographs hadn't conveyed their majesty, or how amazing it was in the middle of the Vespugian jungle to see signs of what obviously had been a sophisticated culture.

Esteban spoke to Cook, who told us that the pyramids were estimated to be about three thousand years old, and very little was known about the civilization that built them.

I wondered what would be known about our civilization in three thousand years. I looked around at us all, the women mostly in cotton dresses or pants, many of the men in shorts and T-shirts. By contrast, Captain Nausinio and Esteban were sweltering in their uniforms, rifles slung over their shoulders. Esteban's fair skin was pale, and there were beads of sweat on his upper lip. As well as his rifle, he carried something in a long, black leather case. Another gun? Or maybe it was his oboe.

Esteban, with Cook translating, told us that the pyramids had been discovered by the early Spanish explorers, in the sixteenth century. The monks thought it was a pagan place and smashed many of the stones and statues.

I looked around and saw fragments of stone all around, and on some of the carvings the faces had been mutilated. I suddenly understood the word "defaced."

Cook translated in an emotionless voice, and I wondered what he thought of monks mutilating anything they thought represented a religion different from theirs. But he continued translating for Esteban without changing expression. "The monks, Esteban says, felt that the pyramids were sacrilegious, and after they had done their damage they went away and the jungle took over again, completely. The pyramids weren't re-discovered until the nineteen-sixties. The largest has four staircases of ninety steps each, adding up to three hundred and sixty days, which was their calendar year, so whoever built the pyramids was mathematically and astronomically literate." He listened to Esteban and told us that if we had the energy for the climb, there would be a beautiful view from the top.

"Come on!" Sam called to me, and started to climb. If Sam could do it, so could I, and when he stopped to rest I paused with him. We were both streaming with sweat. The thought that we'd be seeing icebergs in a few days was incredible. The sun was searing, hotter than it ever gets at home, and the insects were finding me delicious. Sam said, "They ignore me, I'm so old and stringy. And my cigar is protection." It was clamped in his mouth, slightly chomped on, and, as usual, it wasn't lit.

I had my backpack on, so I'd have my hands free for climbing. Most of the others were climbing, too, and there was lots of complaining about the bugs, and people who'd thought to bring bug repellent were passing it around. The two soldiers were also climbing, their rifles banging against their sides. Esteban kept glancing at me, but did not say anything. It was the first time I'd encountered this kind of language barrier that kept us from speaking to each other without an interpreter.

When we arrived at the top, the view was indeed spectacular. We could see other pyramids, and many smaller buildings spreading out in all directions, until the jungle took over. Sam told me that there was still excavation going on. At least there had been under the old president, El Zarco, but General Guedder was not putting money into archaeology.

Having given me this information, through huffs and puffs, Sam lowered himself onto one of the high steps to either side of the shallower ones we'd climbed. I sat down by him. What a great guy! I was pretty much out of breath myself. My shoulders were itching, so I slipped off my backpack and put it in my lap. Sam was still breathing heavily, and I wanted to give him time to catch his breath, so I reached in my backpack and pulled out Adam's letter about the pyramids. I was reading intently and didn't realize that the two soldiers were near us until I heard the older one snap out some kind of order, and suddenly Esteban turned to me, speaking urgently. I couldn't understand a word. He kept pointing at Adam's letter and then at himself. Finally he touched the letter, tugging it gently.

My fingers tightened on the page. "Hey, that's mine!"

Why would he want a letter he obviously couldn't read?

He spoke incomprehensibly to me again, then reached for the letter, and suddenly I felt myself falling, losing my balance, and pitching backward off the steps.

Sam yelled.

And then I was grabbed, shoved, and I fell on one of the wide steps, trembling. Esteban stood by me, and he was trembling, too, and gabbling in Spanish.

Sam said, "Quick work, lad!" Then he asked me, "What happened?"

"I don't know." I was pretty sure I had been pushed. Not by Esteban, who was standing below me, but by the older soldier; I couldn't be sure, and it was a terrible accusation. Why would anyone want to push me?

Esteban's skin looked grey, and his blue eyes were dark with horror. Captain Nausinio scowled. People crowded around.

Cook was coming up the last of the steps. "What's the matter?"

Sam said, "Vicky started to fall. This young lad, here"—he indicated Esteban—"managed to catch her."

My heart was pounding with fear and relief. I said, "I was looking at a letter from Adam—it was in my backpack—I think Esteban wanted to see it—"

Captain Nausinio spoke to Cook.

Cook said, his voice level, "Captain Nausinio tells me his young colleague collects postcards from America. It was a postcard he was hoping for, not the letter."

Had the postcards even been visible? I hadn't pulled them out.

Cook and the soldier talked again, while Esteban hung back, and finally Cook said, "They are terribly sorry there was nearly an accident, Vicky. Lieutenant Esteban is apologizing profusely, and hopes you will forgive him."

"But he's the one who saved me!"

Sam stood up and stretched and yawned. "All's well that ends well."

Shakespeare again. My teacher said that Shakespeare and the King James translation of Scripture have permeated our language and our very being.

"Going down is going to be even worse than climbing up," Sam said. "I'm doing it backward, Vicky, and I think you'll find that easiest, too."

I grunted and started down beside him. When we'd gone about halfway, he stopped and asked, "What was that about?"

I stopped, too. "What?"

"The way you nearly fell. I wasn't looking at you, but—"

"But?" I really wanted to know what Sam's "but" was about.

"You don't strike me as the kind of kid who'd be careless of your own safety."

"I don't think I am."

"Vicky, I do not think that handsome young soldier collects postcards. My Spanish is just adequate enough so I could hear the older man telling him to take something from you."

"Why on earth—"

Sam shrugged. "I don't like it."

I didn't either. "No. But Cookie said they were sorry . . ."

"I'm glad you're with Cookie," Sam said. "I think you should talk to him about this."

Five

Stay awake, Vicky. Stay awake.

I moved slightly away from the tall tower of ice against which I was leaning, and swayed on my feet. Even with my eyes wide open, my mind seemed to slide the way it does just before you go to sleep, when you're not actually dreaming but you aren't thinking ordinary, rational thoughts, either.

Actions have consequences. But what had I done that would lead me to an iceberg in Antarctica? Times and places slid in and out, maybe the way they did for Aunt Serena when she was tired. The seal said that the past and present converged in——

I jerked awake. The seal was still off, fishing. If I lay down and slept, I would die. As long as I stayed awake, there was a possibility I would be rescued. I'd put my family through enough grief, and as for Aunt Serena, she'd given me the tickets to Antarctica, the trip was her gift to me, and if anything happened to me, she——

She'd had enough grief. I couldn't add to it. I shaded my eyes and scanned the horizon, keeping up hope.

When we reached the ground Captain Nausinio came up to us, lugging a case of Coke, which Cook and Sam and I helped him pass around, and we all drank thirstily. Then we were handed cardboard boxes with sandwiches and an orange, and Cook said the sandwiches had been prepared by the hotel and were okay to eat, and of course the orange could be peeled. Esteban and Captain Nausinio stood near us, looking hungry. Although they had carried the lunches to the pyramids, they evidently weren't on the list for lunches, only the tourists were.

Esteban spoke to Cook, who then told us that the people who built these pyramids had not discovered the wheel. He spoke again, and Cook translated. "It seems they were fairly advanced mathematicians. Esteban is very interested in this culture."

Esteban then pointed to some stone slabs, which Cook said were stelae, carved with pictures of men and women in elaborate headdresses. When Esteban had finished giving Cook his information, he squatted down near me.

Captain Nausinio came up to us, barked out something, and Esteban turned to Cook, who explained that Captain Nausinio was going to lead the way to a sort of outhouse, and if anyone wanted to follow him, the privy was only a few hundred yards away. A few people got up and went after him. Esteban watched until the group had turned a corner past one of the smaller pyramids. Then he reached in his pocket and pulled out a postcard and handed it to me, a rather crumpled one of the largest of the pyramids, the one we had climbed. I thanked him and because he still looked very hungry I gave him half my sandwich. He smiled, and his cheeks were pink. I wished I could speak Spanish so I could ask him why he'd wanted my letter from Adam. I looked at Esteban's friendly face, and none of it made sense.

Then Esteban reached for his black case and carefully pulled out his oboe. So I had been right, and it was not another gun. He put it to his mouth to wet the reed, then began to play—a soft, haunting melody.

Not at all to my surprise, Siri came hurrying over to us and knelt on the rough grass, listening intently. When Esteban had put down his oboe, she asked, "Rodrigo?"

He shook his head. "Juan Ormondan. Vespugian. Ours."

"That was a lovely piece." Siri clapped her hands in applause to explain her words. Then, in Spanish, "*Más, por favor.*"

Esteban lifted the oboe and began to play a strange, minor melody, not quite our own scale. I watched his face, fascinated by his dark hair and immense blue eyes. He put his oboe down as Captain Nausinio and the others returned, and we were called to get back on the planes. As we walked across the rough grass, Siri said, "He's a real musician, that young soldier. I wish we could hear him play more."

Sam nodded. "He's okay, that kid. He was doing his best to apologize for whatever it was that happened up on the pyramid. Playing his oboe for you was the only gift he knew how to give you."

"It was wonderful," I said.

Siri suddenly shivered. "The music was superb, and the

pyramids phenomenal, but there's a feel to this place, something unsettling. I can't put my finger on it, but I'm glad we're leaving."

A lot of people were audibly upset about getting back in planes which really appeared unsafe, but our plane, at least, took off smoothly, and there was no turbulence in the air.

I sat next to Cook, who asked, "Are you okay, Vicky?"

"Fine. Thanks."

"How did you happen to fall?"

"It didn't just happen. I think somebody pushed me."

"By mistake?"

"I don't know."

He took quite a while before replying, "It was crowded on those narrow steps at the top. Someone could easily have bumped into you, inadvertently."

I shook my head. "It was all part of Esteban's wanting the letter. It scared me."

Cook sighed. "Yes, Vicky, I'm sure it did. Let it go, if you can."

My backpack was shoved under the seat in front of me. I pulled it out, put it on my lap, reached in, got the two warning cards from my locker at school, and handed them to Cook.

He looked at them, turning them over, reading and rereading the messages, then asked sharply, "Where did these come from?"

"They were stuck in the door of my school locker."

"Recently?"

"Yes." In showing Cook those cards, I'd committed myself.

I reached into the backpack again and got Adam II's unfinished letter, but I didn't hand it to him directly. I said, "Cookie, remember I gave you an air letter addressed to you, one I found up in the attic? An old one that had never been mailed?"

Cook was always quiet, but an added stillness seemed to fill him. He turned slowly to look at me.

I gave him Adam II's unfinished letter. "Did it have anything to do with this?"

He read, slowly. His hand shook, slightly. "Miss Vicky." Then, "Vicky, this is old trouble. It was long ago. It has nothing to do with you."

"Somebody doesn't want me to know about it. Or tell anybody about it."

"Who?"

I could not tell him John's suspicion. "That's the question, isn't it?"

He put the letter down on his lap. "This all happened—before you were born."

I asked, "Did Adam II's letter—the one I gave you—did it maybe make you feel he might not have been killed if you had been there?"

"Of course. But that is a foolish way of thinking. We can't rewrite the past. What happened, happened."

He had answered the question I had not actually asked. "But you think he was killed."

"It is hard to avoid that conclusion."

"What happened?"

"Adam got word to Washington and to the UN that Guedder and his son were planning to use heavy explosives on the

Antarctic continent to try to see what was beneath the ice cap. Once the plans were made public, it was possible to stop them."

"And so they killed Adam?"

"We do not know."

"It would stop him from spying on them, finding out what their other plans were, wouldn't it?"

"It is possible."

"How much does Aunt Serena know?"

"She knows what there is to know. Those of us who loved Adam wanted him avenged, but there were no facts, nothing to go on. Madam said that some judgments are best left to God. And that is where this should be left. It was long ago. It has nothing to do with you. Nothing."

"What about those cards in my locker?"

"They must be part of some practical joke."

"Why?"

"There's no other explanation."

"I wrote Adam about them," I said. "And about Adam II's journal and letters."

He looked troubled. "Perhaps it would have been better if . . ." His voice trailed off.

"Cookie—if somebody pushed me—"

"There's no reason. No reason you should be a threat to anybody."

"But if they're planning something new—"

"It still has nothing to do with you."

"I could tell people."

"It's far-fetched."

"Is it?"

"Did you show this letter to anybody?"

"John. He didn't say anything. He promised. John keeps his promises."

Cook handed me back the cards and the letter. "Don't show these to anybody."

"Of course not."

"We'll be out of Vespugia tomorrow. By late afternoon you'll be on the *Argosy*, and you'll be safe there, no matter what this is about."

"You do think it's about something?"

"I don't know." His voice was low.

I put everything in my backpack. I had not told Cook about the tiny piece of Scotch tape I'd put on my suitcase zipper which had vanished. But that could well have been my imagination. The Scotch tape could easily have dropped off by itself in that steamy weather.

But. But. I turned to him. "Esteban did want Adam's letter. And what about Adam's weird postcards? They were warnings, weren't they?"

"It would seem so. I'll be glad when we're on the ship. I want you out of this, whatever it is."

I reached for his hand again, and he clasped his fingers around mine, reassuringly.

But he was worried. He took what I said seriously. As Adam had written, there was something rotten in the state of Denmark, something miching mallecho, but I had no idea what.

We landed bumpily but safely. In the bus on the drive to the hotel we were told to put our bags outside our doors when we went to bed, and we'd see them again when we boarded the *Argosy*.

I took a swim to cool off before dinner. There were only a couple of other people in the pool, so I swam laps, not pushing, just swimming back and forth, back and forth, enjoying the water. I used to think that the farther south anyone traveled, the hotter it would be, but I forgot that once you crossed the equator and headed down, you'd be aiming for the South Pole. Antarctica is the southernmost part of the planet. Bitter cold.

My rather chaotic thoughts were broken by the sensation that someone was swimming beside me.

Esteban.

He beamed at me. His hair was wet and slicked back, showing the modeling of his face, which reminded me of pictures of Greek statues. Obviously, Esteban wasn't Greek; he was descended from the Welsh colonists. Still, there was something classical about his looks, and his eyes were bluer than the sky.

"Vickee?"

I stopped my stroke and dog-paddled until he came up to me. He frowned, as though troubled, and said, "Ad-am?"

"What about Adam?" I looked at him questioningly.

He frowned again, frustrated by our inability to communicate. "Ad-am *amigo?*"

Amigo. That means friend. I nodded vigorously. "Good friend. Good *amigo*."

We were face-to-face, paddling in the warm water. "Adam *amigo*—Guedder *amigo*—Guedder—" He said something that sounded like "virtue," and "honor," but I didn't quite get the words, and I didn't know much about Guedder, one way or another, though my conditioned reflexes make me suspicious of dictators.

He spoke again, and I caught "Vespugia" and "Guedder," and I think he was praising the General. I nodded, vaguely. Conversation between Esteban and me could not get very far. Then I looked around and Siri was standing at the side of the pool, wearing a sundress and sandals. "Will you and Esteban join me for a Coke?"

Coke is evidently an international word. "*Sí, sí*." Esteban beamed.

"Sure," I called. "Love to." I was thirsty from the heat, and it was hard not to be able to turn on the tap in our room and drink the water.

As we turned to swim to the shallow end of the pool, Esteban stopped me, looking at me with an expression of distress. Spoke. I was sure it was some kind of apology. For what had happened on the pyramid? Did Esteban, or Captain Nausinio, know that the letter I was reading was from Adam? Even if they did, why would they want it? As Cook had said, Adam II's death was long ago. There was no connection between the two Adams.

We climbed out and joined Siri at an umbrellaed table. Esteban got me a towel. Our Cokes were brought. Conversation was pretty much zilch; Siri spoke a few words of Spanish, but she certainly wasn't fluent. Esteban wanted to talk, but though he waved his hands a lot, I had no idea what he was trying to say, and neither did Siri. We all laughed, and it was pleasant to sit there and let the light breeze dry us off.

Sam came and joined us, and I thought he might be able to translate for us, but suddenly Esteban stopped and swiveled to look at Captain Nausinio, obviously come to get him. Esteban stood up, smiled at me, then at Siri and Sam, saying, *"Muchas gracias,"* and other words that sounded like even more enthusiastic thank yous, and left.

Sam grinned at me. "I think that kid is smitten with you, Vicky."

Siri smiled. "He's a nice young man. Too bad to take him away from his musical studies. He's really good, and two years of military service at this time in his life is a lot." She emptied her glass and set it on the table.

Sam said, "Jorge was talking to me about him. He's evidently a cousin of Guedder's, and the General doesn't want to show any favoritism, but they're not letting Esteban do anything which would hurt his hands. Vespugia would be happy to brag about a world-class oboist."

Siri stretched luxuriously. "I'm hungry. We didn't have much of a lunch."

I was hungry, too. After all, I'd given half my lunch to Esteban.

Siri, Sam, Cook, and I ate together. Dick and Angelique had gone to a restaurant high up in the mountains where they were told the view was magnificent. Cook remarked, "The view may be worth it, but the food is mediocre. The best chef in San Sebastián is right here."

While I was eating carrot-and-ginger soup, I thought I heard my name and turned to see who was at the next table. To my surprise, it was Jorge Maldonado with two other men.

One had brown hair turning grey, and was dressed like a cowboy, in tight jeans and tooled-leather boots with high heels. The other was young, maybe even as young as my brother John, and absolutely spectacular. He had hair pale as wheat, and skin which was tanned to gold, and he had golden or maybe amber eyes, somewhat the same color as Aunt Serena's, but hers were firelight and his were sunlight. He wore brown corduroy pants and a bottle-green silk shirt, open in front just enough to show the brightly curling hair on his chest. Sexy, but not overdone.

I guess I was staring pretty obviously, because Jorge looked right at me, gave me a big smile, rose, and came over to our table. "I hope you enjoyed your time at our pyramids?"

"Fascinating," Siri said.

"And still a mystery," Sam added.

I had thought Jorge was going to stay with his family. Evidently Cook had, too, because he said, "It's a surprise to see you, Jorge."

"The trip from my ranch to San Sebastián is dependent on the plane schedule. I took the last plane from the pyramids. We'll be leaving for the *Argosy* early tomorrow. It was too brief a visit at home, but better than nothing. So now I am enjoying a meal with two of our fellow passengers."

The two men stood up, bowing. "Prince Otto Zlatovitcx," Jorge introduced, "and Mr. Jack Nessinger."

Prince Otto had to be the golden one. The man in the cowboy clothes took my hand and shook it heartily. "Jack Nessinger, Miss Vicky Austin. How fine to know that you will be with us on the *Argosy*. We seldom have anyone so young and lovely." He spoke with a Texas drawl, which I suppose explained his outfit.

The golden young man took my hand, but instead of shaking it, he kissed it. "I am enchanted," he murmured. "I look forward to many pleasant times together." He had a crisp English accent.

Jorge said, "Prince Otto was educated in England. I'm sure you two young people will find pleasure in each other's company."

"Thank you," I murmured. "I'm sure we will." I think even Suzy would have been dazzled. She'd certainly have fallen for his looks, if not his title. But, unlike me, she'd have known exactly what to say. Or what not to say. I looked at my hand where Prince Otto had kissed it, then dropped it. Just as I'd forgotten that there was still a world where people had chauffeurs and cooks, I'd forgotten that there were still places with princes.

Prince Otto said, "I arrived only an hour ago from Zlatovica. It took four planes and two days and I am in jet lag. A couple of good nights' sleep and I will be ready to enjoy myself and"——he smiled at me——"you."

Otto and Esteban were both strikingly handsome. Adam was not. Adam's looks were perfectly okay on the outside, but it was his inside looks which got to me. Adam's dazzle was inner, not outer.

Jorge smiled at us. "I hope you have had an enjoyable time in my country."

Cook replied in his most courteous voice, "Vespugia is beautiful and full of interesting history."

"Did you see our museum, and the Inquisition wing?"

"It is very well done," Cook said.

"And quite horrible," Siri added. "Missionaries did no good service to either South America or religion."

Again, I wondered how Cook felt about this.

Sam said, "I heard about a Sunday school class where the kids were asked who the pagans were, and one child put up a hand and said, 'The pagans are the people who don't quarrel about God.'"

We all laughed then, and Jorge, Prince Otto, and Jack returned to their table. Sam saw me watching Prince Otto as he pulled out his chair and sat down. I couldn't help staring. To cover my embarrassment, I asked, "How did he get that suntan in January?"

Sam said, "Zlatovica, his little principality, is well known for its ski slopes. It's mountainous country and quite magnificently beautiful. I used to ski there quite often."

"Is it still a principality?" Siri asked.

"Again," Sam said. "When it was under the Soviet umbrella the prince, Otto's father, managed to go underground. Once the Soviets realized he wasn't going to give in to torture and become one of their puppets, they'd have got rid of him, if he hadn't managed to escape. His wife was killed, but somehow he got Otto off to England, and nobody knows where he was hiding. Now he's back in power, and an able ruler, and determined to make Zlatovica a viable small nation."

Cook asked, "Is he as democratic as he seems?"

Sam said, "He uses very good P.R. Basically, we don't know much about him, and he wants it that way."

"How old is Prince Otto?" I asked.

Sam raised his bushy white eyebrows, "Oh, late teens or early twenties, I think. This fish is superb. I wonder if it comes from one of the local lakes?"

"I enjoy fishing," Cook said, "largely because it is such a quiet pleasure."

I glanced at the other table, where Otto was leaning back, looking weary, his long legs stretched out. Had I really heard Jorge say my name before he introduced Prince Otto and Jack Nessinger to us?

We went to our rooms right after dinner. While I was brushing my teeth, using my own spit and not tap water, I heard Siri stroking the strings of her harp.

"Are you going to play?" I asked hopefully as I came back in.

"Just checking the strings. They don't like this heat. Is something on your mind?"

Was I that obvious? "When I was swimming, just before we had Cokes with you, Esteban was trying to ask me something about Adam."

"Who's Adam?" Siri looked at me questioningly.

"Oh, I'm sorry. Adam Eddington's a friend I'm looking forward to seeing when we get to LeNoir Station. Adam, my friend, is an intern there, and last month when he was in Vespugia, Esteban was his guide."

Siri kept plucking one of her strings, tuning it. "Does Adam speak Spanish?"

"Yes, though he said in his letter that he found the Vespugian accent a little difficult."

136

"Well, then"—Siri started on another string—"they could probably communicate a lot more easily than you and Esteban and I."

"True. But something about Adam seemed to bother Esteban."

"Oh?" Siri swept her fingers across the strings in a minor arpeggio.

I sat on the edge of my bed and watched her fingers moving gently on the strings. Finally I asked, "Did you see Esteban on the pyramid?"

She looked at me over the harp. "No. I was on the other side. But Sam told me you nearly fell. He seemed very concerned."

"Esteban kept me from falling."

Siri put her harp in its case. "Thank heavens. I didn't like the pyramids. Too hot, too many mosquitoes. And where there's been a long history of violence there's usually a residue in the atmosphere. I'm glad we're leaving here tomorrow and heading for Antarctica. Did you remember to put your bags out the door?"

I nodded. "Siri, you've been in Vespugia before?"

She got into bed. "Once, as part of a trip to the Galápagos. Guedder the younger had just taken over and there were soldiers everywhere, far more than now. It's a beautiful country, but—" She shoved down her blanket.

"But what?"

"I don't like police states. We had to show our passports everywhere and our group leader warned us never to let them

137

out of our hands. People who knew Vespugia before the coup were horrified. They said it had been peaceful and pleasant, and now it was totally changed."

"Why would Guedder want to change it? Wouldn't that be bad for tourism?"

She shrugged. "Vespugia is a small country, hot in summer, bitter cold in winter, and over the centuries its borders have been nibbled by Argentina and Chile. Vespugia has only one port city left, and Guedder wants to get back the slice of land Argentina took nearly a century ago."

"Do you think he might go to war for it? Like the Argentineans with the Falklands?"

"I doubt it. Proclaiming world peace and dismantling nuclear stockpiles is very popular right now, and I think he's smart enough not to start something he couldn't finish."

"The Argentineans did. They didn't get the Falklands."

"I'm sure Guedder remembers that. But he took over his own country with a bloody coup, and dictators tend to be fearful despite their fierce fronts. Guedder scares me. I think he has a case of missile envy. Enough. What I'm really interested in is music, and I'd love to hear Esteban play his oboe again. But we're off to the *Argosy* in the morning."

"Esteban seems to think Guedder is terrific."

"Maybe to the Vespugians he is. Who knows? I like Esteban. Sleep well."

"You, too."

In the morning we had a five o'clock call, and by six-thirty we were heading for Santiago. It was only an hour's flight. We were given seat assignments before we boarded, and I sat next to Jack Nessinger. He was in the oil business, though, he said, things were pretty tough right now.

"Is Prince Otto in the oil business, too?"

"He's from Zlatovica, and after tourism, which helps give them the hard currency they desperately need, oil is their only hope. Otto's father is working hard for peace, but it's an uphill road."

"Have you known Otto long?"

"I met the kid only last night, but Zlatovica's been in the news fairly often since the Soviet Union's dissolution."

I felt very ignorant. I know all that part of the world has been overturned, but there's been so much change I haven't been able to keep up with it, and I haven't tried very hard to keep up. Suzy's right about my political illiteracy. I may know enough about *Hamlet* to recognize 'miching mallecho,' but Suzy's not the only one to think that a passion for English literature leaves me a little one-sided.

Suddenly my ears felt plugged up and uncomfortable, and Jack Nessinger said, "We're starting the descent. Good. We're on our way to the *Argosy*. I'm really looking forward to some R and R."

In Santiago we changed to a Chilean plane for Punta Arenas. Someone remarked that at least it would be cooler there, not cold yet, maybe fifty degrees.

On this plane I sat between Cook and Siri. The flight attendants had beautiful long black braids, so it wasn't just Vespugian women who wore their hair like that. I thought fleetingly about letting my hair grow. But it's just ordinary brown hair and I like being able to wash it and towel it dry and not have to worry about it.

We landed in another crowded, noisy airport, and had to go through long passport lines. Again we were told not to worry about our bags, that they'd be delivered to our cabins. There were two buses waiting to take us to the *Argosy*.

We climbed in and sat where we could. I headed for a window, and to my surprise Prince Otto sat down beside me and Cook took the window seat behind. Otto was carrying a large leather camera case.

"Not mine," he said. "Jorge Maldonado's. Mere princes cannot afford this kind of state-of-the-art equipment. Are you excited about getting on the *Argosy*?"

"Very. Are you?"

"Equally very. You have done a lot of traveling?"

"This is my first time outside North America. A couple of years ago we took a tent camping trip all across the continent."

"My father and I sometimes play a game about guessing where people come from by their speech. Of course I know you are American. Not from the Southern states. Or the Midwest. I'll guess New England. Am I right?"

"You are!"

"Jorge says you are traveling with Cookie, and he has me baffled. English but not quite English. Not Australia or New Zealand. Not South Africa. Where? Tell me," he wheedled.

"The Falklands. Our first stop on the *Argosy*."

"Somehow when I visualize the Falklands I see sheep and ancient shepherds in sheepskin coats."

"Penguins, too," I reminded him.

"Penguins, too. Where you live, are there sheep?"

"A few. It used to be dairy-farm country, but the small farmers are having a hard time."

"Your father farms?"

"No, he's a doctor. But we live in what used to be a farmhouse, and for our country it's old, over two hundred years."

"Would you like to see where I live? Part of it was built in the ninth century."

"Sure, I'd love to."

He pulled out his wallet and opened it to a snapshot encased in plastic. It was a picture of a castle, with turrets and what looked like a moat, high up on a mountain. Behind it was an even higher snowcapped mountain.

Otto made a face. "In the winter we freeze. There is no way to put in central heating or modern plumbing. I would much prefer a nice, cozy little cottage."

"It's right out of a fairy tale!"

"There are no fairies or gnomes or goblins to keep us warm on a cold winter morning when the coffee has started to freeze before it even gets to the table." He grinned at me. "But really, I love it. It has been my home and that of my family for hundreds of years. We even managed to survive being swallowed by the Soviets." He gave a harsh, unhappy laugh. "We are so small that they scarcely noticed what they had swallowed, and now we have been regurgitated." Then he pointed out the window. "Look, Vicky, at those wild purple lupines. They are the largest I have ever seen."

"Gorgeous."

"The economy here is not good. See these little houses—it

141

looks as though the wind would blow right through them in bad weather." He yawned, holding his hand up to his mouth. "I needed several hours more sleep this morning. On the *Argosy* I plan to catch up."

"Prince Otto," I started, but he cut me off. "No, no, please call me Otto. Now look at that lush bougainvillea on that wall. And already we are cooler. It never gets hot in Zlatovica the way it does in Vespugia. Look! I think we're nearly there."

I got my backpack out from under my feet and pulled out a warm sweatshirt. Otto was wearing a beautiful rust-colored pullover that must have been hand-knit.

He said, "All my heavy stuff was sent from Zlatovica directly to the dock. Forgive me, Vicky, if I dash out and check everything to see that it's all here."

The bus pulled up at the dock and as I looked at the waiting *Argosy* it didn't seem much bigger than the ferry we used to take to the Island, but of course it was completely different. Our bags were being taken from carts and piled up on the dock, and I was relieved to recognize mine in one of the piles. Otto was running up and down, checking his luggage, which included wooden boxes as well as a couple of small trunks. He turned to Jorge for help in communicating with the dock-hands, and the men, sweaty from heaving luggage, nodded and called over a couple of extra men to help them with the boxes.

We went up the gangplank onto the main deck, where we waited for our cabin keys. I heard one of the *Argosy* people calling out that the wooden boxes were to go to Prince Otto's suite, and should be handled with care.

While I was waiting for my key, Otto came over to me. "I hope you have a pleasant cabin, Vicky. I'll see you later."

Finally the line at the desk dwindled and it was my turn, and a smiling, uniformed man handed me a key. "This is for your cabin, Miss Austin, and you'll find some information and a few other things there. Welcome."

I had the marvelous luxury of a cabin to myself, thanks to Aunt Serena's generous planning. I had enjoyed sharing the hotel room with Siri. It was sort of what I imagined boarding school would be like, and Siri and I had become really good friends in a very short time. But on the *Argosy* I was grateful for my own cabin, and that Cook and Sam were next door. When Cook left, Sam would have that cabin to himself. The cabins, with the exception of the suite, which Otto was in, were all identical, and not that big even for one person. There were two narrow bunks with a small chest of drawers between them, two very narrow closets, and a tiny bathroom with barely room for toilet, washbasin, and shower.

On one of my bunks was a bright red parka, which my packet of information had mentioned; all the passengers would be issued parkas, which would make us easy to identify. I used one of the drawers for my notebooks and other books, which I couldn't have done if I'd had a roommate. I knew that the water would be rough, especially in the Drake Passage, and that it wasn't a good idea to leave anything loose when the ship was rolling. We had just time to unpack and settle in before we sailed, after which the whole group was to meet in the lounge, one deck up, the same deck where we'd been given our keys.

The ship's whistle blew, and I could hear the throbbing of engines, so I rushed up and out on deck. Everybody else had the same idea, but Cook was looking for me, so I hurried over to him. He turned away from the crowd of people at the rail, with their cameras and camcorders, taking pictures as the ship slowly eased away from the dock.

"Come," he said. "I'll show you a better place." I followed him back into the ship, through the lounge, and out a door to a deck where there were only a few other people. "The fo'c'sle," Cook said. "My favorite place. The moment before we sail is always exciting. I never get jaded."

Otto was there before us, and beckoned us to come stand by him at the rail. He put his hand briefly on my arm and smiled at me. "Every minute, I find I am more and more looking forward to this trip."

The door to the lounge opened and Sam came out, followed by Jorge with his enormous Hasselblad.

When the *Argosy* was clear of the shore and heading out to sea, an electronic bell rang, ding-dong (and ding-dong was what we quickly learned to call it), and a loudspeaker summoned us into the lounge. A lot of people were already at the tables, and Cook and I found seats with Angelique and Dick.

I saw Otto being beckoned to join a group of men at a table near ours, with Jorge Maldonado and Jack Nessinger. They were not speaking English, and I wasn't sure what language it was. Dick remarked at the large group of foreigners on this trip, and that they were a rich mix, from Argentina to Zlatovica. A to Z.

"A real United Nations," Sam said, coming over to us and

pulling up a chair, which could move only a short distance because it was attached to the floor by a chain so that in rough weather the furniture would not crash about the cabin. "Many Europeans still smoke," Sam said, "and we're going to be divided into smokers and nonsmokers here and in the dining room. Okay if I sit with you as long as I don't light my cigar?"

Dick laughed. "Feel free."

Angelique said, "We're delighted to have you with us."

Cook ordered a Coke for me and joined the others in a glass of wine. I looked around the room, which had shelves stuffed with books on one side and a bar on the other—port and starboard sides, I guess. In the middle of the fore wall was the door that led to the fo'c'sle. Ropes were strung across the ceiling for holding on to when the sea was rough.

At Otto's table several men, including Otto, lit cigarettes, and one of the crew came up and I could hear him saying that this was the nonsmoking section. "Of course," Otto said, "sorry," and stubbed out his cigarette. He was very nice about it, and so was Jorge, who was explaining to a couple of men who didn't speak English. One of the men scowled and said something that sounded cross, and Jorge spoke to him, smiling, and they all began to laugh. For some reason they gave me an odd feeling, maybe because I couldn't understand what they were saying. I thought of Suzy's joke: "Just because I'm paranoid doesn't mean I'm not being followed."

I was on the *Argosy*. No reason to be paranoid, or to let my imagination go on running away with me. I was out of Vespugia. I turned my attention back to my table and my Coke and a dish of nuts, and listened to what was going on.

A youngish man in blue jeans and a bright red sweater came in and introduced himself as Quimby Forrest, known as Quim, and welcomed us. He was, he explained, more or less the master of ceremonies, and he would be outlining our schedule for us each day. He introduced us to the captain, who greeted us and then left to go back to the bridge. The four lecturers came up, one by one. First, Benjy, the penguin specialist. I looked at him with interest, because he'd be looking out for me after Cook left at Port Stanley. He had sun-bleached hair and a rough, ruddy complexion, as though he was out in the wind and sun a lot, and eyes that were bright chinks of green. Then came Gary, the paleontologist, tall and thin, with glasses with thick horn-rims. Todd, whose area was mammals, with an emphasis on whales, was next. He was short and stocky; and he was followed by Jason, the geologist, who was well over six feet tall, big-boned, with dark brown hair and big brown eyes. They all seemed knowledgeable and easy and ready to like all of us passengers. I immediately liked them, and recited their names to myself: Benjy, Gary, Todd, Jason.

When the introductions were over, Benjy came to our table and sat by Cook, putting an arm affectionately around his shoulder. The two of them were obviously good friends.

Quimby explained that when we got back to our cabins after dinner we'd find a schedule for the next day, but schedules wouldn't be available ahead of time, because the decision of what to do wouldn't be made until he and the captain had considered the weather and then decided what would be the most interesting places for us to go. And we were reminded that this was a research boat rather than a cruise ship, and that would affect our itinerary.

Quimby told us a little about efforts to make Antarctica a completely international community, designated as a demilitarized zone. "What we really hope for is a planetary international preserve."

"Is such a thing possible?" Dick asked.

"Don't be a pessimist," Angelique remarked, as though this was a regular refrain.

"Now," Quimby said, "let me explain your manifest numbers. You've probably noticed the big board just outside the lounge, here on the main deck, full of small yellow chips with your numbers on them. For all our shore excursions, you'll turn your numbered chip from the yellow side to the red, and when you get back on the *Argosy*, from the red side to the yellow. That way we always know who's left the ship, and we'll know whether or not everybody has returned. Okay?"

Otto leaned over from his table and said to me, "That is a wise precaution. It is good to know everybody's safe."

Dinner was in a large dining room with open seating. There were wide windows on both sides of the ship, so there'd be beautiful views of wherever we were sailing. Cook held my arm as we went in, so we wouldn't get separated. Sam was right: as I looked around, he was the oldest and I was the youngest passenger.

Siri and her roommate, whose name was Greta, were at our table. Greta was from Germany and spoke excellent, if heavily accented, English.

"Siri and I have much in common," she said, "both of us

147

being university professors. But I am tone deaf, alas, and cannot share her love for music."

Although it was eight in the evening, we were eating in daylight, with the sun slanting across the water. As we moved south, the days would get longer and the nights shorter, until we reached the Antarctic continent, where there would be hardly any dark at all.

By the time we went to bed, we were still far enough north so that we were moving through a long twilight into night, and the curtains were drawn across my porthole. I took a shower and got into my bunk. I was still tired from jet lag and all the travel, though my jet lag must have been nothing compared to Otto's. The boat was rocking slightly, like a great cradle. We were on the *Argosy* and Cook had relaxed. I went right to sleep.

I woke up feeling refreshed and ready for the day. At ten o'clock we had a boat drill, followed by a lecture from Benjy. All four of our lecturers really knew their stuff and had spent months at a time in Antarctica, living in tents or huts. Benjy had been there during the Antarctic winter, when it is always night and the cold is bitter and without relief. But he waxed absolutely lyrical, saying that his wife had decided he must have a mistress in Antarctica, he went so often. So he took her with him for one trip, and she understood that the land itself was the mistress.

He showed us slides of emperor penguins and their adorable chicks, and then slides of Adélie penguins, named for someone's wife. "Yes, they have feathers," he answered, and I heard the echo of Aunt Serena's voice: "If it has feathers, it's a bird. Anything with feathers, no matter what it looks like, and whether it can fly or not, is a bird."

I took notes, thinking that Suzy would have loved such items of information as that Adélie penguins have seventy feathers per square inch. That's a lot of feathers, but the penguins need them both in the water and for belly-flop landings when they ride the waves into shore.

Lunch was a buffet of all kinds of salads, cheese, breads, fruits. I sat with Cook and Sam, and three older women from Alaska. Otto was on the other side of the dining room with the smokers.

"Is Benjy's wife with him on this trip?" Sam asked.

Leilia, the eldest of the three Alaskans, shook her head. "She died a couple of years ago. He'd have wasted away with grief if it hadn't been for his penguins. He's raised a lot of chicks from secondary eggs or eggs which were hatched too late for the fledglings to survive in the wild, and taking care of the eggs and the chicks is what's kept him going."

One of the other women nodded. "If you want to feel loved, all you need is a baby penguin. They are the cuddliest creatures imaginable."

"What's a secondary egg?" Sam asked.

Leilia explained. "Penguins lay two eggs, a large one and then a much smaller one, in case something happens to the primary egg."

"You seem to know a lot about penguins," Sam remarked.

"We"—Leilia looked at her companions—"worked with Benjy for a few weeks the year his wife died. He's a fine scientist and one of the nicest guys you'll ever meet. This is my third trip on the *Argosy*. I teach science in the high school in Fairbanks. We're all teachers."

Leilia's two companions nodded. They were nice women, with sort of weathered faces, not ruddy like Benjy's, but crinkly and creasy with lots of smile lines. All three had frizzy permanents, as though they'd given them to each other and not bothered much about them because their minds were on other, more important things. They looked comfortable and competent and as though they'd be good teachers who'd know what to do in a crisis.

After lunch I curled up on my bunk to write in my journal and fell asleep. I think most people took naps. When I woke up, the postcard Esteban had given me had slid out of my journal onto the floor, and I picked it up. At least I wasn't likely to see either the pyramids or Esteban again, though he had really seemed nice, despite everything. Or maybe because of everything. Smitten with me, Sam had said, and he'd added later, "Don't worry about Esteban, Vicky. Just remember that Vespugia is at present a fascist country and be grateful that you live in a democracy." I was. And grateful that we'd left Vespugia and were on the *Argosy*.

At three we had another lecture, about whales and seals and other mammals. Todd, the mammal specialist, told us that the lecture room was familiarly known as the Womb Room, because it was low-ceilinged and warm, and darkened so that slides could be shown, and no matter how good the lecture was, people tended to fall asleep. He was right. I heard a couple of snores, even though Todd was fascinating, and not only about mammals. He talked about how important

150

it was to declare Antarctica a global park. It's the fifth-largest continent on the planet, much bigger than the U.S., and it's the last totally free continent on earth, and Todd was passionate about having it stay that way. His controlled intensity over what he cared about reminded me of Adam.

He talked about the pack ice, which can freeze far beyond the tip of the Antarctic peninsula and out into the Drake Passage. When the Southern Ocean freezes, it's a major planetary event. "The patterns of ocean circulation change," he told us, "and affect the earth's climate by shifting the direction of the atmospheric convection currents. If the planet's weather warms too much, we won't have the sixteen million square kilometers of pack ice we have now. That's one-third of the continent which freezes and thaws every year."

Someone asked, "Have you ever been here when the pack ice freezes?"

"Oh, sure. And it freezes audibly, with crackles and snaps." Yes, I'd heard the ice in the brook at home freeze with a sound like a shot.

Someone else asked, "Do you know people from different national research stations?"

"Oh, yeah. We Antarctic freaks of numerous nationalities all get along pretty well together. We go to each other's parties, visit each other's stations, rescue each other in time of need. But our various countries bicker with very green eyes. See this map of Argentina?" The projector flashed a slide onto the screen, and he pointed with his wand. "See? It includes the Antarctic." Click. "Chile. It includes the same prime piece of the Antarctic peninsula. Vespugia. The same. The British

151

claim a lot of it, too. I wish governments didn't think they have a right to own parts of the planet."

A hand went up. "But hey, Todd, what about the U.S.? Don't we want our share?"

"Sure, but we don't include it on our maps, and we're willing to let the work that goes on at the stations be internationally monitored. The more enlightened leaders in most countries remember that the planet is home to all of us, and if we don't take care of it, we'll be in trouble. Big trouble."

Angelique said, "My mother used to say that if we abuse the planet overmuch she will turn on us."

Todd agreed. "Your mother's right. The planet has been sending us multiple messages, and the powers that be have ignored them. So it's up to us, and my guess is that when you finish this trip you'll feel as protective of this amazing land as I do."

Then he explained how the great ice fields of the enormous continent reflect sunlight up into space, and that this is what keeps the planet from overheating. "If the ice fields should melt, the whole planet might turn into a tropical jungle, so hot that most life would turn to death. Or, conversely, it could start another ice age."

Someone asked, "Is that likely?"

"I wish it weren't. I'm not crying doom"——he shook his head——"but I want you to love Antarctica, this remote continent, strange as one of the outer planets, as inhospitable as Mars. Only a little over two percent of the land is ice-free, and that for only the few weeks of summer. Of all the continents, it's the coldest, the highest, and the driest——which may seem contradictory, since it contains so much of the earth's water. But it's true, the interior is as dry as the Sahara. No snow has fallen there for a million years."

To my surprise, because I found all of this totally interesting and was trying to get it down in my notes, my eyelids began to droop and I jerked my head up as I started to fall asleep.

Six

*T*he light was so brilliant, sun sparkling off water, off ice, that my eyes were dazzled and I began to see black spots, and when I tried to blink them away, I saw what looked like snow on a bad TV set. It was a while before I realized that something black on the horizon was really there.

It was moving, it was coming closer to me and my iceberg.

Was it a whale?

What if it bumped into the iceberg?

Whales don't bump into icebergs. They use echolocation, the way dolphins do.

It wasn't a whale. It was a Zodiac. I thought I could see red, the red of our parkas.

I began jumping up and down and yelling.

I took off my parka and waved it like a flag and shouted at the top of my lungs, "I'm here! Here! Help! Come get me! Please come get me!"

I thought the Zodiac was coming nearer. I kept on shouting,
"Help! Help! Come get me!"

Then the Zodiac veered, as though whoever was running it saw
something, and it headed toward a very large iceberg on the horizon,
far away.

It was going away from me.

Nobody saw me. Nobody heard me.

I sank down on the ice in despair. Cold ate into me.

I pulled myself together, scrambled to my feet, put on my parka.
Even if the Zodiac hadn't seen me, even if it was now disappearing
over the horizon, it meant that there were people looking for me. My
manifest number was still turned to the red side, so Quim and the oth-
ers knew I wasn't on the Argosy. They were looking for me. When they
got to the iceberg they were heading toward and didn't find me, they'd
turn around and come back.

Please come back!

Please!

The next day we anchored off New Island, one of the Falklands. We were up early. Breakfast was at six-thirty. While I
was waiting for my oatmeal, I said to Cook, "Just a little while
and you'll be leaving."

"You'll be fine here. I can leave comfortably, knowing that
you're on the *Argosy*, and Benjy will take good care of you."
He held out his coffee cup for a refill.

"Did you tell Benjy anything about what happened in
Vespugia?"

"There really isn't that much to tell." Cook poured milk

155

in his coffee. "I've told him what little there is, and it's behind us, thank goodness."

I added a big spoonful of raisins to my oatmeal. "I'm looking forward to meeting Seth when we get to Port Stanley, and I hope he's going to want to meet me."

"I hope so, too," Cook said. "He was terribly mangled by the seal, and he's been more than a little eccentric ever since, not wanting to mix much with people. He sings well, and oddly enough he enjoys performing, and he's made quite a reputation with his songs. He's worked hard at the little museum in Port Stanley, which we'll probably have a chance to visit, but he often takes off whenever a ship docks in town."

"Even if he knows you're on it?" I asked.

"Even then. Seth is really very erratic. Sometimes he dresses like a penguin. He's my brother and I love him, but I feel I have to prepare you for how odd he is."

The Alaskans joined us then, and we started talking about the rockhopper penguins we'd be seeing that morning.

After breakfast we lined up to get in the Zodiacs, all of us bundled in our red parkas, with rubber pants over our jeans. There were double doors leading out to a metal ladder going down to a small landing platform where a Zodiac was bobbing up and down. When it came my turn, I jumped down into the Zodiac and sat on the black rubber side.

The Zodiac's outboard motor started and off we went. I looked around at the other passengers. We were all wearing small life preservers over our parkas, much smaller than the bulky ones we'd worn for the boat drill, thank heavens. These orange oblong donuts would inflate if they were in the water, and I hoped we'd never have to test them. I was going to be in a Zodiac at least once a day, and usually twice. I'd better get used to carrying around all that heavy equipment.

The captain himself ran our Zodiac, pulling us to shore with a flourish and a scrape of rubber against pebbles. We swung our legs over the inflated rubber sides and sloshed ashore, the water almost to the top of our boots. The sun was beating down, and I saw some of the others taking off their life preservers and placing them on the beach, so I did the same. Almost everybody followed this by taking off their red parkas and dropping them down by the orange donuts.

We had a tramp of about a mile across pastures of tussock grass, where we saw sheep wandering, with penguins hopping all around them—and I mean really hopping in the most amazing way. A penguin would be on the ground, and suddenly he'd be what seemed at least six feet up on a rock. Rockhoppers are well named. And they smelled. We smelled and heard them before we saw them. They chittered, squeaking and squawking at each other, at the day, at the sheep. Just being noisy in general.

Benjy had warned us not to go closer to the penguins than fifteen feet, and never under any circumstances to block a baby from its mother, or get between a penguin and its access to the water.

But the penguins hadn't heard that announcement. Otto came up to me, saying, "When we arrived in the Zodiacs, all of us still in our red parkas, I could almost hear the penguins thinking, 'Hm. Big red birds. They don't seem to be a threat. Let's investigate.'"

I laughed with him. "First time I've been mistaken for a

bird." Even with our parkas off, it seemed to me that the penguins still thought of us as another species of bird. Benjy ambled over to us and told us that if we sat down on the ground and kept very still they might even come and peck at our backpacks to see if we had any food in them. At least the penguins here had never been threatened or hurt by human beings.

Siri spread her parka on the rough beach and sat on it, then took her harp, which had been slung over her shoulder with a wide canvas strap, out of its canvas carrier. She began to sweep her fingers over the strings. Then she hummed a little, softly, and finally began to sing. I'd half slept through the words when she sang in our hotel room in San Sebastián, but now I was paying attention.

> *All things by immortal power,*
> *Near or far,*
> *Hiddenly*
> *To each other linked are,*
> *That thou canst not stir a flower*
> *Without troubling of a star.*

Her fingers on the strings reprised the melody. Then she sang the last two lines again.

> *Thou canst not stir a flower*
> *Without troubling of a star.*

As I was drawn closer to Siri and her harp, so were the penguins, and three of them waddled right up to her.

"Hush," Benjy warned as a couple of people began gushing over how cute the penguins were. It wasn't cute. It was wonderful. It was so wonderful that I felt a lift in my heart, a brightening as I responded to the beauty of the song, the penguins, the sky, the gentle air. I wanted the moment to go on forever, and even though I knew it couldn't, while I was in it, it *was* forever.

Benjy kept people back, and finally we all followed him, away from Siri and her music and the penguins. Greta said wistfully, "I wish I had a better ear for music. I think the penguins got more out of Siri's song than I did." She walked on to catch up with Jorge and Jack.

I stayed mostly with Cook and Benjy. Each moment I was coming to like Benjy more and more. I had seen his face while Siri played for the penguins, and it reflected the same joy I felt.

Otto walked along with us until we arrived at a vast colony of rockhoppers with their young. Benjy said they were about five weeks old, grey balls of fluff huddled together in their crèche, so many and so close to each other that I couldn't begin to count them. For the chicks, company was safety; an isolated chick could easily be picked off by a skua.

The weather, Benjy announced, was extraordinary for the Falklands. It was hazily sunny, and the thermometer must have been in the low sixties. Of course, January in the Falklands is summer, but Cook agreed that this was unusual, and all of us were sweating in our winter clothes. Some of the baby penguins had their "hands" stretched out to catch the breeze and cool off. Penguin flippers, like those of dolphins and whales, have the bone structure of an arm and a hand, not

159

a fish's fin. A few of the fluffy little babies were flopped over on their sides as though they were dead, but Benjy assured us they were only resting against the heat. Their metabolism is geared for cold weather.

"Cookie"——Leilia, the Alaskan teacher, looked at him questioningly——"I've been meaning to ask you——when I was in Port Stanley before, there was a man who looks very much like you."

Cook nodded. "He's my brother. I'm here on my biannual visit."

"Fascinating man," Leilia said. "I hope we'll see him when we go to the museum in Port Stanley. He's really put a lot of effort into that place."

On the beach and up on the cliffs there were yellow flowers, which Leilia said were sea cabbages, and the tussock grass grew in coarse clumps and looked as though it had survived heavy winds and salt water. It was indeed an alien landscape, unlike anything I'd ever seen, but it had its own stark beauty.

Otto loped along beside me, chattering, informing. "A lot of this sod can be cut up for peat. It's used a lot for fuel here."

"How do you know so much?" I asked.

"In my country we're seeking alternate forms of energy. But I don't think peat would work for us. Oh, look, Vicky, look!" In the midst of the rockhopper colony was a nesting black-browed albatross. "They have the longest wingspan of any bird in the world. Now, look over here!" And he pointed to two enormous vultures waiting on a promontory, looking sinister.

I shuddered. "I don't like vultures."

"Most carrion eaters aren't pleasant. But here, where it's so dry that nothing biodegrades, they're useful for disposing of garbage."

In the notebook I was keeping for Suzy, I'd jotted down, "Rockhopper penguins," and now I added "albatrosses" and "vultures."

Cook had reminded me to put on sunscreen, and I had on the safari hat he had given me, because the sun was glaring. Otto remarked that a few of the men who had baldish heads and who weren't wearing hats were going to be sorry.

Otto veered off to talk with Jorge. I wandered along, clumping in my heavy boots, thinking of the words Siri had sung.

Benjy had warned us not to bring anything ashore with us, not to leave anything behind, not a tissue, not an empty film box, not a plastic bag, and not to take anything away with us, not even a pebble. He explained the precariousness of the ecology, and that anything we did could upset it. "I'm not sure we should be here at all," he said, "but it is so beautiful that I know none of you will ever be the same again."

If I picked one of the yellow sea cabbages, that casual action might result in trouble to a star millions of light-years away. It isn't just that if you fall off a roof the consequence will likely be a broken leg because we live in a universe where gravity plays an important role, but that all actions have consequences far beyond anything we can imagine.

"Vicky!" I heard my name. "Earth calling Vicky!" And there was Sam, standing next to Cook and laughing.

"Oh. Sorry. I guess I was off in another world."

161

Sam asked, "What was going on in the other world?"

"Consequences," I answered. "Little things like leaving debris here. And maybe big things, bad things, but also good things, like Siri's music."

Sam chomped on his cigar. "The penguins loved her."

"Did they ever!" Benjy came up to us. "I've never thought of experimenting with music with the penguins before. Tomorrow I'm going to take Siri to a crèche and see how the fledglings react to her music."

"She plays well," Otto said.

"And what a gorgeous voice," Benjy added.

Siri had a nice voice, I thought, but not really a gorgeous one. What Benjy was reacting to was the whole experience of Siri and the music and the penguins, and yes, that was gorgeous. And maybe he was reacting to Siri, herself. I walked along between Benjy and Sam. Cook and Leilia were behind us, chatting away. When we got back to the beach and the Zodiacs, Siri had her harp slung on her back again, and was walking with Greta. They seemed to get along very well, despite Greta's musical lacks.

In my head I began to write a poem, sort of inspired by what Siri had sung and remembering what Aunt Serena had said about penguins and intimacy. While we were waiting to get in the Zodiacs, I sat on the beach and scribbled, and waited for the last Zodiac, so I had something more or less finished.

> *High lifts my heart in warmth and cold,*
> *Moonlight and starlight, cloud and sun,*
> *Sea spray and salt and the land's fold,*

Lamb and fledgling, and love begun
In the heart that dares not warm
But cannot chill. Stars! Stay my heart
And keep my borning love from harm,
For love will start, oh, love will start.

When we got back to the *Argosy*, there was a big tub of water
and a brush with a long handle at the top of the metal steps,
and we were to step in the water with our boots on to wash
the guano off. We certainly didn't want to bring that smell
onto the ship. I cleaned my boots, went to my cabin, and took
off all my heavy outdoor garments, and then the bell rang for
lunch and I was starved.

The lunch line on the *Argosy* reminded me of the lunch
line in the cafeteria at school. Jorge and Otto stood near Cook
and me, and Jack Nessinger joined us, and Otto left the smokers' side to sit with us at lunch. Jorge and Jack questioned him
about Zlatovica, and remarked on how it's not much bigger
than Rhode Island.

After lunch, there was a German-language lecture. Ger-
man seemed to be the common language of the European
contingent, though I heard some French, and there were
some other languages I couldn't identify. During the lecture
the rest of us were given a tour of the ship; the others would
be given the tour later. We went to the engine rooms, to the
kitchen, where a very young chef in a high white hat was bak-
ing vast quantities of wonderful-smelling bread; we went up
to the bridge with all its instruments, and I looked through
the depth sounder and the captain pointed out his new sonar

and some other instruments I knew John and Adam would understand but which were too technical for me. We were shown the captain's quarters. The cabin with his bunk was even smaller than our cabins, but he had a large cabin for a living room, where sometimes he entertained dignitaries. There were two wide and long bunks which were piled with pillows to make them couches. There was a round table in the center of the room with a beautiful, hammered-copper top, and a couple of heavy, comfortable chairs.

After the tour I went down to my cabin and described what I had seen, and then copied out the poem in my journal and caught up on the letter I was writing to Aunt Serena. Maybe I'd copy the poem for her, too, when I'd worked on it a little more.

"You didn't prepare me for the guano smell," I told her. "It's a smell, not a stink, because it isn't decaying or putrid, but you certainly don't want to bottle it and bring it home.

"There are some interesting people on the *Argosy*. Cook and I usually sit with Sam and Siri, but we've also got to know Leilia, a teacher from Alaska, and I'd really like to be in her classroom. Then there's Dick, the ship's doctor, and Angelique, his wife. Dick's an orthopedic surgeon who walks with a cane, and Angelique is a librarian and one of the most glamorous women I've ever seen. And I've met a prince who lives in a fairy-tale castle on top of a mountain. The staff is terrific. Quimby is the one who tells us all what to do. Benjy is the penguin expert, Gary is the paleontologist, Todd knows all about whales, and Jason is a geologist. They're all good-looking and couldn't be nicer. I'm learning a lot."

As soon as the German-language lecture was over, we got back in the Zodiacs and set off for Carcass Island. Again we smelled the penguins before we heard them, and heard them before we saw them. When we landed, we had a two-mile walk, each way, over terrain that would have been lots easier in sneakers than in heavy boots. Otto walked with me, and talked about being in boarding school in England and spending holidays with school friends because it wasn't safe for him to go home. It was nice being with him and enjoying the rock-hoppers with the funny tufts on the crests of their heads. The day was like an early April day at home, with a fresh breath of spring, before all the snow has melted. There was no snow here, but Otto said there was often sleet and icy drizzle.

I had time for a shower before we gathered together for Wrap-Up and instructions for the next day. The Alaska teachers were sitting near us, and Leilia told us how much it had meant to them to hear Siri playing for the penguins, and how excited Benjy had been. "I use a lot of music with my kids at school. I try to expose them to as much variety as possible, and to expand their tastes. How about you, Vicky? What kind of music do you like?"

I smiled. "I've got pretty eclectic tastes. My mother vacuums to Beethoven and Brahms, and my sister Suzy and I wash dishes to rock or country. I thought Siri's song was marvelous."

Quimby, beaming, said that we'd be going to Volunteer Beach in the morning, where we'd see Magellanic penguins, gentoo penguins, and probably king penguins. We'd come back to the *Argosy* for lunch, and then in the afternoon we'd dock at Port Stanley, where the governor's wife had invited us for tea, thanks to an elderly lady in the States who was a friend of the governor's mother. Yay, Aunt Serena! Cook and I looked at each other and smiled, and he winked.

And then I would get to meet Cook's brother.

"Penguins aren't all alike!" Otto exclaimed the next morning at Volunteer Beach. The Magellanic penguins there were very different from the rockhoppers. For one thing, they didn't hop. "See," Otto said, "they have holes in the dunes for nests, completely different from the little circles of stones the rockhoppers use."

Benjy said, "Rockhoppers tend to steal each other's stones. Sometimes they get so reckless about it they get picked off by a skua."

Greta was carrying one of Jorge's big camera cases for him. I wondered if Sam would notice that she appeared to be smitten with Jorge. Like some of the other women, she wore full makeup. I heard one woman explaining that it protected her skin.

We climbed up cliff-like dunes. Angelique and Jason helped Dick, who was having a hard time because the dunes were slippery. Cook was with me, and occasionally took my elbow as we walked over green peat and clumps of tussock grass and more yellow sea cabbages to an amazing scene of gentoo penguins among sheep and lambs. Benjy pointed out how to distinguish gentoos from rockhoppers by the flashing of white across their foreheads from eye to eye.

We walked along in shifting groups. Jack Nessinger took

Otto off, pointing out something ahead of us. Jorge and Greta were well behind, and Jorge did not seem to be taking pictures, despite all the equipment he was carrying. The two of them did not keep up with the rest of us, but turned back toward the beach. We plowed on, farther inland, past a lake, and there we saw a colony of king penguins, considerably taller than the rockhoppers or the Magellanics, with a hornlike toot. Benjy called it a bray. He told us that you can tell what penguins have been eating by the color of their guano. "If they've been eating fish, it's white, and if they've been eating krill, it's pink." What we saw was mostly pink. The wind blew the guano smell in our faces. Pink rhymes with stink.

We tramped across rough terrain to a large crèche of baby king penguins, most of whom were making their funny, chirpy, whistling sounds. They certainly didn't look undernourished. Their little bellies were round from all the regurgitated food their parents had fed them, and I watched one mother bending over her fat baby, whose beak was wide open, waiting for food. Not the way I'd want to be fed.

Benjy tapped me on the shoulder, indicating that I should follow him and Siri. We walked away from the others, around to the far side of the crèche, until Benjy stopped. Siri got her harp out of the canvas case and began to play. Nursery rhymes this time, "Jack and Jill," and "Little Bo Peep," and "The Man in the Moon." She had placed herself the recommended fifteen feet from the crèche, but before she had sung for more than a minute, several little ones crowded up to her, and then two of them crawled onto her lap. One of them began pecking at her harp, so she lifted it high above her head, and Benjy took it. Siri kept on singing, and the little chicks cuddled in to her, and she put her arms around them, still singing, and held them close.

Benjy turned away, as though to protect Siri's harp, but I thought I saw tears in his eyes.

Well, it was pretty amazing. And I felt enormously privileged to have been part of it. Otto would really have liked it, I thought, but he was off with Jack Nessinger, and, anyhow, Benjy didn't want a crowd.

He said, "We'd better get going before we're discovered. Quim will be gathering us at the Zodiacs." Gently he lifted the chicks from Siri's lap and put them back in the crèche.

Siri put her harp in its case, and we started back. I walked a little behind, not wanting to butt in, but they included me in the conversation.

Siri laughed, a pure little bubbling of joy. "Benjy, thank you. I don't know when I've had such a glorious time. Now I can't wait to see them in the water."

"People think penguins can't fly because they're such waddlers on land," Benjy said. "But they're made to fly in water, not air. When we get a chance, we'll go off in one of the Zodiacs and maybe you can play for them while they swim. They use their flippers to paddle at amazing speeds, up to fifteen miles an hour. They steer with their feet and their funny little tails, which they also use for balance when they sit. A lot of the penguin's life is at sea, so its sea skills are more important than its land ones. When you've looked at enough of them, you'll understand how they've evolved over the centuries the way they have."

The wind had come up and the water was rough, and Siri cradled her harp rather than slinging it across her back. When we sidled up to the ship, the Zodiacs were going up and down, up and down, so I was glad of sailors waiting by the ladder to help us. Sam had not come ashore; he said he was saving his energy for Port Stanley, and I thought it was just as well. Quim had taught us to reach for the helping sailor's forearm, rather than hand, which would give us more purchase, and when the Zodiac dropped into a trough just as I was leaping from the rubber side to the metal stairs, I needed a strong heave to keep me from falling.

Cook came out of his cabin as I left mine to go to the fo'c'sle. "Had a good time this morning, Vicky?"

"Wonderful."

"Feeling comfortable with Benjy?"

I nodded vigorously. "He's wonderful. Thanks for letting me go off with him and Siri."

"In this case, three was company and four would have been a crowd. I wanted you to get to know Benjy without my hovering presence."

"You don't hover."

"No more than necessary. But I'll be leaving you this afternoon, and I want to make sure you're not worried."

I had almost forgotten my anxieties about those anonymous warnings and Adam's ambiguous ones, though they lurked just under the surface. "I'm okay."

"If anything bothers you, anything at all, go straight to Benjy. He will take whatever you say seriously."

"Thanks."

"Not that I expect any problems, not on the *Argosy*. I just want you to feel secure."

"I'm fine, really."

"Good."

"Yesterday—you heard Siri's song?"

"Beautiful."

"Do you think it's true? Every action has inevitable consequences?"

"I'm not sure about inevitable. Actions do have consequences, and not all of them are bad. Some of them are miraculously good."

I looked at him questioningly. We went out onto the fo'c'sle and stood at the rail.

He said, "I believe in a pattern for the universe, a pattern that affirms meaning, and perhaps especially when things seem meaningless. Everything we do has a part in the weaving of the pattern, even our wrong decisions. But I believe that the beauty of the pattern will not be irrevocably distorted. That is a hope we learn to live with."

I looked out at the water, thinking.

He glanced at me briefly, then back out to sea. "When the pattern is torn, there is a healing power that can mend. Let me make a metaphor. Sometimes our angels come and give us a nudge and we go in a direction we might have missed otherwise, and so we are helped to make a right step, or to avoid doing something which might have terrible consequences. Sometimes we are not able to or choose not to heed the nudge. We are creatures who have been given the terrible gift

170

of free will, and that means we are responsible for our actions and have to suffer the consequences. Without our angels, I believe we would be in a worse state than we are."

I thought of Aunt Serena and Owain both asking angels to watch over me.

I looked at Cook and he smiled. "I believe in angels. I can't give you any proof or any further explanations, because angelic guidance is not to be understood by our finite minds. But I believe in it."

"Okay. Thank you. I get it. Sort of."

"Sort of is good enough."

When we anchored off Port Stanley, the wind had dropped and the weather was calm and beautiful. We lined up to go ashore and Quimby handed out several letters. I had one from my mother. Everybody was fine, and they missed me. She'd have a letter waiting for me when we landed in Puerto Williams. I gave Quimby some cards to mail. I didn't exactly miss my family. I just felt that I'd traveled further away from them than in ordinary space and time.

There was nothing from Adam.

The short trip in the launch was smooth. We were able to wear ordinary walking shoes because this would be a dry landing and we wouldn't have to wade in through the water in our big boots. I wondered if Seth Cook might be at the dock, but no one was there except a couple of sailors to help the older people.

I looked at Cook, who seemed to know what I was thinking. "Don't worry, Vicky. Seth won't come to meet us in a crowd. Wait."

Angelique and Dick walked together, arm in arm. Dick was leaning on his cane, and Angelique carried their parkas; she wore a cream-colored shirt which accentuated her dark skin, as did the thin gold chain. Her beauty fascinated me because it was casual and unflaunting.

I heard her remark on how very British Port Stanley is, with small houses with flower-filled gardens, and many superb lupines, like the ones Otto had pointed out to me in Punta Arenas. I love lupines, and we have them at home, but these were much larger than the ones in our rock garden. One man who was out digging in his front yard stopped to speak to us and said that the weather had been sleety and horrid for weeks, and this lovely weather had just moved in the day before, and everybody was out taking advantage of it. Nothing we heard or saw reminded us that we were at the bottom of the world just above the tip of South America.

We wandered around for half an hour until it was time for our tea at Government House. As we got up to the big white house, I thought it looked pleasant and rambly. A glassed-in conservatory ran the length of it, and we peered through the panes to see absolutely glorious flowers. There were comfortable garden chairs and tables, and Cook remarked that it was very pleasant to sit there when the outside weather was nasty.

The front door was opened by a white-coated butler, and then we were welcomed by the governor's wife, Mrs. Leeds. We left our parkas in a large dressing/bath room; we really didn't need them, but Quimby had told us it was likely to be cold on the trip back to the ship and advised us to bring them along.

We were led into a spacious parlor, even larger than Aunt Serena's. Mrs. Leeds was tall and slender and gracious and was clearly used to hosting gatherings.

We had been divided into two groups, so we wouldn't be overwhelming, and Cook and I were in the first group. We sat in comfortable chairs and Mrs. Leeds told us a little about the island, and about the Falklands war, and how shocking it was for people to wake up one morning and find armed soldiers in the streets telling them they were now Argentinean and had to speak Spanish. I already had a sense of this very English town, and I tried to imagine the Argentinean invasion happening in Thornhill, and being told we weren't Americans anymore. I didn't think any of our neighboring Yankee farmers would take kindly to having to speak a strange language.

"People are just beginning to feel safe again, after all this time," Mrs. Leeds said.

Out of the corner of my eye I saw a uniformed maid in the doorway. She caught Cook's eye and beckoned. He turned to me, and she nodded. "Vicky," he said softly, and I followed him out of the room into the hall.

"Sir, Miss Austin, the governor expects you in the sitting room."

We followed her and saw Otto coming out a door. He looked solemn, if not angry and upset, but when he saw us he broke into a great golden smile. "Vicky! Cookie! Hi! Rusty's expecting you."

He waved, and we went past him into a small, comfortable room, much less formal than the grand parlor. The governor—I knew it must be he, because he had rusty hair

173

and a rusty mustache—rose from a leather chair, holding out his hand. "Greetings, Adam."

For a moment I was startled. Then I remembered that Cook's first name was Adam. The governor took my hand. "And this must be Vicky."

We shook hands, and Cook said, "Good to see you, Rusty." I tried to imagine Mr. Leeds in the musical-comedy uniform in Aunt Serena's album and decided he could get away with it without looking idiotic.

He offered me a chair near the fireplace, where there was something faintly glowing and smelling somehow cozy and comforting. "Peat," Mr. Leeds said. "This is where my wife and I like to sit and read in the evenings. It's really too warm for a fire today, but if we let it go out completely, it's hard to get started again, so I have it banked."

Otto had talked about peat, and I'd read about peat fires in novels set in England or Ireland, but I'd never seen one before. I could picture the Leedses sitting there with books and cups of tea and relaxing together. I wondered what it would be like to govern a small series of islands like the Falklands where a lot of your constituents would be penguins and sheep.

The governor leaned toward me. "Serena Eddington has written about you most glowingly, Vicky. Are you enjoying your travels?"

"Very much indeed, thank you."

"I wish you could stay and visit with us for a few days, but I understand that going on south to the Antarctic is the main point of this trip. There's not a great deal to see, but what there is, is spectacular."

"I'm looking forward to it."

"Pleasant fellow passengers?"

"Very."

"An interesting group," Cook said. "Vicky's already made friends with several of them."

The governor smiled at me. "Why don't you join your fellow passengers for tea? Adam Cook and I have a few things to talk about."

"Okay. Thanks. Very nice to have met you, sir."

I went into the big room just before the last of the cucumber sandwiches vanished, and had a cup of smoky tea, the kind you put milk in. I looked around, but I didn't see Otto. I wondered why he'd been with the governor. Well. If he wanted to tell me, he would.

I heard Mrs. Leeds suggesting that after tea we visit the museum, which was down the street. There was a bus if we didn't feel like walking. Then she said she had a treat for us.

In came the most extraordinary man I'd ever seen. He was very tall and he wore a full-length cape of black-and-white feathers, so that he looked like an enormous penguin. He didn't waddle like a penguin, however, but walked around the room, bowing and smiling, then stood with his back to the fireplace and surveyed us all.

I looked at him. He had a deep white scar slashing across one cheek. Otherwise, the face could have been Cook's. This was Cook's brother, Seth.

"Welcome. My name is Papageno." He smiled and looked directly at me. "Now, then, Vicky, do you know why?"

175

We were all wearing our name pins. Even so, it surprised me. He looked at me.

It's a good thing I have a mother who loves music, and whose favorite opera is *The Magic Flute*. "Papageno's the bird man in Mozart's *Magic Flute*," I said.

Sam said, "Bravo, Vicky," and I blushed.

Papageno—Seth—took the attention off me by beginning to sing. He had a wonderful deep voice, and I could have gone on listening for hours. Siri was sitting across from me, and her mouth was slightly open as she listened. Benjy stood behind her, one hand lightly on her shoulder.

After a few ballads Papageno said, "One last song. The words may be familiar to you," and he sang:

> *I am the root and the offspring of David,*
> *and the bright and morning star.*
> *And the spirit and the bride say, Come.*
> *And let him that heareth say, Come.*
> *And let him that is athirst come.*
> *And whosoever will, let him take the water of life freely.*
> *For I am the root,*
> *And the bright and morning star.*

I thought of Siri and her song, "Thou canst not stir a flower without troubling of a star." When I am at home I love to go out after dinner with Mr. Rochester and look at the stars. On the *Argosy* we wouldn't be seeing stars as we sailed farther south because the sky would be light until long after we were asleep. I wouldn't want to live for half the year in

176

perpetual daylight and never see stars, each one a flaming sun, and each one light-years away. Some of the nearest stars are only seven or so light-years in the past, and some are hundreds and thousands, stars long dead before their living light ever reaches us. If what we do troubles a star, is it in the star's own time, who knows how many thousands of years ago, or is it in our time, when we are seeing it?

"*I am the bright and morning star,*" Papageno finished, and bowed, to much applause. On his way out he paused by several people, usually saying something in a soft voice. When he came to me, he bowed and said, "You may call me Papa," and slipped a small piece of paper into my hand, very unobtrusively. I opened my hand and looked at the paper, trying to be equally unobtrusive. I expected to see something about meeting Cook, or some kind of greeting, but what I read was: FIRST MAN STILL SAFE NEEDS HELP.

What on earth?

Who needed help? First man?

First man! Adam! Adam was the first man. Was he talking about my Adam? And if he was, why did he give the slip of paper to me, not to his brother?

I looked around and I didn't see Cook. He must still be in the little sitting room with the governor. Was I supposed to give Papageno's message to Cook? Or could the Adam who needed help be Adam Cook rather than Adam Eddington?

Deep in my thoughts, I followed along with everybody else while we were given a tour of the house, which rambled comfortably from one wing to another. I wasn't listening to Mrs. Leeds until I heard her say, "Papa," and then my ears pricked up. She was laughing. "Oh, don't tell him I called him that. Papageno is very slow to offer his nickname to people. He's not often willing to sing for strangers, so you really had an unusual treat."

"Isn't his real name Seth?" someone asked.

"It is. But he says Seth was killed by the seal, and indeed it is a miracle that he recovered, largely thanks to his brother, who came from America to nurse him."

"Cookie," Sam said in a satisfied voice, and Leilia smiled and nodded.

Mrs. Leeds said, "If you go to the museum—and I do hope you will, it's truly charming—you may see Papageno there. He's done a lot of work on the exhibitions, and he has some magnificent photographs of penguins. He's a unique person, and he does care passionately about these islands and all of us who live here."

We said goodbye and thank you to Mrs. Leeds, and as we were leaving, the second group was arriving. I was glad we'd been in the first group, especially if, as Mrs. Leeds had implied, Papageno had gone to the museum and wouldn't be singing again.

As we started out the front door, the butler stopped me. "Miss Austin?"

"Yes?"

"I have a letter for you." He handed me an envelope, not postmarked, with no address, only my name on it. I took it and followed after the group, several yards behind.

I looked at the envelope, which bore the Government

House crest and return address. I opened it and pulled out a sheet of letter paper and saw Adam's writing.

I scanned it quickly, then went over it slowly, not believing what I'd read.

> *Dear Vicky,*
>
> *Thank you for your letters. I think it's probably best if we don't write anymore. We're too young to have a serious involvement, and now that I'm finally off to LeNoir Station I have to put all my energy into my work here. I will always consider you Austins good friends. When you stop off at the station, we'll at least have a chance to say hello. But I hope you agree that we'd better cool it.*
>
> *Sincerely yours,*
> *Adam*

No.

I felt as though I had been kicked in the stomach.

Adam's first letters had ended with "Love." What had happened? What had I done?

I was too hurt even to want to cry.

Seven

I was hallucinating. At least I knew that I was hallucinating, so that meant I had not completely lost touch with reality. I was in Aunt Serena's kitchen and Cook had the freezer door open and it was snowing and it was terribly cold. Cook took the penguin-feather cape off a hook and put it on.

"Cook," I said, "dear Cook, if you and your brother are crazy, then so am I."

"We are not crazy," Cook said. "We are the voice of sanity in a crazy world."

"Where are your angels?" I asked. "Where are their feathers?"

I jerked awake as I realized I was talking out loud. But I wasn't in Aunt Serena's kitchen. I was still on the iceberg. If I kept on hallucinating, I didn't know what would happen to me. I had to keep sane.

If the Adam who needed help was my Adam, how did that tie in with this letter?

180

There was a horrible finality to Adam's words. I shoved the letter into my pocket.

Then I realized that Sam was waiting for me to catch up with the group.

"Vicky?"

"Hi." I tried to sound normal.

"What's up?"

"Nothing. Sorry I got behind. Are we off to the museum?" Sam slipped into step beside me. "Want to take the bus?"

"No, thanks, I'd rather walk. You take the bus."

"Not me. It's much too nice a day, and it isn't that far."

We saw some passengers climb on to a small white bus. The rest of us straggled along the harbor road. "Look at those houses," someone said. "I feel I'm on the route from Heath-row into London."

"Certainly doesn't look even vaguely Hispanic."

Jorge, who was walking just in front of us, said, "You know a lot about music, Vicky."

That was something safe to talk about. "No, it's my mother. She says she'd never do housework without music. She loves *The Magic Flute* and she was playing it last month when she was washing the woodwork and getting ready for Christmas. I guess music has sort of seeped into me without my realizing it." My voice, which had started out galloping unsteadily, sounded almost normal when I finished.

Sam suggested, "Say, Papageno expected us to recognize that last song he sang. What was it?"

After a pause, Siri said, "The words were from John's Revelation, and I think he made up the melody."

"John who?" someone asked.

Sam looked at me. "I'll wager Vicky knows."

I wished he hadn't put me on the spot. "John, from the last chapter of the Bible. My grandfather used to love it. It's full of all kinds of poetry."

Sam smiled at me approvingly.

Adam's letter was burning a hole in my pocket. But I thought I was acting perfectly normal.

Angelique asked, "Did any of you notice how much Papageno looks like Cook?"

Sam said, "He's Cookie's brother. That's why Cookie's leaving the *Argosy* here at Port Stanley, to visit with his brother, and the rest of us will have to look after Vicky."

Jorge said, "It will be a pleasure."

"Not that she needs much looking after," Leilia said, "but we'll be around if you need us, Vicky."

"That crazy man sure could sing," Jack drawled.

Sam gave a short laugh. "Crazy like a fox."

"You think?"

Jorge cleared his throat. "He's a well-known and well-regarded character in the Falklands. But he is eccentric."

Greta said, "Mrs. Leeds did seem to have affection for him when she talked about him. By the way, did anybody else get a little note from him, slipped into your hand?"

Greta's words stopped me in my tracks.

Angelique cleared her throat. "I did. I thought it was some kind of joke."

"What's it say, Angel?" Dick asked.

182

She shrugged. "It just said, BRING NOTHING IN TAKE NOTH-ING OUT."

"Standard orders," Dick said. "Benjy and the other lecturers have all emphasized that."

"Greta," Jorge asked, "did you say Papageno slipped you a note?"

"Yes."

Everybody looked at her, and several people stopped walking and we stood in a cluster on the sidewalk. Jorge prodded, "What did it say?"

"IF YOU WANT TO HURT SOMEONE GIVE HIM SOMETHING HE WANTS."

"What?" Leilia questioned.

"Not so dumb," Sam said.

"Explain, Sam," Greta said.

"Some people are of the opinion that drugs were introduced into America as a most effective secret weapon."

"What's that got to do with it?"

Dick said, "It's feeding into the present feeling that we're entitled to have whatever gives us any kind of pleasure. We've become a pill-popping population."

Leilia asked, "Drugs a problem in your school, Vicky?"

"Sure." I remembered my grandfather saying, "One definition of hell is having your own way all the time."

"Did anybody else get a note?" Jorge asked.

I didn't speak. I don't know why. I couldn't.

"Remember," Siri warned, "Papageno will probably be at the museum."

"Wearing all those feathers?" Greta asked.

"Who knows?"

"Don't Maoris wear feathered capes?"

"Papageno's from the Falklands, not New Zealand."

Papageno's message to me was in my pocket with Adam's letter. Maybe I wasn't the only one to keep my mouth shut. At least this conversation had shifted Sam's attention from me. All I wanted was to go away from everybody, crawl into some small cave, and lick my wounds.

But I had to endure going to the museum, which was a small frame house filled with Falklands history, mostly focused on Port Stanley. All kinds of artifacts had been saved: teacups, chamber pots, primitive dentist's instruments, kitchen utensils; mostly, someone remarked, things which would have been found in any house in rural England a hundred or so years ago. There were photographs of the ships on which people had arrived, and of some of the early farmhouses on the "camps," as the islands with the sheep were called. Lonely, terribly lonely.

I put myself on automatic pilot, and noted a stuffed fox, and a strange fish mounted in a glass frame, a fish which seemed to have no red blood corpuscles at all. It was completely colorless and slightly transparent. "It has to be, to survive the Antarctic waters." Sam was beside me, and I had a feeling he was deliberately staying with me.

He took me by the arm. "Look. Here's Papageno." We walked to a room which was a combination office and lab, where Papageno was standing by a wide work shelf, mounting some beautiful photographs of penguins. His feathered cape

184

was hanging on a hook in the corner, and he wore ordinary jeans and a blue knit vest over a white short-sleeved shirt. I could see that his arms were raked with scars.

"Well, Miss Vicky," he said softly, "it is good to see you."

I was about to ask Papageno about his note, but several other people came in. Leilia asked Papageno if these were new pictures he was mounting, and he answered that he'd taken them only a week ago, and went on with his work.

Angelique commented, "We've seen a lot of penguins in a couple of days. I'm far more entranced by them than I'd expected to be."

Papa nodded. "Um."

Siri asked, "They're doing okay, aren't they? I mean, holding their numbers?"

"Increasing." Papa looked up from his work. "Anybody know why?"

Leilia replied, "Whales. There are fewer whales than there used to be. They're a frighteningly endangered species."

"What's that got to do with the penguin population?" someone asked.

Leilia said, "Fewer whales means more krill for the penguins to eat."

Papageno asked, "Why do you think cetaceans gave up the hand with its opposable thumb and the ability to pick things up and look at them, and went back to the sea?"

Jorge said, without hesitation, "Food. Food was more plentiful in the water than on land, and there were fewer predators."

Papa said, "A reasonable answer. But possibly not the only one."

Leilia smiled at him. "Agreed. Whales and dolphins seem to me to be way ahead of us on the evolutionary scale. But I guess nobody'll ever know."

"Not unless we learn the way they think," Papageno agreed. "And probably not then. We human beings, for instance, will never know what made us choose to get up off all fours and stand on our hind legs, thus freeing our forepaws to pick up something."

Leilia nodded. "And so we have the hand with the opposable thumb."

Papageno took another photograph and started work on it. "It is a good and chastening thing that the human being knows a great deal less than we thought we did a hundred years ago."

Jorge and Dick challenged that, and I heard Angelique whisper to Leilia, "That's something doctors are afraid to admit. Granted, medicine has come a long way, but . . ."

I turned away and lost track of the conversation, because I'd shoved my hand into my pocket, and my fingers touched Papageno's slip of paper and Adam's note.

When I tuned in again, it was into a discussion of waste disposal, not only in Antarctica, but all over the world. Someone mentioned hypodermic needles that had been washed up onto beaches a few summers ago. Someone else talked about sewage.

Dick asked, "What about sewage at the research stations?"

"It is collected in large containers," Papageno said. "It doesn't pose the danger of other waste."

"Such as?"

Papageno shrugged. "Materials with long half-lives."

"You mean nuclear waste?" Leilia asked. I thought of Suzy talking about Ned's concern over disposing of nuclear weapons because of the plutonium and uranium.

"Um."

"Right," Leilia said. "In Alaska we don't want any leftover nuclear matter dumped on our glaciers."

Papageno bent over his photos, held up one of what looked like tiny dolphins leaping in unison.

Angelique exclaimed, "I've never seen such small dolphins."

"Chinstrap penguins, not dolphins," Papageno corrected her. "But you're not far off, because it's called porpoising. I think that porpoises leaping should be called penguining."

I'd seen pictures of chinstrap penguins at Aunt Serena's, well named because they have a black line like a chin strap below their beaks.

Siri said, "Your pictures show us what Benjy meant when he talked about penguins flying in water."

Angelique asked, "Were penguins like porpoises, land animals that went back to the sea for food? That's where they get their food, isn't it, not on land?" Papa nodded, and she went on, "Are they land animals or sea animals? They breed on the land, but eat from the sea. They waddle on land, and fly in the water."

"If penguins swim like porpoises," Greta suggested, "and get their food from the sea, are they cetaceans?"

"Penguins are birds," Papageno said.

Quimby came in and told us it was time to get back to the

ship, and herded us all out like a bunch of sheep. As we left, Papageno said softly, so I think only Sam and I could hear, "The world's waste cannot be disposed of easily. Nor can greed, nor lust for power. It is nausinious."

Sam whispered to me, "What did he say?"

I whispered back, "I thought he said nausinious, but he must have meant nauseous." Or was it another warning?

"Where's Cookie?" Sam asked.

"I don't know." I hadn't seen him since I'd left him with the governor. I needed to talk to him. I couldn't just get back on the ship without saying goodbye, without telling Cook about Papageno's note.

"Don't fret," Sam said.

And then I felt a hand on my shoulder and Benjy was behind me. "Get on the launch, Vicky. Cookie'll see you later. Don't worry." He nodded affirmatively, and I got into line, Sam standing right by me. Greta and Jack were in front of us.

She turned to smile at me and asked, "What was Cookie doing with Governor Leeds?"

"They're old friends," I replied.

"I noticed them as we walked past that little sitting room."

For some reason I prickled. Greta's curiosity was perfectly normal. I said, neutrally, "Cook grew up in the Falklands. He knows everybody."

"So how does it happen that you're traveling with Cookie?" Jack asked.

"He's a friend of the family." That seemed the easiest explanation.

"Isn't he leaving the ship here?" Jack asked. "You'll miss him. But you'll have a shipful of other uncles."

"Move up," Quim said. "Move up. Fill up the front."

Greta and Jack went all the way up front to sit with Jorge. Jack's cowboy clothes were visible again; on our Zodiac excursions they were covered by rubber pants and the red parka, though he usually wore his cowboy hat rather than his parka hood, and he was tall enough so he was easily spotted.

I found a seat somewhere in the middle of the launch, on a wooden bench, between Otto and Siri. I could not understand why Cook had not come to say goodbye, or how he was going to see me later. I looked at the dock as we pulled away, but Cook was not among the small group of people standing around.

"Quimby is such a dear," I heard Siri saying. "Did you know there was a man called Phineas Quimby who was a pioneer in mental healing?"

"Really?" Otto quirked his brows. "I like that. Not many men with Quimby's job have that tolerant calm." Then he turned to me. "Where's Cookie?"

I tried not to show how concerned I was. "He's staying here in Port Stanley, to visit with his brother."

Siri said, "Remember, my cabin's just one door down the hall from yours, Vicky. If you need anything, I'm here."

"Thanks, Siri."

Angelique leaned over from the seat behind. "Me, too. And I speak for Dick."

"Thanks. I really appreciate it."

Jorge beckoned to Otto, who moved to the front of the launch.

Siri yawned. "I don't know why I'm so sleepy. That was fun, this afternoon."

"Delightful." Angelique nodded, and then said to me, "Cookie said you're looking forward to seeing your boyfriend at LeNoir Station."

Not my boyfriend. Not anymore. No matter what I'd thought.

I hoped my voice didn't sound brittle. "I'm not ready yet for a serious boyfriend. Too much school still ahead of me."

Siri said, "I gather pressure's being put on Otto to look for a wife."

Angelique said, "Not many princesses aboard the *Argosy*."

Siri smiled. "Fairy-tale princes do marry princesses, don't they? I hope Otto will do better than the British royal family."

She and Angelique chatted until the launch pulled up beside the *Argosy*.

I turned my red manifest number to the yellow side and went to my cabin. I took Adam's letters and cards, Adam II's letter, and the warning cards from school, and spread them out on the second bunk, adding the letter from Adam I'd been given at Government House. None of it added up. Something was definitely miching mallecho, and I had no idea what.

Where was Cook?

I put the letters and cards away and went out to the fo'c'sle. I felt too horrible even to cry. I listened as the anchor was pulled up. The ship's engines throbbed, and we began to pull away from Port Stanley. John's warning about Cook throbbed in my ears, echoing the rhythm of the engine.

I still couldn't quite believe that Cook had just gone off

and left me in Port Stanley, though it was no more strange than Adam's brusque letter, tossing me away as though we'd never meant anything to each other.

Several passengers came out with their cameras, and there was lots of general talk about how pleasant the afternoon in Port Stanley had been. I listened as Leilia described Papageno's penguin-feathered cape to one of the passengers who had not been in the first group. I turned and saw Angelique touch Dick's cheek in a gesture of tenderness. I noticed that Sam was standing not far from me, looking at me. I pretended not to see him.

Gradually, people began to leave the fo'c'sle. It was time for Wrap-Up, for people to gather together in the lounge for drinks.

"Coming, Vicky?" Sam asked.

"Sure," I said. "In a few minutes."

"I'll save you a seat. Shall I order you a ginger ale?"

"Please. Thanks."

He left, looking back at me once, and went into the lounge. I stayed at the rail, staring at the grey expanse of water widening as we left Port Stanley. Then I saw something moving toward us. At first I thought it was one of the launches, coming back for some reason, because it was about the same size. But then I realized it was a different kind of boat, blue and shabby, with PORTIA painted on the side. Cook was standing on the foredeck, waving at me and calling, "Wait right there, Vicky."

I nodded and the boat turned to go to the portside of the *Argosy*. I thought I saw Papageno at the wheel, and remembered that Cook had told me his brother had a seaworthy old boat.

After about five minutes, a side door opened and Cook came out. "Seth and I are taking off this evening, and I wanted to talk with you first. You had a chance to visit with him at the museum?"

"With lots of other people."

"I know, Vicky. I'm sorry. This is not exactly turning out to be the quiet trip we'd planned."

"Cookie—" I drew in my breath, let it out. "You really wanted me to come with you on this trip?"

"Very much. But I think it's just as well I'm leaving you here."

"Why?"

Cook looked out to sea. His head was covered with an old fur-lined cap with earflaps which were dangling. "Rumblings. Suspicions. It may be nothing. Seth is eyes and ears for the governor, going about in his little boat and seeing what other people don't hear and see."

"Like—?"

"Unrest. It's all over the planet, there's no denying that. But there's something new afoot, we're not sure what." Then he looked at me sharply. "Vicky, are you all right? Is something upsetting you?"

I was not, *not* going to tell him about Adam's letter. "While we were at Government House, Seth—Papageno—"

Cook smiled. "He's usually called Papageno around here, but I've known him as Seth for too long to think of him as anything else. Go on."

"He slipped me a message."

"Do you have it?"

"Yes." I pulled it out of my deepest parka pocket and handed it to him.

He studied it.

"Which Adam?" I asked.

Cook closed his eyes for a moment, than said, "He's referring to young Adam."

"Adam III."

"Yes."

"Why?"

"He's a smart but innocent kid, and he seems to have antagonized someone while he was in Vespugia, someone who is as irrationally upset and angry as a disturbed fur seal. Adam may have given Esteban, or perhaps Captain Nausinio, the idea that he knows more than he does."

"Esteban called him *amigo*." I did not add that Esteban called Adam *amigo* with a question. "And Cookie, what about me? What about someone at home not wanting me to come on this trip?"

Again he closed his eyes. I thought he was not going to answer me, but finally he said, "Perhaps I should have taken those messages you received at school more seriously. I took them to be some kind of prank."

"And now?"

"I'm not sure. I still have no idea where they could have come from, or why. What happened in the past has no connection with you whatsoever. *I* am connected with the past. You are not."

"What about Adam? Adam III?"

Cook shook his head.

I said, tentatively, "I wrote him about those messages I found in my locker. I don't know if he got my letter or not. Maybe I'm the one who's put Adam in danger?"

"No." Cook's voice was firm. "I don't think either you or Adam is in any danger, but there are serious issues at stake, and I want you and Adam to stay out of them."

I thought of the pyramid in Vespugia, but said only, "Cookie, you can't ignore the warnings."

Cook sighed. "I have no idea what Adam's Shakespeare cards are about, and my hope is that this is a lot of sound and fury signifying nothing." He laughed, ruefully. "Now I'm quoting Shakespeare. It seems to be catching. If you see Adam before Seth and I do, tell him to mind his p's and q's. Okay? And you do whatever Benjy tells you to do, all right?"

"All right."

"Seth and I are going to do a little quiet investigating. He may play the fool, but he isn't one."

"I know that."

"I've got to go. Quim left the ladder up for me." He took a deep breath. "Seth has a good radio on the *Portia*. He checks in with Rusty or the Coast Guard daily, and we'll keep in touch through the radio room on the *Argosy*. Benjy will be expecting my calls. Even if you don't hear from me for a while, you will be very much in my concerns."

"Thank you. And you in mine."

He pulled me to him in a quick hug. "Angels watch over

you." Then he was gone, slipping like a shadow through the side door.

Benjy escorted me in to dinner, and through the wide windows I could see the *Portia* becoming no more than a shadow as it moved away from us. We sat with Siri and Sam, Angelique and Dick. Dick was definitely grouchy, and Angelique murmured that his leg was paining him. Dick growled and began talking about the movie we were going to see that night, about Admiral Scott's 1903 expedition.

When we finished eating, Benjy got a call to go up to the bridge. "You okay, Vicky?"

"Sure."

"There's about an hour before the movie——"

"I'm going down to my cabin. I'll see you up in the Womb Room."

In the cabin I simply sat on my bunk, trying to think, and feeling instead numb, dumb, stupid. I looked at all my "exhibits" once more. Nothing. In the drawer where I kept my books was the paperback book of quotations Suzy had given me for my birthday, and I pulled it out and opened it to the Shakespeare section. The first quotation I glanced at was not encouraging. Rather, it made my heart sink.

> *Alas! 'tis true I have gone here and there,*
> *And made myself a motley to the view,*
> *Gor'd mine own thoughts, sold cheap what is most*
> *dear——*

I knew some people would do anything for money. People turned traitor for pieces of silver. But who? John's warnings again rang in my ears, and again I did not, would not believe them. Not Cook.

And not Adam. Certainly not Adam. Maybe he was dumping me for another girl, or just because I'd never really meant anything, but he wouldn't do anything dishonorable. Or cheap. He would not sell anything that was dear to his heart, not for any amount of money. And who would give money, and for what?

I put the letters and cards away again and headed up to the lounge to wait for the movie. As I went into the big room, I saw Sam and Otto and several others at a table near the door to the fo'c'sle, drinking after-dinner coffee or tea. I overheard something about Papageno, so I slipped in quietly and sat at a table in the corner by the bookshelves, where I was moderately inconspicuous.

Yes, I've been taught about eavesdropping, but I was quite visible if anybody had turned to look my way. They were talking about Papageno's encounter with the fur seal, and then Otto asked what had happened to Dick's leg.

Sam said, "It was shot to bits while he was a medic in one of those internecine African wars where the U.S. Army went in supposedly to bring food to the starving."

"Supposedly?" someone asked.

Sam said, "Like Dick, I sometimes have a suspicious nature. I don't think everything we do is eleemosynary. Angelique says he nearly lost his leg, and it still gives him a lot of pain, which, as we saw tonight, he does not like to admit."

"No wonder he tends to be pessimistic," I heard Otto say sympathetically.

I started to move away from my corner, but then I heard "Cookie" and pricked up my ears again.

". . . seems very thick with Rusty Leeds," Otto was saying. "Cookie's a charming chap, but there's something secretive about him as well as charming."

"Private," Sam said. "Private, rather than secretive."

"Rusty, too," Otto said. "Stubborn as a mule."

"One would have to be, in order to govern someplace like the Falklands." It was Leilia's voice.

"There's no place like the Falklands." The slight accent told me it was Jorge. "That string of islands is unique, and the islanders can be troublesome, adhering to their English ways as though they're more British than the British, and refusing to speak the language of the part of the world they live in."

"Rusty speaks perfect Spanish," Otto defended.

The ding-dong rang for the movie, and I got up from my corner and waved at the others before heading up the steps to the Womb Room. Benjy was operating the movie projector—it was an old-fashioned one, not a video—and I sat on one of the side benches. Siri and Angelique joined me, and Sam came and sat nearby. The room was darkened and the only light came from the machine, with which Benjy was fiddling. I felt very tired. I leaned back and closed my eyes. Siri and Angelique were talking about folk music, and Angelique promised to teach Siri some of the songs from her home island. "The melodies are beautiful," she said. "Full of sorrow and joy all together."

197

Jorge was sitting a few chairs away and turned toward us. "Well, Vicky, looking forward to the movie?"

I opened my eyes. "Sure."

"And to getting to LeNoir Station on Eddington Point?"

"Yes."

"And to seeing your friend, also named Eddington, isn't he?"

—You know that, Jorge. What's this about?

But he smiled disarmingly. "We started to talk about this once before, didn't we? In my old age I tend to get repetitive."

"Come on, Jorge," Angelique said. "You're far from being old."

"And Vicky's too young to have known the explorer Eddington." Jorge shook his head. "It's the very young who make me feel old."

Angelique patted my shoulder. "Nonsense, Jorge. Vicky makes me feel young all over again."

"A remarkable man, the first Eddington. Highly respected. If the present Eddington takes after him, he must have many special qualities." He smiled at me.

"He does." That was still true. I couldn't wipe Adam out just because he'd wiped me out.

Angelique asked, "Are you blushing, Vicky?"

Sam's voice was unusually gentle. "Don't tease Vicky." He smiled at me.

Jorge said, "I didn't mean to tease, Vicky. But young love is always attractive to us old fogies."

198

When the movie was over, Otto was waiting for me at the foot of the steps and suggested that I come into the lounge with him for a cup of mint tea.

"Sure," I said. "I'd like that."

There were only a few people in the lounge, and Otto took me to the table in the library corner where I'd been sitting earlier, a little isolated from the other tables. He ordered our tea, then leaned toward me. His eyes were amber, a little lighter than his tanned skin.

"Are you missing Cookie?"

"Yes."

"I promised him I'd keep an eye out for you."

"Thanks."

"Some of the passengers—well, those you have come to know best—are okay for you. But there are those who may be part of multinational groups which have more interest in Antarctica than they should."

I sighed. "I know a lot of countries want what they think is their share."

"It is more than that," Otto said, "but I think it will not be a problem for you. I will see to it."

I looked my unspoken question at him.

He replied with another question. "Why did Cookie bring you with him on this trip, Vicky?"

"He didn't exactly bring me with him. Aunt Serena gave me the trip for a birthday present."

"That is an amazing birthday present."

"Aunt Serena is an amazing person."

"Who is she, this Aunt Serena?"

"She's not really my aunt, at least not biologically. She's what we call a love-aunt, and she's old, even older than Sam, and wonderful." I took a swallow of my tea, which was getting cold, and asked my own question. "Otto, are you on the *Argosy* purely for a vacation?"

He smiled, shaking his head slightly. "Not entirely. Wherever I go, I am an ambassador for Zlatovica, and I have some business here."

"What kind of business?"

"It is confidential." His voice was harsh. Then it softened. "You are intelligent and perceptive, Vicky. I told you that Zlatovica, though no longer under Soviet domination, still has Russian silos up in the mountains, silos which hold a deadly load. Perhaps even more dangerous, we still have a Chernobyl-type reactor, and while it appears to be functioning smoothly, we are aware of the potential horrors it poses. As you have observed, there are passengers from many countries on the *Argosy*, and it is possible that I may be able to do a certain amount of negotiation. I am not the only traveler to Antarctica who is here for more than pleasure." He paused, looking at me. "For instance," he said, "Jack Nessinger may be helpful to me in finding a source of affordable oil which my country desperately needs."

"Is Jack here just on vacation?"

Otto shrugged. "Who knows? Perhaps the *Argosy*, like a golf course, is a good place to do business."

The world of business was a total mystery to me. "You've spent a good bit of time with Jorge . . ."

"Jorge is a person of considerable knowledge and authority,

200

at least in South America. Can you think of anybody else who may be on the *Argosy* for purposes other than pleasure?"

"Otto, I don't know. Thinking that way is not—not within my frame of reference." Certainly none of the lecturers, not Siri or Sam or any of the people I usually hiked with or sat with at Wrap-Up or for meals.

But Otto suggested, "Sam?"

"Sam! Sam's eighty-three."

"So? We Zlatovicans do not have the American cult of youth. Sam is what I think you call savvy."

"Sure he's savvy," I said. "But I don't think he's into any international-intrigue stuff."

"Ah." Otto laid his finger briefly against my wrist. "That's why he's such a natural. He's experienced. He knows how to act like an innocent old codger."

I thought this over. I didn't like it. I didn't believe it. Not Sam.

"And what about Angelique and Dick?" Otto continued. "Angelique comes from a country as small and poor as mine, and surely her beauty and sophistication open doors for her."

I laughed, but it was a faint laugh. "I know Angelique is gorgeous, but I really don't think she's a Mata Hari."

"You watch old movies?"

"Sometimes, with my brother John. But, Otto, why would all these people with—with special interests—be coming to Antarctica?"

"It is neutral territory. That is important."

If they were all after a piece of the pie, would it remain neutral? "Tell me a little more about Zlatovica."

"We are, as you know, a small country. Landlocked, but with the benefit of many beautiful lakes. Now that we are again open to tourism, that has become one of our major industries, but I would not like to become another Monaco or Luxembourg. It is my dream that we become not merely a playground for the rich and idle of this planet, but that our mountains and lakes be available to the ordinary people of our land. You understand?"

"Yes. I think that's marvelous."

He bathed me with his smile. "Ah, Vicky." He reached out and touched my hand gently. "You have such good understanding. I have been trained all my life, even when we were in hiding, to be a prince. It is a heavy responsibility."

One I could not comprehend. So I just nodded.

"Too many small countries, such as Vespugia, are burdened by debts to American and European banks. We, the Zlatovicans, are poor, desperately poor, but we are not under that burden, and now we have a rapidly evolving middle class. It is my deepest desire that our peasants all sit under their own vine and fig tree."

I looked at him. He wore a pale blue shirt and a heavy blue cardigan. No rings on his fingers. Nothing to indicate that he was royalty. He continued, "Now that we in Zlatovica have reached a measure of independence I seek for true freedom, despite our many problems. Our economic growth is the envy of many emerging countries."

"Otto, I'm really sorry to be a dunce about your country. I should know a lot more about Zlatovica than I do."

He reached out and ran his hand lightly over my hair.

"Most people don't, Vicky. The iron curtain, which imprisoned us, also helped us to survive. Nobody knew what was going on inside. No one knew when my mother died under torture. Her body was too fragile for what they did to her, and it killed her."

"Oh—Otto—"

"It is the way of the world. It is not only that torture is a useful way of eliciting information from the unwilling; it is also that it is enjoyable to the torturer."

I put my hands over my eyes. Otto gently pulled them down.

"I wish you could stay innocent forever, Vicky. But there are not many good places or people left." He sighed. "My father is no longer young, and the years under Soviet dominion were hard on him, desperately hard. He had to go from one hiding place to another. He has paid a heavy toll, physically. I must do what I can to help." He looked at his watch, finished his tea in one gulp. "It is late, and I think the crew would like us to leave so they can clean up here." I hadn't realized he had his red parka with him on the seat until he handed it to me. "Put this on and we'll go out on deck for a minute."

"But you'll be cold."

"I have on a very warm sweater, knit for me by my ancient nurse, who was my mother's nurse before me, right out of a fairy tale. Come on."

I shoved into the parka and followed him across the room and out onto the deck, zipping up as the cold wind bit into me.

We went up to the front and suddenly Otto's arms were around me and he was kissing me, not roughly, searchingly.

Why was I astonished?

He'd sought me out. He'd made it clear that he liked me. Nevertheless, I was totally surprised. His lips felt a little salty. He tasted slightly of cigarette smoke. If it hadn't been for Adam's total rejection of me, I might have pulled back. But I didn't. It was a good kiss; I moved into it, feeling a wonderful tingling through my whole body.

Finally he turned away. "Thank you," he said. "Sleep well, my dear Vicky."

"You, too, Otto." I wanted to say, "My dear Otto," but couldn't quite manage it. Otto did not think I was too young. Otto trusted me.

He walked me downstairs, waiting courteously until I opened my cabin door. I took off his parka and gave it to him. "*A demain*," he said softly.

"*A demain*." At least I knew enough French for that.

Till tomorrow, Otto, till tomorrow.

I sat on the edge of my bunk. Otto made me feel beautiful. Otto put salve on the wounds Adam's letter had made.

I pulled out my notebook and began to doodle, and slowly the words of a lament kind of poem came.

> *Penguins play but do not love.*
> *Does a penguin's heart go cold*
> *When a skua flies above . . .*

That was terrible. Stupid. It didn't begin to say what I felt about Adam's rejection. Why couldn't I write about it directly? I pushed my mind into writing something different, something that had nothing to do with my pain, something maybe I could show to Siri for her to sing. Something maybe Otto could listen to.

> *Tell me, oh tell me, the one who sings,*
> *Do angels really and truly have wings?*
> *Do they call out with a cry like a bird*
> *And then fly low to see if we've heard?*
> *When they make their energy manifest*
> *Do they put on wings to be fully dressed?*
> *Is it really true, what I have heard,*
> *That if it has feathers, it is a bird?*

That was plain silly, and probably equally bad poetry, but later I'd probably copy it out for Siri.

I sat there, my head on my hand, and thought again of my conversation with Otto, and that not everybody on the *Argosy* was there for a vacation. Was Otto telling me more than I could understand? Surely Otto felt responsible to the entire planet as well as to his own small country. He had pointed out that the *Argosy* was neutral territory, and that was why it was a good place for representatives of various nations to meet and discuss plans, quietly. Quietly.

Surely Otto hadn't kissed me just to keep me from suspecting him of some kind of international skullduggery. That was not consistent with the Otto I had come to know during these few days. Maybe he wasn't the golden fairy-tale prince he appeared to be, but I certainly had no political importance which would draw him to me. In Otto's world of international

diplomacy, I was nobody. I had to believe that he walked with
me ashore and sat with me on the ship and kissed me on the
deck because he liked me. Me, Vicky, and not just because the
two of us were the only people under twenty aboard.

I had thought my heart belonged to Adam in such a way
that I would not, could not, respond to anybody else. But
Adam had rejected my heart. And I had responded to Otto.

I pulled the book I was reading off the chest between the
two bunks. I had put Esteban's pyramid postcard in the book
to mark my place. It was not there. And it had been there. I
was certain of that. I looked around, and finally spotted it under the second bunk. I opened each one of the three drawers
of the chest. I am not the tidiest person in the world and I
couldn't tell whether or not anything had been touched. I
checked my backpack. Adam's cards and letters, the cards
from school, Adam II's letter were in their place in the inside
zippered pocket. Nothing looked different, but I was sure
someone had opened my backpack, checked everything, and
put it all back.

Why?

What were they looking for?

In the morning, things would be clearer.

They weren't. I felt as vulnerable and naïve as ever.

Eight

*I*t wasn't vulnerability that had me on an ice floe. Maybe it was naïveté, though I don't think so. It was power and corruption and paranoia. I knew that people who are motivated by power are ruthless. I've known that for a long time. It's a kind of global insanity, almost like a virus. I'd met it in New York, but it isn't confined to big cities. It's everywhere, and little people get caught in it the way they always have.

On TV the good guys always win. But this wasn't TV. Unless somebody came soon, the bad guys were going to win this one, and nobody would know anything except that Vicky Austin had disappeared. Just as Adam Eddington had disappeared. But Adam Eddington, Adam II, had sprung an information leak which had stopped disastrous experimenting in Antarctica. Was that action affecting only what went on in Antarctica a generation ago, or was it touching the present? Had I been incredibly foolish to set off for Antarctica without telling about those two warnings in my school locker? If I never got off the ice floe alive, that would affect not only me but my family, my

207

parents and John and Suzy and Rob; it would affect Aunt Serena and
Stassy and Owain and Cook. No. Not Aunt Serena. It did not seem
possible that fate, never mind how blind, could deal another blow
from the Antarctic to Aunt Serena.

When I went in to breakfast, Jorge was at an otherwise empty table and beckoned to me to join him. I sat down across from him and was brought coffee and my usual oatmeal. Not only has my mother emphasized the virtue of hot oatmeal, but I like it. The sea looked choppy and cold. Maybe we'd see icebergs.

"Good morning, Vicky." Jorge nodded at me. "It is good to see you looking fresh and ready for the day."

"I'm ready for icebergs," I said.

"Maybe you'll be the first to spot one. It is tradition on the *Argosy* that the first person to see an iceberg gets a bottle of champagne as a prize." He passed me the rolls. "You still have schooling ahead of you?"

"One more year after this of high school, and then college; that is, if I can get a good scholarship. We've all been putting money away for our education since we were little kids."

"College, rather than marriage?"

"Couldn't I have both?" I asked. "I do want a good education which will give me a chance to decide what I want to do to earn my living."

"Ah." He nodded approvingly. "You don't expect it all to be handed to you on a silver platter. Otto, too, has a sense of responsibility about all he is inheriting."

I smiled. "At least I don't have a whole country to worry about, just myself."

"You enjoy school?" he asked.

"Pretty much. I have a very good English teacher."

"Do you learn languages? French? Spanish?"

"I took French in school a year ago. My sister is taking Spanish this year."

"And science?"

"We have a good science teacher. My sister's the scientist, not me."

"It is literature that you enjoy?"

"Yes." I was polite, but I couldn't see why he was interested.

Jorge leaned across the table toward me. "Captain Nausinio told me you had an accident on the large pyramid, not long after I left to go to my ranch."

"It was only a near-accident."

"Nausinio said that it was Esteban's quick reflex that kept you from a bad fall."

"I'm very grateful to him."

"A good lad, bright and talented. I, too, am grateful. It would have put a cloud on the whole trip if you had been hurt."

—Or killed, I thought.

"I'm sure it must have frightened you."

"It happened so quickly I didn't have time to have hysterics."

Jorge smiled warmly. "You are a lovely young woman, Vicky. I hope life will treat you as kindly as you deserve. I know that whatever you decide to do, you will do it well."

"Thank you." He meant it sincerely, and that warmed me.

He said, "I didn't mean to embarrass you about your friend Adam Eddington last night. I have long been an admirer of his uncle."

Adam II had always seemed special and private to me, but that was naïve, again. Jorge's interest in him still jarred.

"It is pleasant for you that you will have a friend waiting for you at the station. And, Vicky, please excuse me, but—if I may—Otto is very taken with you."

I tried to laugh. "We're the only teenagers on the *Argosy*."

"You're a charming girl, and you yourself do not know that, do you?" He pulled back his chair. "See you in a little while."

I watched him leave the dining room. He meant the nice things he said. But I didn't know what I thought of him. I was not born with a suspicious nature. I grew up in Thornhill. But too much was going on that I couldn't understand. I thought of the postcard on the floor, instead of where I had left it in my book. I thought of all the warnings, and I was afraid. I do know that there is evil, real evil in the world, and nobody is safe. Jorge hoped that life would treat me as kindly as I deserved. But did Otto's mother deserve to be tortured and killed?

Leilia came into the dining room and sat down by me, and was followed by Angelique and Dick, and I relaxed. There are still a lot of good people in the world. "Good morning," I said, and they all welcomed me with their smiles.

We had two lectures that morning. I took notes dutifully, setting down bits of information like "90% of all the ice in the world is in Antarctica, and 60% of the world's water."

Gary was lecturing, and he was passionate about how important Antarctica is for the world's water.

"A slight exaggeration," Jorge murmured to Sam.

"Is it?" Sam asked.

One thing Gary said I really enjoyed was, "Mammals groom. Birds preen." What about people? Suzy preens.

Between the lectures, several of us stayed up in the Womb Room. With the curtains pulled open instead of drawn across the windows, and with the door to the aft deck propped wide, the room was reasonably light, and cooled off quickly.

Several people went out on deck, including Otto and Jorge. Angelique, shrugging into a sea-green cashmere cardigan, came and sat down by me. She wore jade earrings which swung against the rosy darkness of her skin. Siri joined us, saying, "I did get sleepy, even though Gary is a fascinating lecturer."

"Womb Room, indeed," Angelique agreed, stretching. Her neck was long and slender, and her earrings showed it off. I used to think I wanted to look like Suzy, but Angelique's beauty was deeper, and it seemed to shine out of her from the inside as much as from the outside. Every instinct told me that Angelique could never be a Mata Hari. She said, "Dick is down in our cabin, napping. He's really enjoying this voyage, but he does get tired."

Sam strolled over, his unlit cigar in his mouth. "Has he had many patients?"

Angelique shook her head. "A couple of people arrived with *turista* from eating unwisely in Vespugia. But this seems to be a healthy group, and the Meclizine pills are good for preventing *mal de mer*."

Someone began drawing the curtains, and Jorge came in, looking back at Otto and Jack Nessinger, who were in the rectangle of light by the open door, putting out cigarettes. Jorge

211

said, smilingly, "Todd's about to give his famous lecture on the virtues of guano."

Angelique laughed. "Don't knock it, Jorge. I come from a very little nation, and about our only valuable export is guano—not from penguins, we've too warm a climate for penguins—but we have many other seabirds. Guano is a valuable fertilizer. We're also learning to use it for building material. It looks rather like stucco and it does not, I assure you, smell like penguin guano."

Otto came in, pulling off his heavy sweater. "I am looking forward to this lecture. Todd has a good sense of humor. At home I do not often have the opportunity just to relax and laugh." He sat down beside me. "You've been taking so many notes, Vicky."

"I promised to," I said.

The lights were dimmed as Otto said, "Not everybody cares about honoring promises."

Benjy found me before lunch and we went into the dining room together. Benjy was taking care of me, but not hovering. I wondered if I should tell Benjy that I was sure someone had been in my cabin. I trusted Benjy.

But not only was there someone in Vespugia I didn't trust, there was also someone on the *Argosy*.

It didn't add up. Who would have had access to my locker at school? To my cabin on the *Argosy*?

My brother John is a scientist, and he believes in verification by repetition. An experiment performed once is not enough. It has to be repeated, over and over, to be taken seriously.

212

That was Adam's theory, too. Adam III. But I did not want to think about Adam. I had thought I trusted Adam completely. Did his rejection of me constitute a breaking of trust? To me, it did.

Benjy gave me a small shove; the people just ahead of us in line had reached the buffet table. Among other delicious salads spread out before us there was a large bowl of hydroponic lettuce from the Falklands. Small countries can do large things with very little. I told Benjy about Angelique's buildings made of guano. He said he'd seen a couple, and they were white and clean and architecturally quite handsome.

This was a day at sea. No Zodiacs. After lunch we had a couple of hours to relax, and then more lectures. I wondered if the lectures I was hearing on the *Argosy* were the kind of thing I'd get in college—not that I planned to major in any kind of science. But there'd be lecture courses, and I hoped the lecturers would be as good as the ones I was hearing on this trip.

Between lectures the beautiful, clement weather deteriorated, and the ship began to roll. I went out to the fo'c'sle to look at the birds, and Sam followed me. We saw Southern giant petrels, Cape pigeons, Wilson's storm petrels—I wrote the names down for Suzy. I could be a lot fonder of Suzy with several thousand miles between us than I could at home.

Benjy came out and told us we were crossing the Scotia Sea, and the Antarctic Convergence, and that was why it was so rough. "You don't get seasick?"

"Not yet."

"Then I doubt if you will. Dick's got several miserable patients this afternoon."

By late afternoon we began to see icebergs.

Icebergs!

Pictures simply do not do them justice. Color, for instance, the incredible, burning blue! The majesty of floating ice, some of it millions of years old, ice that has broken off from glaciers!

At last I was seeing the world Adam II had written about in his journal.

That night at Wrap-Up, everybody was talking about icebergs. There was a new feeling of excitement in the atmosphere, good excitement.

Quim talked to us about Elephant Island, which we'd be passing the next day, and where we'd take the Zodiacs if the wind and waves were quiet enough. Then he said, "We have a nice surprise for you. Siri has promised to play her harp and sing for us."

I hadn't realized that Siri had her harp in the lounge with her, leaning against her chair. She picked it up and went to the center of the floor. Benjy brought her a stool, and she sat and played her "Troubling a star" song. I would never hear that song without thinking of the penguins coming to her as she sang. She followed this with a couple of folk songs, and then, totally to my surprise, she began to sing the silly song I'd copied for her and slid under her cabin door.

> Tell me, oh tell me, the one who sings,
> Do angels really and truly have wings?

When she came to the last two lines, she reprised them.

Is it really true, what I have heard,
That if it has feathers, it is a bird?

Everybody laughed and applauded, and then Siri asked me to come up and sing it with her. She'd written out the melody on a sheet of paper and it was simple. I could read music fairly well, so, although I was embarrassed, I sang it with her, and she sang a descant, and wove in and around the melody with her harp. When we went in to dinner I felt happy, with my anxieties far below the surface.

The next morning we were threading our way among thousands of icebergs, from little ones to enormous tabular icebergs, bigger than a football field. They were staggeringly beautiful, glowing blue and sometimes green. They seemed to have an inner light, to contain deep within their ice the fires of the sun from the days when the planet was young and still forming. On many of the bergs were what at first looked like shadows but were sleeping seals.

Siri sat by me at breakfast.

I said, "I'd like a picture of you sitting on an iceberg and playing to the seals."

She reached for the cream. "I'll sing for them when you write me a seal song, and also when we're closer to land."

"Siri, that song you sang about troubling a star, who wrote the words?"

"Francis Thompson, an interesting nineteenth-century poet, maybe not a great one, but he had a good and loving mind."

"Your music to his star poem is lovely, too. You're a fabulous composer."

"Thanks. I love making music."

"Will you sing it again?"

"Sure. It's one of my favorites, and I think the penguins like it, too. I'll play them your angel song and see how they respond to that. What gave you the idea for it?"

"A conversation I had with Cookie before we left home, about angels and feathers." I found myself telling Siri about Aunt Serena and her gift of this trip, and about Cook.

"So he was once a monk? Not surprising, somehow."

All day at sea, the waves worsened, and quite a few people didn't make it up to the Womb Room for the lectures. Todd gave us a lecture about whales, and the disastrous effects of whaling. The figures on remaining whales of various species made me shudder. "Whale oil was used for everything, from dog food to jet turbines. The high temperatures for the turbines required lubrication that was hard to refine from petroleum, but during the Second World War it was discovered that it was much easier to use sperm-whale oil. It is especially tragic to me that the oil of these peaceable creatures should be used for war." He had a picture of the Antarctic blue whale on the screen, and was silent for a moment, letting us look at it. Then he said, "However! In the 1970s it was discovered that the jojoba bean, a desert shrub found in the American Southwest, had oil that was an ideal substitute for sperm oil. But the whale population had already been decimated. We can hope that there will be enough calves so that the population will increase, but it is easier to destroy than to create, and greed pays little attention to destruction." Then he tried to cheer us up by showing slides of whale flukes, each one unique.

By the time we went in for dinner that evening, there were quite a few empty places. Jorge ate about half his dinner, then said, "I took a Meclizine pill, hoping it would keep me from being seasick, but I have a feeling I would like to lie down. Excuse me."

Suddenly Greta put her hand to her mouth and hurried out. I was glad seasickness didn't seem to be one of my problems.

Sam looked at me, then at Otto. "You two okay?"

"Fine," I said.

Otto smiled. "Happily, like Vicky, I do not get seasick." He looked up as the ding-dong sounded for an announcement. Quim told us we were about to sail by Elephant Island, and the captain would make the decision as to whether or not we would be able to anchor and take the Zodiacs in. I was sitting by the window and the water was rough, with large white-caps, and I didn't think getting in or out of a Zodiac was a good idea. But Elephant Island as we sailed by was awesome. Glaciers. Snow-topped mountains. Blue ice, white ice, yellowish ice, strange shadows and shapes, clouds that looked like part of the glaciers but suddenly swirled and roiled.

"Look!" Angelique cried, and pointed out a large petrel battling the wind.

"My advice as ship's physician is that we should stay right

where we are," Dick said. Certainly, getting in or out of a Zodiac bobbing up and down was not easy for him.

Angelique leaned against him affectionately. "I'm quite content to see Elephant Island from here."

Otto put down his knife and fork, asking, "Do you realize that several of Shackleton's men spent—how many months?" He looked at Sam, who shook his head, then at Leilia.

"A long time, right there"—Leilia pointed out the window—"under two upturned lifeboats, waiting to be rescued, and believing they *would* be rescued."

"Were they?" I asked. Elephant Island looked wild and hostile.

"They were," Leilia said. "Their faith in Shackleton was justified. I have a not very good video documentary of Shackleton I play for my kids, to teach them something about promises and honor."

The ding-dong sounded, and the loudspeaker came on. Quim's voice told us that there was no way the Zodiacs could be launched in these seas. Angelique gently touched Dick's knee and gave him a quick, loving smile.

Quim's voice continued, telling us that the portholes on starboard were being covered, but this was normal procedure, nothing unusual or worrisome.

The sense of awe I felt as we sailed past Elephant Island was deeper than Aunt Serena's photographs or even Adam II's journal had prepared me for. What we saw as we looked out the windows was stranger and more alien than pictures of the moon. Not many people nowadays see the planet like this, pure and serene and ruthless.

"Would it happen today?" Angelique asked.

"What?" Dick raised his eyebrows.

"Caring about your colleagues enough to risk your own life for them."

"It's anybody's guess," Dick said. "We've become deeply entrenched in uninvolvement."

"Not you," Angelique said.

Leilia shook her head. "Quim or Benjy—or any one of our lecturers—I think they'd care enough, be responsible enough."

"Let's hope they're never tested," Dick said.

"Are you seasick?" Angelique asked him.

"Because my pessimistic side is to the fore? I don't like the water when it's this rough. I'm off to my bunk."

"Me, too," Otto said, and bid us all good night.

In the morning we moved out of fog into sunlight as we sailed through a turbulent sea full of ice floes and spectacular icebergs. Even more than the day before, I felt as though we had sailed back billions of years. The blue coloring in some of the icebergs was so brilliant it made the sky look pale. The water was rough and full of whitecaps, and Siri, who was sitting across from me at breakfast, announced that she was very glad that our ship had radar and depth sounders and that the double hull was ice-hardened. Quimby came on the intercom and told us we'd be sailing south all morning, passing to the east of Joinville Island and the Danger Islands en route to Paulet Island, where there should be thousands, literally thousands, of Adélie penguins.

219

Otto came into the dining room and joined us, and so did Sam, Angelique, and Dick. Despite the rough sea, we saw several groups of penguins porpoising, incredibly graceful in the water in comparison to their clumsiness on land. Benjy was right about their flying in water. While they were leaping in swiftly graceful arcs, they did look like cetaceans rather than birds. No wonder Benjy found them so fascinating. I wondered if Adam was studying penguins at LeNoir Station.

——No, Vicky. You aren't thinking about Adam.

Todd, our mammal lecturer, came on the intercom to tell us we might see some whales, and maybe a few dolphins, though not many here at this time of year. "Keep a lookout, though," he urged us, "and if a whale flukes, take as many pictures for me as you can. I'm studying flukes."

After breakfast, while I was putting on my heaviest sweater, red parka, boots with two pair of heavy socks, Benjy knocked on my door and poked his head in to make sure I was all right. We went together out to the fo'c'sle, to look in all directions as we sailed through seas so full of ice that some of the smaller floes hit against the sides of the ship with a sound like distant thunder. Benjy said the channel had opened just a week before, and there was no way we could go through it without bumping into floes. In another week or so, it would close up again with solid ice.

Todd came out, his parka hood pulled close about his face. He stood with us, and we saw many seals sleeping on ice floes, crab-eater seals, Todd told me, though there are no crabs in these bitter waters. The seals were lazing on the tabular ice-bergs in larger numbers than the singletons or doubletons on the floes, snoozing away because they hunt at night. For a while we sailed through a veritable city of icebergs. Benjy said we were seeing a far greater colony of bergs than usual. Then he excitedly pointed out two snow petrels. Benjy had taken this trip many times and had never lost his excitement.

The wind was so fierce that, even with our hoods up, we were driven in. I hadn't seen Otto, but I had tried not to look for him. It was quite easy not to see somebody, because our red parkas made us all look alike.

To my surprise, the ding-dong rang and the announcement was made that we were going ashore. About half of us lined up to get in the Zodiacs. When my turn came, the Zodiac seemed to leap up at me and I dropped in and sat on the side beside Leilia. Getting out was not bad, because the rubber boat was pulled partway up onto the beach and we just had to swing our legs over the side and slosh in. And there were indeed thousands of Adélie penguins. I was surprised to see one languid Weddell seal lying among the penguins nearest the shore, and others on ice floes no more than a few feet away. Papageno's experience had made me a little leery of seals, but Todd assured me that Weddell seals wouldn't harm either me or the penguins.

"What about your harp?" Greta asked Siri.

She shook her head. "I didn't bring her this morning. The water's pretty rough, and I don't want her getting wet. She's hard enough to keep in tune as is."

I reminded her, "What about singing to the seals?"

She assured me, "There'll be other opportunities, I promise you. Today let's concentrate on penguins and birds."

Benjy said, "One seal doesn't make a stink, but wait till we get close to a bunch of them. They dribble yellow mucus from their noses to get rid of excess salt, and while the stuff is functional, it's also smelly. Hoy! Look up there on the cliff at that albatross nest!"

Sam let me use his binoculars. "That water's getting mighty rough." He didn't sound happy. "Once we get back to the ship, the Zodiacs aren't going to stand quietly while we disembark. They're going to go up and down like jumping jacks. It's going to be even harder on Dick than on me."

"The sailors'll be there to help." I tried to sound comforting, but leaping out of the Zodiac onto the small metal platform of the ladder wasn't easy in clothes that made you weigh double your normal weight and in boots that made your feet twice their normal size.

"I hope they really check our manifest numbers," Sam grumbled.

"We do," Benjy assured him. "On one of our trips, when we checked the board, one manifest number hadn't been turned over, so Quim and I got in a Zodiac and went back to the part of the peninsula where we'd been that afternoon, looking for the missing passenger, who'd climbed high up on a cliff where he shouldn't have been. He was an amateur ornithologist and was trying to take pictures of albatross babies in their nest, and he slipped and fell and knocked himself out. He came to after all the Zodiacs had left for the *Argosy,* and he was mighty glad to see Quim and me, I can tell you. And look—"

High above our heads an albatross was flying, riding the current, its great wings outspread, and I thought of Adam II's description. The great bird glided serenely, with no motion of the wings, sailing on wind and sky and sun. I watched for so long that I had to run to catch up with Siri and Benjy. If Greta hadn't been with them, I'd have continued to lag behind, but she was chattering away about some zoo in Berlin, ignoring a colony of gentoo penguins.

"My ex-husband liked that zoo," Siri said.

"Ex?" Benjy asked with what I thought was considerable interest.

"Very ex. He's married to a fifty-year-old heiress so he can live in the life-style to which he always wanted to become accustomed." Her usually gentle voice was sharp.

"Where'd the heiress's money come from?" Benjy asked.

Siri made a face. "Deodorants, I think."

"And where does your money come from?"

"It doesn't come. I work for it."

"My point entirely," Benjy said, though I wasn't sure what his point was. Whatever, it was meant to make Siri feel better. "I enjoy my work and I think you enjoy yours, right?"

Siri's voice and smile were back to normal. "Right."

Sam and I were in the same Zodiac on our way back to the ship. It seemed to me that, wherever I went, Sam was apt to be there, too. Not exactly shadowing me. Not exactly hovering. Just there.

I watched two strong sailors heave him safely onto the landing platform. One thing about Sam, he didn't let anything stop him.

Greta said, as she washed the guano off her boots, "Jorge and Otto stayed on the ship. Business talk."

Fine. I didn't want to get obsessed with Otto. Or anybody.

The next morning we had a very early wake-up call and after coffee and a roll headed for the Zodiacs. Quimby had warned everybody not to drink too much coffee, because we'd have an hour's trip each way in the Zodiacs, and there weren't going to be any johns along the way. The sea was moderately calm, despite the frigid winds—katabatic winds, Quim called them, and I liked the word because it sounded as bitter as the winds.

A few people stayed on board and slept in, but most of us made it. Greta was feeling miserable, Siri said, and was staying in her bunk, and Leilia and her friends, who'd been here before, were catching up on sleep. So was Otto, Jorge told us. Jack was sitting across from me in the Zodiac, and I wished he'd take off his cowboy hat, which was blocking my view. Dick and Angelique were next to me, Dick determined not to miss anything he didn't have to.

It was beautiful in the semi-light of what would still have been deep night at home. The icebergs gleamed as if by moonlight, and there was a pearly quality to the day, as though the planet were a jewel in a great shell. We were heading for an island off the coast of the Antarctic peninsula, where an explorer called Nordenskjöld and his companions had been stranded during the 1902–3 winter. When our Zodiac approached the beach, Benjy let out a startled exclamation, and I could see several bright orange tents.

"Who the——" Benjy started, and then, as our Zodiac was pulled up onto the beach, "Vespugians. What the——"

The second Zodiac pulled up next to ours, and Quim jumped out, saying, "Hey, Benj, they shouldn't—" and then shut his mouth as several tent flaps opened and half-dressed men came staggering sleepily out to see what was going on.

A bulky man who looked like, but wasn't, Captain Nausinio came hurtling toward us, buttoning and buckling his uniform jacket and shouting ferociously, and I thought I heard the word *cientifico,* and then Quimby was shouting back.

Jorge splashed into shore, talking to the bulky man, then to Quim, and they both quieted down, though the bulky man was scowling and Quim looked anything but pleased.

Todd was giving Dick a hand out of the Zodiac, and I heard him mutter, "Scientific, my Aunt Fanny."

Jorge was carrying his enormous camera cases and was slung with two other cases of equipment, which he put down at his feet. He continued talking to the Vespugian in a calm, smiling way. The still-scowling Vespugian officer picked up Jorge's cases and took them into one of the tents.

Quimby said, "Well, this was an unexpected surprise, ladies and gentlemen. We were given no indication that anybody was going to be here."

Benjy muttered to Dick, "Spurious scientists, if I ever saw one. Everybody knows the Vespugians want to be a presence in Antarctica." Jorge, at the same time, was reassuring everybody that the tents represented a small scientific excursion, there was nothing to be disturbed about, everything was fine.

More soldiers were coming out of the tents, and suddenly one of them waved at me, shouting out, "Vickee!"

It was Esteban. I waved back, a reflex of recognition

225

through my startlement. I turned to Jorge. "What on earth is Esteban doing here?"

Jorge went over to Esteban and shook his hand, saying to me over his shoulder, "It is not that surprising to see him. The Vespugian army is very small, as our country is small, and the General wants to give the young men as full and varied an experience as possible during their two years of service."

The other soldiers were not as welcoming as Esteban. Some of them appeared confused by our presence. A couple turned to Esteban with what seemed to be both scolding and questioning, and the one who looked like Captain Nausinio and who seemed to be the leader came up to Quimby again, still exuding belligerence.

Once more Jorge intervened, talking, smiling, laughing. I heard him say something about Generalissimo Guedder as he patted the bulky soldier on the shoulder, and then apparently asked him what he had done with the camera equipment.

The Vespugian pointed toward his tent and Jorge nodded, saying to Quim, "Good, my equipment is very expensive and not replaceable in Vespugia. I'm glad to have it under cover until I'm ready to take pictures of Nordenskjöld's hut."

Jack Nessinger came up to him, and the two of them moved past the cluster of tents.

Benjy turned to me with a grin. "The Vespugians thought—maybe they still think—we're an invading army, come to take over their post. Jorge has been trying to reassure them. I guess being a pal of the General's gives him considerable clout."

"If they weren't expecting us," Dick said, "a whole lot of people in identical red parkas arriving in Zodiacs would seem pretty threatening."

"We weren't expecting *them*," Quimby growled. "I don't think they're supposed to be here. They're certainly not a registered station."

"Thank goodness for Jorge," Angelique said, "and his diplomatic ability. I thought the captain was ready to line us all up and shoot us."

There were half a dozen tents, and some of the emerging soldiers had gone back in and were now fully dressed in their uniforms. It was early, not yet five in the morning, and they must have been sound asleep. Esteban had gone back into his tent, and now he came out, buttoning his uniform jacket. He waved again and smiled at me, and spoke to the Vespugian leader. Esteban was pointing at Siri and me, then at Sam, and nodding and smiling. I think he was explaining that he had already met us. The bulky captain stood with his legs apart, hands on hips, scowling as he listened. He wasn't wearing his gun, though some of the others had picked up theirs. "They've become a gun-happy people," Sam muttered.

Jorge walked over to us. "Esteban will lead you to Nordenskjöld's hut, and I'll get everything here straightened out with the captain."

Quim muttered, "I suppose it's politic, having one of them be our guide. Jorge knows we're perfectly capable of taking the group to the hut, but this gives their being here more plausibility, I suppose." He did not sound pleased.

We followed Esteban, crunching along in our boots. I was walking with Sam, but he said, "Go walk with Esteban, Vicky. I think he'd like that."

Dick, just behind us, grunted assent. "This can't be a pleasant post, no matter what the reason for the Vespugian presence here."

Angelique smiled at me. "Esteban has been casting longing glances at you."

I thought they were exaggerating my importance to Esteban, especially as the language barrier was as high as ever, but I moved up to walk beside him, and he gave me a brilliant smile. Then he handed me another postcard, this one of Weddell seals on a large ice floe. He nodded and smiled and nodded again as though he were trying to tell me something. I turned the postcard over, and on the back was written in pencil: TEN CUIDADO! GUÁRDATE! Even though my Spanish is nonexistent, I was pretty sure it meant BE CAREFUL!

Nine

The Zodiac had come so near that my heart had quickened with hope, and even after I had long given it up, my heart continued to pound. I listened for the sound of the motor as it died away. The Zodiac had gone after something—someone—else. Had left me.

It had been so close. I was sure someone had to have heard me, seen me waving my red parka.

On the Argosy they must know I was gone. My manifest number would be red side up, not yellow. Benjy had told about going back for someone who had not turned his number. They would not sail off and leave me. Benjy would not let that happen. An alarm would have been raised. All I had to do was wait.

How long had it taken for Shackleton to rescue his men? We'd watched a movie about that one evening. He'd tried four times to get to Elephant Island. It took him how many weeks? Months? I had no lifeboat to shelter me. I couldn't catch fish with my bare hands. I wouldn't last many more hours, much less days.

229

. . .

"Esteban." I spoke slowly, enunciating clearly, as though that would help him to understand. "What are you doing here?"

Esteban frowned, obviously not understanding a word.

Benjy, who had been trotting up and down beside our group, herding us like a sheepdog, came over. "Communication problem?"

I nodded. "Esteban was our guide at the Vespugian pyramids, so I just wanted to ask him what he's doing here, and about this postcard he gave me."

Benjy spoke to Esteban in Spanish, stumbling over the words but getting them out. He listened to Esteban's reply, then said to me, "They're here only for a few days, on what he said is a sort of camping trip. But"—he shrugged—"like I said, the Vespugians want to be a presence in Antarctica, and my bet is that's why they're here. I can't see any signs of science."

He didn't say anything about the postcard with what I took to be a warning, and I didn't push it, though it gave me a definitely chilly feeling.

I needed Cook. If anything else happened, I'd have to get Benjy alone. I had to talk to someone.

Siri came up to us then, shook hands with Esteban, then made motions with her fingers, like playing an oboe.

Esteban smiled at us, and his eyes were the color of the blue in the icebergs, not cold, but radiant. He spoke to Benjy, rather apologetically.

Benjy translated. "He says he can't bring his oboe here because—something about heat and cold. It doesn't make much sense."

Siri said quickly, "It makes a lot of sense. When he plays the oboe, the warmth of his breath heats it, while the cold outside air chills it, and the opposition of heat and cold would probably crack it. That's tough. He needs to practice regularly."

We had reached the hut we had come to see, and that's all it was, a hut built of smallish stones, barely still standing. It was interesting if you knew the history behind it, but not in itself.

Angelique said, "We're on a comfortable boat. It's summer. What do you think this hut would have been like in the Antarctic winter?"

Sam said, "As an explorer, I've sometimes wondered which is preferable, freezing to death or broiling."

Dick leaned on his cane, smiling rather grimly. "Surgery in the jungle when your hands are so slippery with sweat you can hardly hold the instruments isn't much fun."

Angelique put her mittened hand on her husband's arm. "Not to mention bombs and machine guns."

Dick jerked in reflex as we heard engines above us, and three helicopters began circling. They flew over our heads, and we could see down the slope of land to the water, and the helicopters dipped low over the *Argosy*.

"Vespugian helicopters." Sam pointed his camera skyward.

Dick relaxed. "Just checking out all these redcoats in their little black boats zooming in from their little red ship."

Siri asked, "Why're they so nervous? Do they really think we're an invading troop?"

Leilia smiled at her. "Vespugia's been invaded quite a few times. I don't blame them for checking us out."

231

"Maybe," Angelique said, "they're nervous because they aren't supposed to be here."

Esteban, who of course hadn't understood a word we were saying, indicated that it was time for us to go, and we followed him back toward the Vespugian tents. The helicopters circled a few times and then disappeared over the horizon.

Benjy came up to us, explaining, "Jorge thinks the captain here is probably upset by our presence because he realizes he's violated the Antarctic Treaty by being here with weapons. The treaty prohibits 'any measure of a military nature, such as the establishment of military bases and fortifications.' Jorge says the poor man is so worried by our unexpected arrival that he's not thinking clearly, and he's forgotten that the treaty goes on to say that it does not prevent the use of military personnel or equipment for scientific research."

"Hm," Dick said.

"Hm, indeed," Benjy agreed. "But that's why he radioed his base, and why we were checked over by their helicopters. Never a dull moment."

Most of our group had taken pictures of the hut, and still had their cameras out, and Leilia asked Quimby if it was all right to take pictures of the Vespugians and their camp. It ended up with our red parkaed gang taking pictures of the Vespugian soldiers, and the Vespugians taking pictures of us, and finally everybody relaxed.

Quim called us to come to the Zodiacs; it was time to go back to the *Argosy*. As I climbed in one of the Zodiacs, with

232

Sam right behind me, I noticed Jorge going into a tent and coming out with all his camera stuff.

At lunch, Otto sat with us on the nonsmokers' side. We had to tell Otto all about the morning's adventures, and he laughed as though the whole thing were totally funny, and I suppose it was.

"So Jorge calmed everybody down?" he asked.

"With great diplomacy," Sam said.

Leilia lavishly buttered her roll. "If Jorge is such a bigwig, I wonder what he's doing on a funny little ship like the *Argosy*?"

"Fun," Dick said. "People in his position need to get away and have a rest periodically. That's why I'm here—love of travel and a need for stress release from working with little bones."

"Have you forgotten you're ship's doc?" Sam asked. "What about big bones?"

"I've set a couple on previous vacations," Dick acknowledged, "but it's very different from the constant pressure of my everyday life."

Angelique laughed. "So take good care of yourself, Sam. Dick would be very cross with you if you fell."

"Never fear," Sam said. "I'm a cautious bloke. That's how I've survived for so long. As for Jorge, I agree with Dick. And he obviously loves the Antarctic."

Leilia leaned back in her chair. "As Benjy says, this place is contagious. A lot of my friends think I'm nuts, leaving Fairbanks for the Antarctic. Mostly we Alaskans try to get away to someplace warm, like Hawaii. But it's so beautiful here I keep coming back, so I can understand that it's equally addictive for Jorge."

"And, thank God," Angelique added, "the big cruise ships haven't taken over. At least not yet."

"Maybe," Sam suggested, "Jorge is here to keep an eye on things for Guedder."

"Why not?" Greta asked sharply. "Aren't you being a little suspicious, Sam?"

Sam raised his bushy brows. "Suspicious? I thought I was making a reasonable suggestion. If Jorge is working for his country, bravo for him."

I thought of Otto and our conversation over the mint tea. This was a world I knew nothing about. I love my country, but I guess I've always taken it for granted. My roots are deep in New England and a democratic government. But I've never had to fight for it, or do anything that demanded courage or sacrifice. Our parents told us that two of our downstairs walls are double thick, with about a foot of space between, and they were made that way long after the house was built, in order to make a hiding space for escaped slaves on the Underground Railroad. I was glad our house had been part of that, but it was a long time ago, and I'd never really thought about the people who lived there then putting themselves in danger for their principles and for other human beings.

Now, having been in Vespugia, having been in the Falklands, having talked with Otto, I was opening my eyes to a new way of seeing. Esteban cared enough about Vespugia to risk his life for it, I thought. And now I was in the strange world of the Antarctic, where Benjy and Quim were as passionate about protecting this amazing land as Otto was about making Zlatovica into a viable principality. Or wasn't it the same?

After lunch we dropped anchor near Seymour Island and got back into Zodiacs. When we landed, there were more penguins than could be counted, some going in and out of the ocean from the crescent of the beach, landing with whopping belly-flops and skidding on their thick padding of feathers as swiftly as though they were flying. Otto was walking with me, and we giggled at a dozen or so who were waddling laboriously uphill, chittering as they climbed the barren mountainside, which really did look like a moonscape. When we reached the top, there were hundreds of fluffy silver-grey chicks, perfect little moon creatures. They were roly-poly from being fed by their parents, but they could waddle after an adult penguin with amazing speed. Otto doubled over with laughter, pointing out a little one as it fell flat on its belly, picked itself up, and ran after a grown penguin.

"Which might not even be its parent," Otto said, "in which case it won't get fed. Adult penguins feed only their own chicks."

Siri, coming up beside us, asked, "How on earth do they tell them apart?"

"By their voices, Benjy says."

Siri cocked her head, listening. "I've a pretty good ear, but it's obvious I'm not a penguin. They all sound alike to me."

Otto and I continued climbing. When we paused to rest,

he looked down at his booted toe, making a mark on the icy shale, and asked, "You have a boyfriend?"

I shook my head. "I do not." I sounded too vehement.

"You've quarreled?" Otto asked.

"I guess. Sort of. It doesn't matter. I'm too young, anyhow, to be really serious about anyone."

"Truly?" Otto asked.

I started climbing again. Carefully and deliberately, I turned my mind away from Adam. Asked Otto, "How's your Spanish?"

He stopped, breathing quickly from the exercise. "I have a little. Not much." He shrugged. "French and Italian help, but I cannot, for instance, read Cervantes."

"But for conversation?"

"What is this, Vicky?" He turned to me, smiling. "Is this sudden interest in Spanish something to do with that young oboist Jorge has told me about?"

Good. Let him think I'd fallen for Esteban. "It would be fun to be able to talk with him."

Otto said, "I should not have stayed in my bunk the other morning. I would like to have met this young man who I am told is very taken with you, and who would obviously like to be able to talk to you." He looked me directly in the eyes. "I'm just as happy that he can't. I want no other young man making eyes at my beautiful Vicky." Then he added, quickly, "I'm sorry. I know you're not 'my' beautiful Vicky, or anybody else's. You are your own. But oh, my dear Vicky, you do delight me."

I was glad my parka hood was up so that my blush was at least partly covered.

"So I have made my inquiries about this Esteban and I have learned that he is related to Generalissimo Guedder. Be careful, Vicky. This Esteban will try to influence your thinking."

"Hey, Esteban doesn't speak English and I don't speak Spanish. He can't do much influencing."

Otto pushed my hood back so that he could see me more easily. "Vicky, this Esteban may be young and attractive, but he is not for you. He is nobody."

"So'm I."

"Vicky, you are young and bright and lovely, but you are naïve politically."

"I know. I can learn."

"Yes, you will learn, but it is not pleasant to learn that there is corruption in high places. On this trip, please, let's just enjoy the penguins and the seals. Forget that there are people on the *Argosy* with conflicting views." He took a few steps up the mountain, taking us beyond the rest of the group. "It is a heaviness on my heart." I looked at him questioningly. He continued, "There are those who do not want Zlatovica to continue as an independent principality. We are an old and ancient land. I love my country, and I will do whatever needs to be done. Enough. I'm sorry. It is just that you are good to talk to."

I said, softly, "I'm glad."

"Vicky, I would not have any harm come to you. I know we have known each other only a short time, and to make true friends takes time. But already—I want you to know that if ever you need me, I'm here for you. At any time." He leaned toward me, taking my hands. His eyes were warm and golden.

He looked around to make sure we were alone, that nobody had followed us up the mountain except a few penguins. Then he kissed me.

It was a lovely kiss. I liked it.

I had liked Adam's kisses. They were not my first kisses, I was not "sweet sixteen and never been kissed." But both Adam and Otto were more experienced than I was.

"We'd better go down," Otto said. "Look." The small group of penguins was leaving us, waddling downhill. Otto took my hand and we hurried to join a cluster of red-parkaed people with Jason, our geologist, in their midst. We looked as he held out his hand. "Petrified wood," he said.

Wood, here in this barren place where there was no vegetation except for a little lichen, a little dried-up moss! Once upon a time there had been trees here.

Jason put one of the pieces of wood no longer wood but stone into my hand. "See, Vicky, those little white things? They're fossils of extinct species of clams."

More people gathered round, exclaiming. Jason, slipping into his lecturer's voice, said, "Even though the petrified wood tells us that there were once trees here, millennia ago, there are no indications of any indigenous humanoids ever having lived on the Antarctic continent." He held out another fossil to Angelique, who took it, looking at it with awe.

Dick reached out with one finger and touched the fossil that lay in Angelique's palm. "You can't escape the great chain of life in this place. Perhaps it's just as well there have never been any human beings around here to muck it up with our bloody history."

Angelique handed the fossil to Jason, put her arm around Dick's bulky parka. "Not always bloody, my darling. Not always."

I was writing in my journal and was nearly ready to go to the lounge for Wrap-Up, when Benjy knocked on my door, came in, and plunked himself down on the second bunk.

"Everything okay?"

"Sure."

"You look a little preoccupied."

I looked down at my journal. "I'm just being a broody adolescent."

"Nothing on your mind?"

"Oh, Benjy, that'll be the day! There's lots on my mind."

"Want to talk about it?"

I looked at my watch. Benjy would have to join everybody in the lounge in a few minutes. What I wanted to talk about would take real time. "Not yet. Soon."

"Otto appears to be taking good care of you."

"Um."

"You know, Vicky, Otto may not be twenty yet, but there's pressure on him in Zlatovica to marry, and there aren't that many princesses around."

"Hunh?" I was so startled I was inarticulate.

"Are you old enough to have heard of Princess Grace?"

"Vaguely. I know she was supposed to be as beautiful as a fairy-tale princess."

"And a commoner." Benjy grinned.

"Benjy, what are you implying?"

239

"Otto is very interested in you. Perhaps I'm letting my imagination run away with me, but remember, Vicky, all that glitters is not gold."

I said, rather stiffly, "Otto glitters, I know that, but——" I stopped. Caught my breath. I'd started to say, "But he's not coming on to me." But wasn't he? I stood up. "Hey, Benjy, I'm only an ordinary adolescent American girl, planning to go to college and do all that stuff. Okay?"

"Sure," Benjy said. "Okay, time for Wrap-Up."

We went into the lounge together, and he headed for the table where Siri was and sat down beside her, giving her a look of love that almost brought tears to my eyes. Because I wanted that. I know not everybody in the world gets it, but I wanted it. Angelique and Dick had it. I think maybe my parents have it, but it probably gets diffused when there are four kids vying for attention.

Otto was sitting at the table next to us, and reached over to grab my hand for a quick squeeze.

Do royals ever have it? Or do they get so mixed up in politics and diplomacy and all that other stuff that the real thing gets lost?

And I am not, definitely not, princess material.

That night I went to sleep right away and then woke up suddenly. I looked at my watch. Just after two. I didn't know what had roused me, probably ice bumping against the hull of the *Argosy*. I was wide awake. I turned over and tried to go back to sleep. I rolled from one side to another. My mind jiggled like a broken kaleidoscope. Vespugia. Antarctica. Adam's letter, cold as ice. Zlatovica and Princess Grace.

If I'd been at home, I'd have gone to the kitchen and made cocoa. I very seldom have trouble sleeping, but it does hit occasionally, usually when I have too much on my mind, and there's no point trying to get back to sleep until I can stop my thoughts from swimming around like fish in a bowl. I remembered that there's always hot water up in the bar area of the lounge, and powdered cocoa as well as tea or coffee, so I got out of my bunk, put on my warm bathrobe and slippers, and opened the door. All up and down the corridor, cabin doors were closed. I thought I heard a snore from the cabin next to mine, which, now that Cook was no longer on the *Argosy*, was Sam's alone.

I went up the stairs to the main deck. Only the dim nightlights were on. The exit light over the fo'c'sle door was lit, but it would be much too cold out on deck. The lounge was full of the dark shadows of round tables and chairs. I put some powdered cocoa into a mug, filled it with hot water and stirred it smooth, then sat on the padded seat at one of the corner tables. I wished someone else were awake, so we could talk.

Suddenly I heard a sharp sound. A bang. Louder and closer than ice hitting the ship.

I ducked down on the seat. There was no reason I shouldn't be in the lounge, but it was a reflex. My face was down on the cushion of the seat and I peered under the table. I could see Otto coming out of his big cabin carrying one of his wooden packing cases. He looked around, as though to make sure he was alone, then went to the fo'c'sle door, pushed it open, and went out.

Why didn't I just say, "Hey, Otto, I'm here"? I didn't. I stayed hidden. I didn't dare try to make a run for my cabin, all the way across the lounge and down the wide stairs to my deck. I didn't know who else might come, or when Otto would return. If someone saw me, I'd be terribly embarrassed. I felt like an idiot, hiding in the corner.

Finally the fo'c'sle door opened and Otto came back, without the box. Where was it? Overboard?

It was after two o'clock in the morning, the time when imagination is most likely to run wild. Zlatovica had Soviet silos with nuclear weapons. Suzy's precious Ned was concerned about the disposal of such weapons.

I knew what I was thinking was crazy, but I still thought it. No, Vicky. Nobody with any intelligence would travel with radioactive material unless it was properly protected from any kind of leakage, and Otto was certainly intelligent.

But what was in the box?

Several people on the *Argosy* had talked about the danger of disposing of nuclear waste in Antarctica. But what about the Antarctic Ocean?

All these thoughts darted through my mind in the time it took Otto to cross the lounge and go into his cabin. I heard him turn the lock on his door. I listened. Heard only the creaking of the ship moving through the waters. Then I heard a loud sound and finally understood that this time it was the ship's hull hitting an ice floe, not Otto coming out of his cabin. Slowly and carefully I stood up. Then I moved as quickly and quietly as possible across the lounge and down to my cabin. Closed the door slowly and carefully so it wouldn't make a noise.

I was sure I wouldn't sleep, but I did.

In the morning we anchored off Half Moon Island and got into Zodiacs immediately after breakfast. Otto was in the Zodiac which followed mine, and he hurried over to walk with me, and suddenly there was Benjy on my other side.

Otto was talking about his need to finish his studies, probably back in England, but he wasn't going to be able to until newly independent Zlatovica was more stable. I was only half listening, because all I could think of was the night before.

Benjy picked up on what Otto was saying. "And this trip? How is it that you have time for Antarctica?"

Otto laughed openly, merrily. "It seemed wise for me to leave Zlatovica for a few weeks. Some of my ideas for educational reform did not sit well with my conservative uncle, who is one of our chief ministers. And my father wanted me to look for options for energy, always a problem in a small, emerging country. But mostly it seemed the better part of valor to make myself scarce until tempers cooled." He took my arm and gave it a gentle squeeze. "This, too, is true."

My green-booted foot slipped on a round stone and both Benjy and Otto steadied me. Others joined us as we came to a large group of penguins, but Benjy was talking to Otto about alternate sources of power. "The sun has all the power we need, and when the technology is worked out, it will be available to us without any drain on the sun itself."

"Ideal," Otto agreed. "The sun is a massive atomic furnace, and if we could simply pick up what it discards every day, we'd have enough energy for the entire planet."

Benjy sounded suddenly severe. "No matter what happens to the earth's energy sources, there's no need to draw on Antarctica."

"Quite," Otto agreed. And then other people began to ask questions, about solar energy, about penguins, about what we were going to do after dinner.

When we got back to the ship, I'd hardly changed out of my boots when the ding-dong sounded and Todd's excited voice told us that there were three humpback whales ahead of us to starboard. I rushed out to the fo'c'sle, and so did almost everybody else. It was awesome, watching those huge bodies swimming alongside the ship, coming all the way up to *whoosh* through their blowholes, going under, then rising slowly until they were grey shadows under the water, then rising to *whoosh* again. They were so enormous and so marvelous that they took my mind off all my questions. Most people had cameras out, including Jorge with his enormous Hasselblad, and Jack with a cardboard throwaway camera.

Benjy and Todd were working with an underwater recorder which played humpback-whale music, hoping these whales would hear it and sing for us, but they didn't. I've heard recordings of whale song, and it's strange and wonderful, and Siri told me of the work of the composer Alan Hovhaness, who was one of the first music writers to use actual whale song in an orchestral composition. That gave me an idea of something to get Mother for her birthday.

The whales stayed with us for over an hour, though it seemed much less. Todd once again asked people to get as many pictures as possible of their flukes, but the whales apparently did not feel like fluking, for every time we thought they were going to dive and show us their flukes they just went under, and Todd and Benjy groaned, and then cajoled, "Come on, whales, come on! Aw, come on! Be good whales! Come fluke for us!"

It really seemed as though these great creatures were teasing us, because there'd be shouts that they were about to fluke, and groans as they dropped down under the water again. Benjy and Todd looked both disappointed and frustrated, and finally, when we'd all about given up, Benjy yelled "Hey!" and suddenly, as a goodbye present, the whales fluked their great glorious tails for us. All kinds of cameras went off, taking as many shots as possible before the whales disappeared. And I felt the same surge of joy I had felt when Siri first played for the penguins.

In the early afternoon we took the Zodiacs to Hannah Point on Livingston Island. Siri and Sam were in the Zodiac with me, and Benjy was at the outboard. Otto was in the Zodiac ahead of us with Jorge and Jack, big Jack standing out as usual, with his cowboy hat making him a head higher than anybody else.

On Hannah Point we saw our first elephant seals— blubber slugs, Benjy called them. They were enormous creatures, lying together in a great, shapeless pile, with steam rising up from their massive bodies. They weren't as big as the elephants they were named for, of course, or they couldn't have moved their great bulks about on land. Even so, they were cumbersome and clumsy. Otto came over to me and pointed, and we watched one great wrinkled body heave itself up and struggle over several prone seals who just happened to be in its path, before flopping down again. And they did smell.

Otto put his arm about me.

Otto, Otto. What were you doing last night?

I said, lightly, "I don't think the elephant seals are much of a threat, not unless we get in their path when they want to move somewhere."

Were there other nights, too, when I was asleep and Otto slipped out of his cabin and threw cases overboard? Cases of what?

Sam joined us, saying, "Unlike some seals, leopard seals, for instance, elephant seals don't eat penguins." The beach was full of penguins waddling about, ignoring the seals.

"Chinstraps and gentoos," Otto said. "Look. The chinstrap has a black line under its jaw, and pale pink feet."

"Um." Sam nodded. "And the gentoo has a red bill and red feet."

If I thought about penguins, I forgot to worry. We climbed a steep, stony hill to see hundreds more, including one lonely macaroni penguin with a funny little topknot on its head. Benjy said that it was like the hairdo of dandies at the time of the American Revolution, and in "Yankee-Doodle Dandy" the "put a feather in your cap and call it macaroni" was a sort of slap at the colonial dandies. "The penguins aren't particularly dandy," he said. He looked at the funny little macaroni and said probably it didn't lay its egg in time, and wouldn't be able to complete raising its chick. There's a lot of infant mortality.

I turned away from Otto, and Benjy was pointing out nesting petrels and gulls on a ledge above us. I felt irrationally sad. And uneasy.

Siri had left the group and gone back down to the beach with her harp. I said, "Siri's getting her harp out of its case. I'm going down."

"Okay," Benjy said. "Take care."

Otto said, "I can take care of Vicky."

Sam hooked his arm into mine. "Vicky and Otto will take care of me."

Together we went down the slippery mountainside. Sam slowed us. "Creaky knees. Thanks for your help."

Siri was already singing when we reached the beach, an old ballad, "I wonder as I wander," and several penguins were clustering about her. As far as I could tell, the seals were paying no attention to the music, but maybe seals are less sensitive to music than penguins are. Elephant seals do look like enormous blobs of protoplasm.

Three of the penguins began to chitter, and maybe I was being anthropomorphic or something, but I was sure they were trying to sing along with Siri. I looked around for Benjy. He was still standing up on top of the cliff, slightly apart from the rest of the group, looking down on us.

Icebergs. Ice floes. Sleeping seals. Sunlight flashing off ice, touching and deepening the amazing blue of the bergs. I sat on the side of my bunk and wrote a sort of song:

I've made myself vulnerable,
I've let myself care.
I've opened my firmly closed heart.
My safety is gone,
It's no longer there,
My protection is falling apart.

Nobody promised
Our hearts would be safe
Or our bodies protected from harm.
A moment can change
All we think that we have,
But still we must welcome the storm.

I wasn't sure about welcoming the storm. Maybe it should be something like "strongly" or "staunchly we'll weather the storm." I'd have to brood on it, so I left it for a while. I'm getting braver about poetry. I wrote some more in my letter to Aunt Serena, then copied the poem for Siri, finally writing the last line as "Hope will endure through the storm," and slid it under the door of her cabin. I was learning a lot from penguins.

I was nervous and restless. Part of me felt I was making much ado about nothing (Shakespeare again), and part of me felt I wasn't taking all the accumulating warnings seriously enough.

I went to the lounge, but for once nobody was there, so I opened the door to the fo'c'sle. It, too, was empty. I wanted to be alone with the wind and water. I leaned on the rail and looked at the horizon. The sky was grey, the water even greyer, but sunlight still seemed to reach the white of icebergs, to touch their incredible blue. I heard the door from the lounge to the fo'c'sle open, and backed away from the rail until I could see who it was. In our winter clothing and bulky red parkas, we all looked pretty much alike, male and female. It was Leilia. Not Otto. I was glad it was Leilia; she exuded practicality and solidity and, yes, trustworthiness. We used to use that word when I went to Scout camp. You don't hear it much anymore.

Leilia came and stood by me. "Beautiful, isn't it?"

I nodded. "It's so beautiful I can't even begin to describe it."

"Interesting group on this trip," Leilia said. "Not that I'm surprised, because Antarctica tends to draw interesting people. But we're all rather old for you, even Otto, who bears the burden of being a prince fairly heavily despite his seeming lightheartedness."

I watched a seal on an ice floe to starboard, so close I could see his whiskers. "I guess I think princes should take their jobs seriously."

"Has he shown you the snapshot of his fairy-tale castle?"

I nodded. "Right out of the Brothers Grimm."

Leilia laughed. "Sometimes the Brothers Grimm can be pretty grim."

The door opened and Jack Nessinger came out. The wind almost took his cowboy hat, but he grabbed it before it blew overboard. "Hey, ladies. Looking for whales?"

"Haven't seen any," Leilia said. "I just like it out here."

"Me, too. But it's too cold for me today. My Texas blood is thin. See you gals later."

Leilia and I stood looking at the majesty of the icebergs for a few minutes longer. Then she turned to go in. "See you at Wrap-Up."

"Sure."

As she opened the door to the lounge, a couple of other people came out. It was Benjy in his tan parka, and Siri in her regulation red one. They walked over to me and Siri said, "Thanks for the poem, Vicky."

"I know it's not terrific," I said hastily.

"I'm not sure about it as poetry," she said, "although I like it. I needed to hear what it said." She smiled at me.

There was a silence as we looked at one especially magnificent iceberg, with turrets and towers and sworls and incredible coloring. Then Benjy said, "Vicky, I think you need to trust us enough to talk to us." I looked at him. Nodded. He continued, "Cookie told me what happened, or nearly happened, at the pyramids in Vespugia. He showed me his peculiar postcard from your friend Adam, and told me about yours."

"What about the warnings in my locker at school?"

"Incomprehensible," Benjy said. "Is there anything else we ought to know?"

I shifted my weight from one foot to the other. I told them about finding Esteban's card on the floor.

"What else? There's something more on your mind."

I told them about Otto and the night before.

Benjy leaned his elbows on the rail, whistling softly between his teeth. "He didn't see you?"

"No."

"Got any theories?"

I said bluntly, in order to sound neither tentative nor hysterical, "I think it's all about dismantling and disposing of nuclear warheads."

Benjy said, "That's a horrendous, universal problem. What's it got to do with all this?"

I asked, "What was Otto dumping last night?"

"Hey, wait a minute," Benjy protested. "You can't believe Otto was carrying anything radioactive aboard the *Argosy*."

"Why not? It could have been shielded in lead or whatever."

"Vicky, sweetie, you're crazy."

I said, stubbornly, "Siri, you said Generalissimo Guedder has a case of missile envy."

"Sure, but—"

"So he needs uranium."

Benjy demanded, "Do you realize how heavily that stuff has to be shielded?"

"I think so."

"After Chernobyl, some workers went in on what was a suicide mission, and they were dead in a few days. You can't take uranium or plutonium and forget it's lethally radioactive."

"I know that. But bombs are being dismantled and . . ."

Benjy turned and flung up his hands. "Vicky. Yes. And no. I mean, it's an unsolved problem, and Antarctica has been discussed as a possible place for disposal, and it's being fought. The thought alone is intolerable. It could have disastrous consequences. But even if some country broke all the treaties and tried to get nuclear waste to Antarctica, it couldn't be done on a small ship like the *Argosy*."

"Okay, but——" Now I was formulating thoughts that had been below the surface. "If Vespugia wanted to make a nuclear warhead, and didn't have any uranium, then, if they had a lot of money, they might try to buy it from another country . . ."

Benjy looked at me with his intense stare. "Are you planning on being a novelist?"

"There are worse things to be." I glowered at him.

"Hey, relax. Sorry, Vicky. I'm a simple guy and I know a lot about penguins and not much about politics. I want to keep Antarctica an international zone free from greed and corruption and power games. I realize that makes me as naïve as——"

Siri said, "As me. I'm naïve, too, and it's not a good thing to be in this wicked world. Something's going on around us on this trip. Vicky blundered into it at the pyramids. Sam was with her when she nearly fell, and he takes it seriously."

"Okay, okay," Benjy said hastily, "so do I. Listen, it's almost time for Wrap-Up and I've got to get in and confer with Quim about plans for tomorrow. Since our suspicions don't add up to anything tangible, let's keep them to ourselves, okay?"

"Sure."

"See you both in a few minutes."

"Sure," I repeated.

Siri looked at me with a slight smile as the door closed behind Benjy. "Vicky, sweetie, handing over a nuclear device from one country to another, more than half a planet apart, is just about impossible."

"Okay." I pulled my parka hood more tightly around my face. "I know I'm no scientist."

"I *am* a scientist. I'm trying to look at all the elements of this puzzle, and I have to admit I can't make any sense of any of it. What do you suppose Otto was doing last night?"

I shook my head.

Siri shook hers. "What bothers me is that it does seem you have been given warnings, and I can't see you as any kind of threat to anybody."

"Neither can I."

"Since my marriage busted up, I've tended to keep my head buried in the sand, and refused to be involved with anybody or anything. Not good. Thanks again for your poem. It really hit me. I think you're right about being vulnerable. If we can't be hurt, we might as well be dead. It's a good poem."

"Thanks, Siri. Thanks a lot. We've talked about Aunt Serena—who gave me this trip—"

"Yes. She sounds marvelous."

"She told me about penguins being communal creatures, but never intimate."

"Yes. Benjy talks about that in one of his lectures."

253

"But we're human. We can't be like that."

"We can try." Siri's voice was low. "As part of a university community, I've been almost as communal as a penguin. But I forbade any more intimacy after getting my heart smashed."

"Are you feeling vulnerable again?" I asked.

She nodded.

After I'd spoken to Benjy and Siri I realized that my suspicions were crazy, just as Benjy had said. There was no way Otto could have had nuclear warheads, mantled or dismantled, in his wooden boxes. But something was in them. Something he went out on deck with, and came back without.

Zlatovica had warheads it desperately wanted to get rid of. Zlatovica, via Prince Otto, would be glad to sell them. But who had the money? And how would they dispose of them?

After dinner there was going to be a movie about whales. While I was finishing my meal, Sam looked at me. "Do you want dessert, Vicky?"

"No."

"Nor do I. Come on out and let's look for whales."

We excused ourselves and went on deck. Sam demanded, "What's on your mind?"

"Am I that obvious?"

"No. I've been talking to Siri. You may be totally off-base in your guess as to what's going on, but something is, and needs to be taken seriously."

"What did Siri tell you?"

"She filled me in where I had questions."

Sam had been with me on the pyramid. Sam took me seriously. I wasn't angry with Siri for talking to him. I was relieved. "Sam, if you wanted to make a great deal of money—I mean billions and billions, what would you do?"

"I suppose I'd sell something people wanted."

"It would have to be more than a better mousetrap, for the kind of money I'm thinking of."

"What kind is that?"

"Enough to buy Zlatovican uranium. Even if Otto has nothing more exciting than—than ski equipment in his wooden cases, he does want to get rid of the warheads that have been left in Zlatovica by the Soviets, and his country does need money, big money."

"Um."

"So I suppose the biggest money, if it isn't munitions, might be drugs?"

"Might be."

"I know there are drug barons in South America."

"Yup."

"Vespugia?"

"In all likelihood. Are you thinking of anybody in particular?"

"Jorge Maldonado is a friend of Guedder's, and Guedder wants missiles, or at least a missile."

"Um." Sam chewed his cigar.

"Jorge has seemed—he has been—so nice."

"He is," Sam agreed.

"But do you think maybe—He talked about cutting back

on cattle because of ecology and all that stuff. Do you think maybe he's growing—well, crops for drugs?"

"Could be."

"Sam!"

"A lot of nice people have done terrible things. There are some people who love their wives and their children and their native land and who have no conscience, no sense of wrongdoing. You know that. You must have learned about the Second World War and the concentration camps."

"Yes."

"People who lived, on the surface, ordinary, decent lives also, without any sense of evil, fed other human beings into gas chambers."

I looked at Sam. His face was unreadable. His cigar was in its usual place in his mouth. I said, "Sometimes people do terrible things thinking they're doing good . . ."

Sam took the stump of his cigar out of his mouth and threw it overboard. "Such as?"

"Well, those monks who found the pyramids in the fifteenth century or whenever it was, and destroyed a lot of what they found—they thought they were doing it for Christ, didn't they?"

"Probably."

"So they did evil and thought they were doing good."

"It happens," Sam said, "too often. We're seldom truly sure of our motives."

The ding-dong rang, calling us into the Womb Room for the movie. "Sam, thank you."

"For what?"

"Listening. Not thinking I'm totally crazy."

"You're not crazy, Vicky. But before you put any judgments on anyone, wait until you have more evidence."

"Yes. Thanks."

Ten

I was still alone. The seal was fishing. The iceberg was empty. So it was still night.

Where was Papageno? I couldn't think of anybody who'd make a better spy. Sound a little crazy and no one pays any attention to what you say or where you go.

Where was he now? Where was Cook? What were they up to? I scanned the horizon, looking for the Portia, looking, hoping. But sea and sky met in a grey, shadowless line.

Aunt Serena's Adam had never been found, Adam II who had so loved this strange and alien land. Ice floes moved calmly past me.

Despair began to seep into my bones like the cold.

While I was getting ready for bed that night, there was a knock on my door. I opened it cautiously and there was Siri. "Benjy thinks it's best if I bunk in with you."

I looked my question marks at her.

"Something's going on, Vicky, even if we haven't the foggiest idea what, and he doesn't want you sleeping alone, and I think he's right. Hope you don't mind."

"I'm glad. Thanks."

"Benjy said, just in case someone saw you last night."

"I don't think anyone did. It was after two o'clock in the morning. Nobody was expected to be up and wandering around."

Siri put a small duffel bag on the second bunk. "I'm all showered and ready for bed. You'll be glad to get to LeNoir Station. Perhaps we can call Cookie from there. Much easier than on the ship's radio. And more private." She shoved her case under the bunk. "I told Greta you weren't feeling well, a little *turista*-type bug, and I'd promised Cookie I'd look after you."

"Thanks, Siri."

We got into our bunks, and read for a few minutes. She looked up from her book. "I talked to Sam."

"He told me."

"Don't be angry—"

"I trust Sam," I said. Then I thought of Otto's suggestion that maybe Sam was one of the people who were on the *Argosy* for more than pleasure. I still trusted Sam.

I dreamed I was in the small colonial church at home. There were a dozen or more stretch limos lined up outside. I was wearing my oldest jeans and a torn T-shirt and Suzy was rushing up and down the aisle wailing, "Where is it? Where is your wedding dress? You can't marry a prince looking like that!"

259

My father said, "A princess is a princess no matter what she wears, but we could at least get you a clean shirt."

Someone was playing the organ, but it wasn't wedding music, it was my "If it has feathers" song.

"I don't want you to be a princess and leave home!" Rob wailed, and he was a baby again, no more than three.

I woke up, and almost laughed at the absurdity of the dream. But then I asked myself: Why did I dream it?

No answer.

I went back to sleep.

At breakfast Siri ordered rolls and cheese and cold meat, "a real Norwegian breakfast," she said. "I treat myself every once in a while, and I feel the need of sustenance today."

I ordered my usual oatmeal. That should be sustenance enough.

She put her elbows on the table and looked at me. There were a few other people in the dining room but we were early, and no one was sitting near us. She lowered her voice. "So you think maybe Jorge isn't as lily-white pure as he'd like us to think?"

"I don't know. I don't like thinking bad things about people." I picked up a spoonful of oatmeal, put it back in the dish.

Siri put cheese and sausage on her roll. "Neither do I. But life has brought out a certain cynicism in me. Drugs have always been a big export in South America. I know they don't see it the way we do."

Since Siri had been talking with Sam, this conversation did not surprise me as much as it would have otherwise. I put a spoonful of raisins onto my oatmeal. "At home a lot of kids are involved. I guess it's everywhere. A kid in my class died from an overdose and everybody was shocked for a while."

"It's big money," Siri continued.

My mind was jumping from thought to thought. "Siri—that night in San Sebastián when we met Otto and Jack, and they were sitting with Jorge—what—?"

"What were they doing?" Siri asked. "I doubt if they were just getting acquainted. They were, I assume, conducting business, but what kind of business?"

I shrugged. "Siri, I don't know anything about business." Where did Jack come into this story? I suspected that Jorge was buying materials for an atomic bomb from Otto with drug money—but surely neither Jack nor Texas needed either money or bombs. So what kind of business was he here for?

My mind continued to bounce from idea to idea. "Siri—what about Jorge's cameras?"

She put down her roll and looked out the window at a petrel flying low over the water. "He doesn't use them much, does he? I've wondered about that."

"When he was smoothing things out near Nordenskjöld's hut the other morning, his cases all got put in one of the tents."

"I noticed. Go on."

"Maybe Benjy'd ask if I'm planning on being a novelist again—"

Siri's voice was calm. "Go on, Vicky."

"Well—I just wondered about it."

Siri asked, "Does the fact that Otto may be involved bother you?"

I could feel myself flush. "Yes. And no. Yes. Otto loves his country in a way I guess people haven't loved America since the early days of the very first states—and yet Zlatovica is centuries older than we are."

People had been coming into the dining room while we talked, but nobody was near us until the three Alaskans came and sat with us. Then Greta wandered into the dining room, looked around, and came to our table.

"Feeling better, Vicky?" she asked.

I'd forgotten that Siri had moved in with me because I was supposed to be feeling queasy. "Oh. Lots better."

"Just a touch of *turista*," Siri said swiftly, "but it kept her up a bit last night, so I think I'll bunk in with her for another night or two."

Leilia said, "Good idea."

"I'm fine, really. And it's lovely of Siri to take such good care of me."

Leilia smiled. "We all promised Cookie we would."

The days got longer and the nights got shorter. Nothing new happened. Greta didn't ask why Siri was still sleeping in my cabin, partly because I think she liked having a cabin to herself.

Siri grinned and suggested that Greta might like to be alone with Jorge. That had occurred to me, too. Mostly, ship's conversation was more or less normal. More or less. There was an undercurrent of tension in everything we said. Wherever I was, I felt watched. I knew Sam was on the alert, and so were Benjy and Siri. But my imagination had me figuratively looking over my shoulder wherever I turned.

We went to Palmer Station, one of the U.S. research

sites. Quim told us that all the water in the ship would have to be turned off while the *Argosy* was anchored, because of some kind of water experiments. I went to the fo'c'sle to watch us draw closer to land.

Jack came out, said, "Y'all right, honey?"

"Sure."

Jack took a couple of pictures with his cardboard camera and went in. As we drew nearer to land I saw a small boat which was anchored closer to shore than we'd be able to go, a small blue boat which looked like a fishing boat. The *Portia*! I was sure it was the *Portia*! While I watched, it began to move, and before we got to our anchorage it had pulled away and was heading in what I figured was a southerly direction.

The second I got Benjy alone, I'd tell him. If it was the *Portia*, it meant that Cook and Papageno had just been at Palmer Station.

The ding-dong summoned us to the Zodiacs, and I had to hurry back to the cabin to put on my boots. Siri wasn't there, and we weren't in the same Zodiac, though Sam was with me, and so were Angelique and Dick. I looked at Dick's kind, lined face, and at his heavy cane, and was irrationally glad he was there.

When we landed I didn't get a chance to speak to Benjy alone to tell him I was sure I'd seen the *Portia*. Everybody clustered about, looking at the buildings, and at some tanks with starfish in them. The young graduate student who showed us around was enthusiastic and hoped to have his stay extended beyond his internship. "It's my turn to be on plankton watch tonight," he told us.

"How do you watch plankton?" Siri asked smilingly.

"We have this floodlight on a post in the shallow water in front of the station. It attracts all kinds of zooplankton."

"Such as?" Dick asked.

"Oh, copepods, hyperiid amphipods, ctenophores, mysids, et cetera, et cetera. Let's go this way." He took us into the building that held the refectory and common rooms. I was walking beside him, thinking that maybe Adam did plankton watch too, when he startled me by saying, "I have a letter for you from your friend Adam."

I took it with a feeling that my heart was thudding. Adam had rejected me. What more could he have to say?

"Where did you get it?" I asked.

"One of the scientists from LeNoir stopped off here for a few days."

I asked, "Was it Cook or Papageno?"

"Who?"

"They left, just before we anchored, in their boat, the *Portia*."

"Oh, yeah, there were a couple of older guys here for a few hours, but I didn't get to see them. Hope the letter is good news."

"Thanks."

The rest of the time at Palmer Station was a blur for me. I slipped away from the group and stood in the shelter of one of the buildings and opened the letter. It was, again, simply addressed to me. Inside was a letter that was a computer printout, not handwritten. I checked the signature. It looked like Adam's. If his last letter had left me feeling devastated, this one produced total confusion. It was all scientific stuff. There was a paragraph about something called self-similarity, and Leibniz's theory that a drop of water may contain an entire universe. Then it got more complicated as Adam talked about scaling phenomena and hierarchies of scales which apparently destroyed the naïve ideas of self-similarity.

Naïve. I certainly felt naïve. I understood a little of what Adam was talking about, because it had come up in conversation with John last summer. But I had no idea why he was writing to me that way.

I managed to get in the Zodiac with Siri to go back to the *Argosy*. I whispered, "I have to see you and Benjy."

When we got back aboard she said, "Go to the cabin. I'll find Benjy."

In the cabin I read the letter again and it still made absolutely no sense to me. Rejection in the last letter, and now a lot of scientific technicalities Adam must have known I couldn't possibly understand.

When Benjy and Siri came to the cabin I handed the letter to them, and they read it together, Benjy holding it, with one arm around Siri. When they had finished, he handed it back. "What do you make of it?" he asked.

I flung out my hands in frustration. "Nothing."

Benjy said, "Seems to me it's an excellent smoke screen if anybody's interested in Adam's mail. He's telling you he's okay, but he's indicating with his scientific gobbledygook that there's more to it than meets the eye."

"But what?"

"Like I said"——Benjy sat on the second bunk and Siri

265

plunked down beside him——"I think he's just telling you he's okay, and nobody reading what he's written will have any idea what he's saying."

"Neither do I."

Suddenly Siri asked, "Do you think there could be a code hidden in the letter?"

Why hadn't that occurred to me? "There might be."

"Work on it," Benjy said. "I've got to go confer with Quim and the captain. There's about an hour before Wrap-Up. See if you can do some decoding."

"Okay."

"See you." He left. Siri had brought her harp to the cabin and now she picked it up and began tuning it, something she had to do constantly. I reread the letter. I had not told Benjy or Siri about Adam's "cool it" letter, but it didn't seem to have anything to do with this. I checked the first letter of every word to see if they added up to anything. John and I used to play at making up codes for each other, so we'd learned all the usual code-breaking devices. In the middle of the letter I got something. I wrote each letter down on my lined pad. THOSECLAMOROUSHARBINGERSOFBLOODANDDEATH. Then I separated it into words. THOSE CLAMOROUS HARBINGERS OF BLOOD AND DEATH.

Shakespeare. It had to be Shakespeare, though I didn't recognize it. I felt cold. Kept on working. Found another phrase: NO MAN'S PIE IS FREED FROM HIS AMBITIOUS FINGER. That made a little more sense. Antarctica was looked at as a huge piece of pie with lots of countries wanting a slice. At the end I found, like a signature, CONSIDERATION, LIKE AN ANGEL, CAME AND WHIPPED THE OFFENDING ADAM OUT OF HIM.

Double gobbledygook. Science and Shakespeare. Something was going on which should not be going on and he was warning me. The problem was that I did not understand the warning. I had given Adam one warning, about those cards in my locker. But his warnings were becoming more and more urgent.

"Siri," I said, and she put her harp down. "I've found something." I handed her the paper.

She read what I'd written out. "Let's show it to Benjy."

"Okay."

"It all ties in with Adam's 'Something rotten in the state of Denmark' card, doesn't it?" She looked at her watch. "We'd better go up to the lounge. It's past time for Wrap-Up, but maybe Sam will have saved a place for us."

He had, with Angelique and Dick. Quim was telling everybody that we were just starting to enter the Le Maire Channel, one of the most beautiful parts of the trip. It is a narrow gorge that is open only a few weeks a year when enough ice breaks up so that a ship like the *Argosy* can push its way through. "A big cruise ship could never make this," Sam said with satisfaction.

We started by looking out the windows, then went on deck to see the full beauty. It was so magnificent that the view broke through my preoccupation and confusion. Benjy stood next to me, looking at the indescribable loveliness, his hand lightly on my shoulder.

I noticed that Jorge wasn't taking pictures, and the Le

Maire Channel was probably the most spectacular water the *Argosy* had sailed in. Jorge's usually pleasant expression was tight, his eyes narrowed as though against light much brighter than the pearly twilight we were sailing through.

When the ding-dong rang for dinner we all turned reluctantly to go in. Benjy put his hand on my elbow and spoke to me in a low voice. "Siri showed me how you broke Adam's code. At least we'll get a chance to ask him personally what all this is about when we get to LeNoir. Meanwhile, try to set it aside. Tomorrow Siri will sing to the seals."

It wasn't until we'd anchored off Paradise Bay and Siri slung her harp over her shoulder that I remembered how much I'd been looking forward to her playing for the seals. We were in a Zodiac with Sam, Leilia, Angelique, and Dick, and Benjy was at the outboard. He'd obviously engineered which passengers were going to be with him. Benjy's driving was unlike anybody else's. We hung on to the ropes that ran along the sides of the Zodiac as he whizzed us through ice fields, past crab-eater seals on floes, on to a small island where there was a colony of gentoo penguins. Then we went past nesting shags, Benjy's word for cormorants, high on some cliffs. Finally he pulled up close to an ice floe where three Weddell seals were sleeping, and cut the engine.

"Okay, Siri, let's try it here."

We were a few yards out from a large crescent of stony land. Beyond us was the tumbled ice of a glacier, filling in the valley and nudging out into the ocean. Clouds covered the top of the mountain, so all we saw was ice.

Siri got out her harp and we made enough space for her on the rubber side of the Zodiac so that she had room to play. Benjy had nestled the Zodiac so close to the floe that she could have stepped out onto it.

She began by running her fingers softly over the strings in a series of chords. Then she played and sang "Speed, Bonny Boat." One by one the seals lifted their heads, their dark liquid eyes looking at her. Benjy suggested, "Play your 'Troubling a star' song. That's my favorite, that and Vicky's 'If it has feathers.' "

Was it just my overactive imagination, or did the seals really move their heads in time to the music? Benjy thought they did, and Benjy is a scientist, accustomed to observing seals as well as penguins. Sam said, "I wish we had Greta's video camera. We really ought to be filming this. Stills aren't enough, and we need sound, too."

Angelique put her arm around me and gave me a gentle hug. "Oh, Vicky, isn't this marvelous!"

Dick took a few stills, and so did Leilia, but I was too focused on watching and listening to think of anything but the music and the seals.

"I wish we had days and days for this." Benjy's voice was wistful. "The humpbacks didn't sing for us when we played their music, but they were with us for not much more than an hour." He looked at Siri. "If you could play for the seals, the same seals, for several days, then we'd have some repeated results to go by. Once isn't enough." He sighed. Then he held his face up, listening.

There was a sudden silence. Benjy pointed and we looked

toward the glacier. As we watched, a great wall of ice detached itself and fell into the sea. Then came a strange roar, like thunder, only more formidable, cracking the air. Water rose like a geyser, then splashed down like rain as the broken-off wall of ice disappeared. Then followed an intense silence.

Angelique asked, "Was that calving?"

"It was," Benjy said. "Glad we were here for it. The others will be green. That was a beauty."

I felt prickles of excitement. It was something momentous to have seen and heard.

"It's getting late. We have to move on." Benjy pulled the rope to start the outboard motor.

Siri slipped her harp into its canvas case and zipped it. "Antarctica is impersonal. Seals or skuas eat penguins; penguins eat krill; krill eats plankton. But it's only because of the basic need for food, and not human lust for power."

Dick said calmly, "All life lives at the expense of other life. There isn't any other way."

The water was smooth during the night, and we reached LeNoir Station shortly after an early breakfast, and got into the Zodiacs to go ashore. As usual, Sam was sticking close to me.

We were in the first Zodiac, for once. We drew up to some large, tumbled-looking rocks. We could see a wooden building on top of the cliff. Jason was at the tiller, and showed us how to get out onto the rocks and climb over them to where they went up almost like a natural staircase that led to a wooden walkway.

Benjy and Quimby were standing at the top of the rocks,

holding out helping hands, but they weren't joshing as they usually did. They looked solemn. And shocked.

There were several people from the station standing around. I did not see Adam.

I tried to help Sam up the slippery rocks. I wondered how Dick would manage with his lame leg and his cane. Sam was game, but it wasn't easy for him; then suddenly Jason was by us, giving Sam shoves in just the right way, and then Benjy and Quim leaned down and heaved him up in one quick pull.

I clambered up and stood by Sam, hearing him ask, "What's up?"

"The Leedses have been calling all the stations. It seems that Papageno has disappeared."

Cook was with Papageno. Where was Adam?

It was apparent that Quim and Benjy were deeply upset.

Benjy said, "They're afraid something has happened."

In my confusion over Adam's last letter, I'd forgotten to tell Benjy about seeing the *Portia*. I blurted out, "But—listen, Benjy, just before we docked at Palmer Station, I saw the *Portia* pulling away."

"Are you sure?"

"Not a hundred percent. But it was an old blue boat. It looked like the *Portia*. And if it was, Papageno and Cook were on it."

Benjy made a thinking-humming noise. "Okay. We know they've been off on the boat for a while, but Papageno always answers when Rusty Leeds calls. Or the Coast Guard. He checks in every day. But for the past forty-eight hours there hasn't been a response. The Coast Guard has a search party

271

out. The *Portia*'s a stable old tub, but even if you saw it leaving Palmer Station, the fact that it hasn't been heard from in two days is going to get out, and I wanted you to hear it from me."

"Where's Adam?" I demanded.

Benjy looked startled. "Isn't he here?"

"I don't see him, and it would be sort of natural for him to come out and say hello when we arrived."

Then I heard, "Vickee!" and Esteban was walking toward me.

I didn't see Jorge to translate for us, but Esteban, talking with Benjy, managed to make us understand that he and Adam were a governmental swap, in mutual appreciation and trust between Vespugia and the United States. Esteban was going to be able to observe what was going on in the labs at LeNoir Station, and Adam would be doing the same at one of the Vespugian stations.

It sounded plausible, but my nose twitched and I smelled something very rotten in the state of Denmark. Or Vespugia. Or wherever. And Esteban seemed to be overemphasizing and at the same time looking embarrassed.

Gary and Todd were helping the last few passengers climb up onto the rocks and the wooden walk, and I was glad to see Dick making it, with Angelique behind him and Jason beside him holding the cane until Dick could reach out for Gary. Benjy and Quim were herding people into a loose bunch, and Quimby said, "We'll divide you into two groups again, and those in the second group will have a chance now to look at the shop. There are some sweatshirts, for those of you who didn't buy them at Palmer, and some other things that might interest you—film for your cameras, for instance."

Jason said, "Benjy will escort the first group, and I'll go with the second."

He had a hard time making himself heard, because several people recognized Esteban and were clamoring to know how he came to be at LeNoir Station, and this time Jorge appeared and did the explaining, so it didn't take too long.

Benjy saw to it that I was in the first group, along with Angelique and Dick, and Siri, who was with Greta. I didn't see Otto. Usually his golden looks made him very visible, and I looked around but didn't catch a glimpse of him. Jack Nessinger's cowboy hat towered over several people's heads.

Esteban walked along beside Benjy, as did another young man from the station, a nice young man who reminded me painfully of Adam, though he was probably several years older. He smiled at me, at all of us, and said, "I'm coming along with you to tell you what we're doing here at the station." First he pointed out the functions of the various buildings: the two labs, the dorm, the refectory and recreation rooms. We went into one of the labs, which looked like a modern version of Papageno's at Port Stanley. There were several graph machines making squiggly lines on paper, and tanks with various kinds of plankton.

I was paying only minimal attention to what was being said, and missed what appeared to be a semi-lecture by Benjy. Where was Adam? Where were Papageno and Cook? Why was Esteban at LeNoir Station? Everybody else seemed to have taken his explanation at face value. I didn't.

Benjy was talking about emperor penguins.

"I hope we're going to see some emperor penguins in real life before the trip is over." Greta moved so that she was standing near Jorge. "Doesn't the male emperor fledge the eggs, or whatever you call it?"

Benjy explained, "The male emperor incubates the eggs on his feet for sixty-four to sixty-seven days, covering them with a flap of abdominal skin."

"Where're the females?" Jack Nessinger asked. He had the hood of his parka pushed back and was now carrying his cowboy hat in one hand.

"Once she's expended her energy laying her two eggs, the female takes off," Benjy said. "The male loses approximately half his body weight during the incubation period."

"Why?" Angelique asked.

"He fasts."

"Why?"

"It's a little difficult to go fishing with an egg on your feet." Benjy smiled. "The males gather together to preserve body heat. Once the egg is hatched, the female returns and the male takes off for the sea and food."

"That would be quite something to see," Angelique said. "Hope you'll have a chance to sing to the emperors, Siri."

People began asking questions as though nothing was wrong. My anxiety translated itself into a white heat of impatience.

Miching mallecho. Miching mallecho. The two words kept repeating themselves in my mind. I could not dislodge them.

We were going to anchor off Eddington Point overnight and go ashore in the morning, up into the strange, stony hills behind the station, where there were nesting albatrosses and more penguins, gentoos, chinstraps, and Adélies.

On the other side of the peninsula from the station, Todd told us, there would be a colony of Weddell seals.

"Terrific," Benjy said. "Siri can play for them."

She looked wistfully at Esteban. "I wish he was able to have his oboe here. The seals might really respond to that." Then she said, "I would like to ask Esteban how this switch with Adam came about."

So she, too, was suspicious.

But Benjy explained that it was not that strange, that there was always some visiting between stations. I looked at Esteban and thought his sparkle seemed diminished. He stood slightly apart from our group, and his shoulders drooped. But when someone spoke to him, a smile lit his face.

Quimby called to us to let the second group have the tour of the station, and most of our group headed for the shack which was also the store, with sweatshirts and T-shirts and coffee mugs, about the only evidence we'd seen that tourists ever came to Antarctica.

I'd bought a mug for John and sweatshirts for Suzy and Rob at Palmer Station, and the shop at LeNoir was so tiny that the few people in there looked like a crowd, so I walked along the wooden planks and then leaned on the rail, looking at the rocks and at the Zodiacs tied up below.

Siri came up behind me. "Vicky—"

I jumped. "Hi."

"You heard about Papageno?"

"That his boat's disappeared? Yes."

She frowned, worriedly. "It's something else unexplainable, and I don't like it. Why is Esteban here?"

I heard footsteps, sounding fairly loud on the wooden walkway, and there was Sam coming up to us. "Hi, guys."

"Hi," we both said, and Siri asked, "Why isn't Papageno answering his radio calls?"

Sam said calmly, "Maybe he doesn't want anybody to know where he is."

"Why would he want to disappear?"

Sam chewed on his cigar, took it out of his mouth and looked at it speculatively, then threw it into the water. "Totally biodegradable," he said.

"Sam?" Siri persisted.

"Not everybody on the *Argosy* is a disinterested passenger. There's tumult in the Balkans, violence in the Middle East, confusion in Africa, disturbance in South America."

"What's that got to do with the *Portia?*"

Sam shrugged. "Secrets. Secrets others want. All the emerging countries. Albania. Zlatovica. Estonia. Argentina. Vespugia. All the struggling democracies and the equally struggling superpowers. Everyone. I don't discount the U.S."

Siri leaned both elbows on the wooden rail of the walkway. "We're not as good and pure as we'd like to be."

Sam said, "We wrestle not only against flesh and blood but against principalities, against powers, against the rulers of the darkness of this world, against spiritual wickedness in high places."

Those words were familiar. Something my grandfather quoted, I thought. I asked, "So where is Adam?"

Sam said, "I have no evidence for this, but it is my conviction that he didn't just change places with Esteban. It is also my conviction, since I'm an old codger, that his disappearance and Papageno's are not unconnected. Until I know more about what's going on, 'nuff said."

I asked, "Do you think they've been kidnapped?"

Sam chewed on an invisible cigar. "It is a reasonable supposition, and a distinct possibility, but some instinct, which I've learned to trust, tells me no."

"Do you think maybe Adam had to make himself scarce?"

"Possibly."

"Do the people Adam and Papageno and Cook have to make themselves scarce from—are they interested in Antarctica?"

"Everybody's interested in Antarctica."

"From two different points of view," I said.

"Hm."

"Some people seem to be interested in what may be in Antarctica," I went on, "and some people may be interested in how to get rid of—of—"

Sam cocked his bushy eyebrows at me. "Rid of—?"

"Nuclear waste?"

"Are you suggesting that some people may be considering using Antarctica as a dumping ground?"

"It's been mentioned, hasn't it?"

Sam said, "It seems to be human nature."

Siri said, "But, Vicky, not from the *Argosy*, you know that."

"Okay. But what about Adam? What about the *Portia*?"

277

Sam said, "As you probably guessed, Papageno is working with Rusty Leeds, trying to see that no country is infringing any of the treaties. He can and does go anywhere in that old boat of his."

"You mean," I asked, "he's a secret agent?" If I hadn't been so filled with anxiety, I'd have laughed at myself for being the romantic again.

Sam pulled another cigar out of his pocket, snipped off the end with a gadget he carried on his watch chain, and smiled at me. "I guess you could call it that."

We turned as Quimby shouted, calling us together to climb down the rocks and get back in the Zodiacs. People were coming up behind us, and the group ahead of us was slithering down the rocks and climbing into the waiting Zodiacs. Gary and Quim were there to help everybody, and it was good that Quim's arms were strong and steady as he helped Sam into the Zodiac.

I didn't want to be frightened. But I was.

When we got back to the *Argosy,* Siri, Sam, and I went out onto the fo'c'sle and stood looking at the water. The wind was whipping whitecaps along the surface. A few other people came out, but a gale was blowing from fore to aft, so nobody stayed more than a minute or two.

"Something else I don't understand," I said, "is, why me? Why is anybody after me?"

"It's not you, Vicky." Sam looked at me. "It may be what some people think you know."

278

"I don't know anything."

"Paranoia is rampant and often accompanies greed."

I shuddered, and not just from the cold. "It all ties in with Adam, doesn't it? Adam III. Whatever he found out, and hints at in his cards and letters. Oh, Sam, do people kill other people for—" I broke off. "Yes. They do. I know that. Otto's mother. It's what you said, about wickedness in high places."

"And some not so high," Sam said, and looked at me.

"What do you mean?"

"Think," Sam said. "Who's had an opportunity to know things that might put you in danger?"

I thought about the cards in my locker at school. I still had no answer. Not Cook. It could not be Cook.

Then I thought about all that had happened since I left home. "You mean Esteban?" I drew out the words slowly. I didn't want to say them.

"Who else would know anything about Adam's letters or cards to you? Why was Esteban our guide at the pyramids? Why was he selected as Adam's guide? Surely you know that simply the fact that Adam Eddington is named Adam Eddington is enough to have him watched, especially if anybody remembers the explorer Adam Eddington." He looked around to make sure we were the only people on the fo'c'sle. Two red-parkaed figures came out the lounge door, were buffeted by the wind, turned, and went back in. The wind was raw and cold and unwelcoming. Katabatic. We were alone, I was certain, but Sam walked slowly around the small space, double-checking. When he was positive nobody else was there, he came back to the rail.

"Sam." I looked at him, calmly chewing his cigar. "When you were with me on the pyramid in Vespugia, did you suspect something?"

"Yes."

Eleven

I *was nearly asleep and I knew I couldn't make myself stay awake*
much longer. I was ready to let go. My will for life was being frozen.

Then I jerked awake, terror leaping from my heart to my throat.
Two huge grey forms were surfacing just a few yards from the iceberg.
Seals. Some seals will attack human beings. Leopard seals. Fur seals.
Papageno had almost been killed by a fur seal. I'd rather die of cold
than be killed by a seal. I tried to sink into the tower of ice that rose
behind me.

Not seals. The shadows were too large to be seals, even elephant
seals. Two plumes of water rose into the air with a great whoosh.
Whales! Two whales! They swam around the iceberg, sometimes sub-
merging, sometimes raising their great bulks out of the water, then
diving down, then blowing great fountains through their blowholes.
Then they dived down, deep, showing their great, patterned tail flukes
before they vanished. I strained to watch for them, and saw them
spouting as they headed for the horizon.

They seemed to be saying, "Hold on, Vicky. Hold on."
I would try.

Everything on the *Argosy* went on as usual. Or appeared to. It was hard, when we all gathered together for Wrap-Up before dinner, to act natural. Otto came in, wearing the green sweater that set off his golden tan, and headed for our table. He bowed. "May I join you?"

"Of course," Sam said, and pulled out a chair for him, between Angelique and me. "Where were you this afternoon?"

Otto grinned. "You put me to shame, Sam. I stayed on the boat and had a nap. I was up late last night, so I'm looking forward to seeing LeNoir Station tomorrow."

Quim came in to talk to us a little about the walk up into the mountains the next morning. Then he said, "So, now, just relax and enjoy the evening."

Jorge came over to our table and stood, his hand on the back of Otto's chair, leaning toward us. "Esteban's delight in seeing you, Vicky, was charming."

"Esteban." Otto made a face. "So he is after my Vicky."

"He's a young admirer of Vicky's, true," Jorge said. "He's a talented oboist, serving his two years in the army. He pulled quite a few strings so that he could see Vicky again here at Eddington Point."

Otto said, "I should have gone ashore to meet this prodigy."

I said nothing. I felt embarrassed.

Jorge looked at me. "I hope you're not too disappointed at not seeing your friend Adam?"

"I am a little disappointed," I said. "Of course." Jorge did make Esteban's switch with Adam seem a little more plausible. But only a little, because I no longer trusted Jorge.

After breakfast we got into Zodiacs and headed for LeNoir Station. I hadn't eaten much. Anxiety had taken away my appetite.

Angelique sat next to me. "Are you okay, Vicky?"

"Sure. Just a little *turista*." I might as well stick to Siri's excuse for sleeping in my cabin.

"Where's Otto?" she asked.

"I think he was in the Zodiac before ours."

"You two seem to have hit it off."

"He's fun. Not at all stuck up."

"Your first prince?"

"Not many princes around our part of New England."

The Zodiac pulled up to the tumbled rocks. "Slippery," Angelique said. "Be careful, Vicky." She looked at me with concern in her dark eyes. "Please be careful."

Benjy was helping people climb from the rocks up onto the walkway. He reached out and gave me a hand, then turned to help Siri, who was a little encumbered by her harp. "Wait for me," he said.

As usual, we took off our orange life preservers before starting on the day's hike. As I was putting mine down next to Siri's, Esteban appeared and stood beside us and reached out to touch her harp case, hopefully. She smiled at him and nodded. Most of our group had already started up the mountain with the other three lecturers and Quim. Otto had his hood pushed back, so I could see the gold of his head as he climbed. Jack had on his cowboy hat; I don't know why he hadn't lost it in the wind.

Benjy came out, looked questioningly at Esteban for a moment, then beckoned to us to join him, and we trudged along the beach for a good half hour, away from the station and any sign of human life. "Tourists like our group," he said, "aren't the menace to the Antarctic continent—at any rate, not yet—that you're supposed to be. The damage done has been by various government-sponsored scientific and pseudo-scientific missions."

I was glad Esteban couldn't speak English.

"And," Siri added, "by commercial fishing and whaling. The number of whales killed is appalling, and to some extent it's still going on."

"We're trying to stop it," Benjy said. "You tourists arrive on ships, take pictures, and leave. So far, you haven't done any damage, left any sign that you've been here." He sounded cross, the way I do when I have something else on my mind, and talk in order not to think about whatever it is.

"What happens," Siri said, "is that we're so overcome by the beauty that we'll do anything we can to keep it from being spoiled. Any way we can help have Antarctica made into a world park, we will." She smiled at Esteban, turned to Benjy. "Clue Esteban in to what we've been talking about. You were sounding very fierce."

"Sure." Benjy fumbled with his semi-Spanish, and Esteban nodded eagerly.

The beach Benjy led us to was slippery with wet stones, not big enough to be called rocks, too big to be called pebbles. They slipped and slid under our feet and made walking difficult. I was with Esteban, and any time I started to slip, he steadied me.

In a few minutes we came to a curve in the beach where a couple of seals were lying, and Benjy signaled us to be quiet. There were more seals on the floes nearest the land. As much as one can tiptoe in heavy boots, Benjy tiptoed down to the edge of the water, near where a large floe rocked gently only a few feet offshore. Half a dozen seals lay on it, steaming slightly. One raised an uninterested head, looked at us, and returned to its nap.

Benjy whispered, "Okay. Here."

Siri took her harp out of its case and began to play softly, the familiar melody of a South American song, and she looked over at Esteban and he began to sing. He had a warm, rich voice, and it was hauntingly lovely. I looked from Siri and Esteban to the seals. One of them let out an enormous sigh that rocked the floe. Several shifted position. As we watched, three of them turned slowly so that they were facing Siri and Esteban.

They were listening!

Benjy said, "I am awed. Totally awed."

Siri continued to play. She looked at Esteban and hummed a melody, and he caught on, and sang, and then he began to weave his own melody to her arpeggios. The two of them were caught up in music, and the seals—the seals were listening as intently as Benjy and I were listening.

The moment was broken by the sound of heavy, running footsteps, and we turned to see Greta hurrying toward us. "Oh, Benjy—Siri—Sam has fallen—"

"Where?" Benjy asked sharply.

"Up the mountain"—Greta was gasping—"near the largest crèche—hundreds and hundreds of penguins—slippery with guano—steep—" She grabbed me by the arm as though she couldn't stand without help.

"Esteban, stay with Siri and Vicky!" Benjy shouted, and he ran perpendicularly along the beach, and then upward, slanting his way toward the penguin rookery. A skua flew by overhead, crying raucously.

Siri started to put her harp in its case, slowing herself down in her hurry.

I tried to shake Greta off so I could follow Benjy, but she clung to me like a terrified animal. "Greta, let go!"

Esteban was looking on helplessly. Of course he hadn't understood Benjy, but he moved a step closer to me, saying something I couldn't understand.

Greta continued to hang on to me. "Wait, Vicky, wait. We're not needed. Benjy's trained in CPR."

"How did Sam fall?"

"He slipped." She panted, gulped in air, continued, "Guano, it's more slippery than ice alone. He went over the edge of a ledge—"

"Is he hurt?"

"Yes—no—I don't know. He lay terribly still."

I jerked away. Started running, Esteban beside me. Siri

and Greta were running behind us. I could hear Siri's harp slapping against her back.

"Vicky! Wait!" Siri panted. "There's no point in getting a heart attack."

"Siri, I've got to run. Your harp——"

"I know. It's slowing me down. But I don't want you to be alone."

"Esteban's with me," I called back to her. I had forgotten Sam's warning about Esteban. "Take your time. We'll be okay." We were lots younger than Siri and Greta. We could run faster.

I heard Greta calling, "You should stay with us! You won't be any help!"

Maybe not, but I had to go. Esteban matched his pace to mine. I wasn't sprinting. We'd come over a mile to get to the seals. The rocks slipped and slid under our feet. We ran at a moderate pace I thought I could keep up. I couldn't see Benjy.

Then I heard the familiar putt-putt of a Zodiac coming in to shore just ahead of us. There were three men in red parkas: Jorge, Jack, and Otto.

Jorge clambered out of the Zodiac and splashed through the water to the shore, calling, "Vicky! They're taking Sam to Palmer Station. Come on, we'll get you there."

I hurried toward him. Sam was more than just a friend. In our short, intense time together he'd become very dear to me. Jack and Otto were pulling the Zodiac up onto the shore.

"All the way to Palmer?" I asked.

"It's not that far as the crow flies—or as the penguin

swims. The *Argosy* has done a lot of zigzagging with side excursions here and there."

Jack came ashore, adding in his soft voice, "It shouldn't take more than a couple of hours, and we have plenty of gas. Quimby assured me of that. Let's go."

Esteban was standing beside me, his hand on my arm, looking with wide eyes at the three men.

We heard footsteps—running silently in boots is not an option—and Greta came hurrying up.

"Greta," Jorge ordered, "you and Esteban go back to the station. Tell them we're taking Vicky to Palmer."

"Siri—" Greta panted, and Siri came huffing up, still slowed down by her harp.

"Siri, too," Jorge said. "There's no hurry. We just don't want anyone to be worried about Vicky."

"Benjy—" Siri panted.

"He's with Sam, and he and Dick will go with Sam in the Zodiac to Palmer." He turned to Esteban. "You will take care of the ladies?" Then he smiled, said, "Sorry," and switched to Spanish.

Esteban's face was pale and worried. He spoke urgently in Spanish.

Jorge replied sharply, obviously telling him to go. Telling him to take care of Siri and Greta. The three of them began to walk up the beach, Greta briskly, both Siri and Esteban slowly, turning to look at me.

I asked, "How badly is Sam hurt?"

Jorge shook his head. "He's asking for you."

But Greta had said he was unconscious.

Jorge continued, "He's barely conscious, just a moan, Vicky, Vicky. Dick thinks it would help if you could be with him. He has a concussion, certainly. We hope nothing more, but—"

I looked at Otto. He was standing by the Zodiac, holding the painter. "Otto—?"

"Come quickly, Vicky," he urged.

I looked up the beach. Esteban, Siri, and Greta had gone around a wide curve and I couldn't see them. "Benjy—"

"Benjy is with Sam," Jorge repeated. "Come, Vicky, time may be important."

"Sweet Vicky," Otto started.

But Jorge cut in, urging me toward the Zodiac. I tried to pull my arm out of his grasp, but his fingers clamped like iron. "Vicky, what's wrong with you?"

"Sweetie—" Jack was standing in shallow water, one hand on the black rubber side of the Zodiac. Suddenly I didn't like Jack's calling me sweetie. "Come along."

"No. I don't want to go with you." Something was wrong. I looked to Otto for help, but he just stood there, letting the water slap against his boots. He looked at me and shook his head, very slightly.

Jorge nodded at Jack, who took my other arm. I was being propelled toward the Zodiac.

"No! Otto!" The wind was blowing my words away, out to sea. I struggled to break free, but Jorge and Jack were far stronger than I.

"Otto!" I shouted.

"Vicky," Otto cried, "watch—"

Calmly and deliberately, Jack slapped Otto across the mouth.

"Otto!" I yelled again.

Jorge spoke sharply to Jack. "No rough stuff."

Otto was rubbing his lips, wiping away blood. "Let me speak to her," he said to Jorge.

"Be quick," Jorge said.

Otto's mouth stretched in a grimace. "Sam needs you—"

No. Something was wrong. Something other than Sam.

"Otto." Jorge's voice was low and commanding.

Otto took a deep breath. "Go with them, Vicky. It's not safe to—"

"Enough!" Jorge said.

I felt myself lifted. My feet were dragged across the black rubber side of the Zodiac and I was dumped, like a sack of potatoes, on the bottom. "Greta and Siri! They'll tell—"

Jack said, "Captain Nausinio is waiting for them."

"Captain Nau—he's not there—"

"Captain Nausinio has a Vespugian cutter. He can be anywhere. Be quiet and do what you are told."

"Are you taking me to Sam?"

Jack raised his hand as though to slap me as he had slapped Otto, but at a look from Jorge he lowered it. They sat on either side of me. "Otto!" Jorge commanded.

But Otto had turned away from the Zodiac. Now he stopped, looking pale, a trickle of blood on his chin.

Jorge said, "You will go back to the station and wait for us there. You are not needed."

"But Vicky—"

290

"You will tell everybody that we are taking Vicky to Sam. You will see to it that everything is under control. You will get what is coming to you. Do you understand?"

There was a double meaning to those words.

Otto drew himself up. "I will stay with Vicky."

Suddenly Jack had a pistol pointed at Otto. "Prince Otto. You will do as you are told."

Jorge pulled the starter sharply. The engine coughed and caught. Jack had one booted foot out of the Zodiac so he could push away from shore. Then we were heading out to sea. Jack put his pistol away.

Otto splashed into the shallow waves, almost up to the top of his boots.

"Go," Jorge snapped. He had the throttle wide open, and the Zodiac was moving rapidly away from shore.

I lay on the bottom of the Zodiac. "Where are you taking me?"

"To Sam, of course."

"Just relax, honey. You've misunderstood everything. The natives were a little restless, nothing more." But Jack was still holding me down on the bottom of the Zodiac. "We're going to Palmer Station, where Sam can have proper care."

"What do they have at Palmer they don't at LeNoir?"

"Vicky." Jorge sighed heavily. "Palmer is twice the size of LeNoir. They have a proper infirmary."

Did they? I didn't remember.

Jorge was silent, steering the Zodiac. We were going at full speed. I tried to get off the bottom, but Jack held me down.

"I'm not going to jump overboard," I grunted.

291

Jorge nodded, and I scrambled up and sat on the black rubber side. The wind whipped viciously against my face. Jorge looked at me pleasantly. Jack patted my knee. I flinched at his touch. "The problem with you, honey, is that you know too much."

"About what?"

"What were you doing in the lounge at two o'clock in the morning?"

"You saw me?"

Jorge merely nodded, smiling pleasantly.

Jack said, "We also saw Otto. He will pay for what he did."

"You should not leave your room at night," Jorge reprimanded.

Jack added, "Otto has talked to you unwisely."

"Otto hasn't told me anything!" I shouted.

Jorge said, "A little knowledge can be a dangerous thing."

Jack said, "Otto is a young fool, jeopardizing everything. You should have kept out of this, sweetie. You're in over your head."

"What's your part in this, anyhow?" I demanded. "What are you getting out of it?"

Jack grinned. "What I came to get."

I had no idea what that was. Whatever was going on, Jack had not seemed one of the component parts.

I could feel the Zodiac slowing. We weren't near land. The shore seemed very far away. But the Zodiac was definitely slowing down. I looked around a little wildly. All I could see in all directions were icebergs, icebergs of various sizes. Jorge sidled the Zodiac up to a middle-sized berg on which a seal was sleeping. The Zodiac bumped against the iceberg.

Jorge gestured and suddenly Jack had me under the arms and I was lifted over the side and dumped onto the iceberg. Jorge backed the Zodiac away until there was about a yard of dark water between the iceberg and the rubber boat. "We mean you no harm, Vicky," Jorge said. "When we are certain that our work can continue, we will come for you."

"How are you going to make certain?" I shouted to Jorge across the widening water. "Shoot everybody?"

"That will not be necessary," Jorge called back.

"And Sam—what about Sam?"

"What about him?" Jorge's voice grew faint as he turned the Zodiac and headed away from me at full speed.

I had been on the iceberg forever. Like Adam II . . .

Then—

I heard before I saw. Heard the putt-putt of a motor, the familiar sound of a Zodiac. I froze. Was it Jorge?

The Zodiac coming toward me was smaller than the ones from the *Argosy*. Someone in a heavy parka was driving it, but the parka was not red. It was a faded blue.

Adam!

He jumped out of the Zodiac onto the iceberg, pulled the rubber boat up after him. "Papageno and Cook are on the way," he said. "The Zodiac's a lot faster than the *Portia*."

"How did you know where I was?" Relief made me light-headed.

"Guesswork. Not that difficult." He had brought blankets,

which he draped over me, and hot sweet black coffee, which I hate, but I drank it anyhow to try to stop my teeth from chattering. He had both his arms around me, warming me, and I did my best to control my shivering.

"S-Sam," I stuttered. "H-how's Sam?"

Adam said carefully, "I don't know. He's sort of vanished, and Papageno thinks Captain Nausinio took him so they could give you that cock-and-bull story about his falling."

"Benjy? Siri? Esteban?" Then I realized that Otto had finally met Esteban, and in all the excitement maybe didn't even realize it.

"Save the questions for later," Adam said. "Cook and Papageno will be coming any minute, and we can get you back to the station, where we can take care of you. Hey, look, here they come!" But he stopped abruptly, his hand tightening on my arm.

Suddenly I was again so cold I felt I'd been frozen into a statue, like the prince with the marble legs in the fairy tale. The boat coming toward us was not Papageno's shabby old *Portia*. It was a gleaming white motorboat, a large one.

Adam swore.

The boat approached us, and I could see Esteban and Captain Nausinio. Nausinio held the rudder, and brought his boat close to the Zodiac.

"See!" Esteban cried out, and said something in Spanish.

Adam said, "He says he promised to come for you. Do you know what this is about? Can you trust him?"

Esteban had given me a warning postcard. Esteban did not wish me evil. If he had been alone, I would have believed him. But not with Captain Nausinio.

294

The small Zodiac from the *Portia* was safely on the iceberg with us. Captain Nausinio urged the motorboat closer, so it scraped gently against the ice.

Esteban was speaking rapidly, and I could tell that he was urging us to get into the motorboat. He was pointing to the Zodiac and I more or less gathered that he was telling Adam he could pull it behind the motorboat.

"Miching mallecho. Miching mallecho." I hardly realized I was saying it aloud.

Then Nausinio was pointing a gun at us, just as Jack had, but it wasn't a pistol. It was the big rifle he usually had slung over his shoulder. Esteban leaped onto the iceberg, again speaking rapidly in Spanish.

Adam looked at me. "I think they want us as hostages."

"No," I said. "I won't go with Nausinio."

Esteban grabbed Adam and began wrestling with him, and the two of them grasped each other, hitting each other, fighting as sometimes boys in high school still fight, and then I realized that Esteban was no high-school kid, that he was trained in fighting, that he was urging Adam toward the edge of the iceberg. If Adam fell into that icy water, it would kill him. Even if he could pull himself back up onto the berg, he would freeze to death.

I pushed myself between them and the water and leaped on them with all my strength, knocking them both down on the ice. Esteban wriggled out from under me.

"Oh, Vickee—" Suddenly, tears coursed down his cheeks.

I heard a shot and saw Nausinio standing in the motorboat, aiming his rifle. Then I heard another motor, and I scrabbled to my feet with an energy I didn't think I had. A

295

black *Argosy* Zodiac was coming toward us. There was another shot, and I heard Adam give a yell, and Esteban jumped up and leaped from the iceberg into the motorboat as Adam fell.

I dropped to my knees by him. "Adam. Adam."

"Stay down, Vicky!" It was Otto in the Zodiac, shouting to me. He had a gun.

Nausinio grabbed Esteban so that he was in front of him, like a shield. The shot cracked the cold white air. Esteban gave a horrible jerk and then he was in the water. He went down like lead.

Adam tried to struggle to his feet, and I rushed to the edge of the iceberg, my instinct being to jump in and try to rescue Esteban.

Otto shouted, "Stop!"

Captain Nausinio was turning the motorboat away and taking off.

Otto raised his gun.

"No." Adam's voice was a groan. One hand was pressed against his shoulder and I could see blood. "Don't. Let him go."

"Esteban!" I cried. "Esteban!"

"Esteban?" Otto asked. His eyes were wide and suddenly without color.

"Yes."

Otto groaned. "It is too late. Oh, God." He groaned again. "He would have killed you."

"Who're you?" Adam asked.

Otto was trembling violently. "Otto of Zlatovica." He sat abruptly on the side of the Zodiac. And then, once again, we heard an engine.

The *Portia*. Cook and Papageno in the *Portia*.

I could hardly see them through the Antarctic whiteout that burned my eyes.

I lay wrapped in warm blankets, propped up on a wide bunk. I was in the captain's sitting room, which I recognized when I saw the great copper table in the middle. The cushions which made my bunk into a couch were piled up behind me.

I was sipping very sweet tea, which Dick said would help me get warm. He and Angelique had rubbed me down with hot Turkish towels until I thought they would burn my skin off, though they told me the towels were not hot, and they were being very gentle, simply trying to get my blood circulating.

The captain's cabin was crowded. Angelique and Dick, sitting by me on the bunk. Adam with Cook and Papageno, on the other couch. Siri was in one of the big chairs, with Benjy perched on the arm, and Sam was standing in the doorway. Oh, Sam.

My voice seemed to have been frozen along with the rest of me. "Sam?"

Sam grinned. "They dumped me up in the hills. Didn't think an old codger like me could make it back to the station. But I did."

"Esteban—"

Suddenly the cabin was silent.

Cook spoke quietly, "Do you remember, Vicky?"

"Otto shot him."

Benjy said, "If Otto had not done that, Nausinio would

297

have killed you and Adam. Esteban would have let it happen. He was helping it happen."

I looked at Adam, sitting between Cook and Papageno, and realized that his arm was heavily bandaged and in a sling. "Adam—are you all right?"

"Sure. Dick fixed me up." But his voice had less than its usual strong timbre.

"Nausinio—"

Benjy said, "Gone to whichever spurious Vespugian station is nearest."

"He just went off and left Esteban . . ."

Cook said, "Even if Nausinio had not been Nausinio, Esteban was beyond saving."

Angelique had her hand lightly on the blanket over my feet as though she were still warming them. She said, "It was brave of Otto to do what he did. He is not a killer. He loves his country deeply and he believed when he came on the *Argosy* that what he was doing was right, that the negotiations with Jorge Maldonado and Jack Nessinger were legal."

Dick nodded. "When he realized what was involved, he could not stomach it."

Benjy said, "He nearly betrayed you, Vicky, but he couldn't go through with it."

"But *Esteban*—"

Dick urged gently, "Drink a little more tea, Vicky."

Sam's voice was level. "Esteban is—was—not an evil person. He, too, believed he was serving his country. He was well taught, but what he was taught was not well."

"He tried to warn me." I took a swallow of tea.

Benjy said, "Esteban was torn between his heart and his mission."

"He——" Words of anguish and grief would not come.

"Hush, Vicky," Dick said. "Sleep now. Talk later."

"Let me finish the tea. Please. Jorge——" I needed to know more before I could sleep.

"Gone," Benjy said gently, "with Greta and Jack."

"Where?" My voice came out in barely a whisper.

"Probably to that alleged scientific station where we surprised them. And from there by helicopter to Vespugia. At least, that's my guess."

I looked at Adam. He was tanned, but underneath the tan he was pale, exhausted-looking. "Adam——you weren't at LeNoir——"

Adam said, "Cook and Papageno picked me up just before the purported Esteban–Adam exchange."

Cook continued, "When Nausinio came to LeNoir with Esteban, planning to take Adam, there was no Adam at the station."

Papageno smiled. "So Nausinio had to leave Esteban and pretend the exchange had been made."

I pushed up on one elbow. "I don't understand."

"Lie down," Dick said gently, putting one firm hand on my shoulder.

"I don't understand about Esteban," I reiterated.

Cook sighed. "Esteban was working for his beloved Vespugia, and working mostly with Jorge Maldonado."

I asked Adam, "How much did you——"

"Nothing," Adam said. "I had suspicions that Esteban was

299

not the simple, friendly guy he tried to seem, but I couldn't pin down my suspicions. Now I know that when I was in San Sebastián, Esteban gave Nausinio the letters he'd offered to mail for me. He told me the mail from his army post was more reliable than the general mail service, and I bought his story."

Papageno nodded. "Nausinio's knowledge of English is rudimentary, and he read into the letters far more than they actually contained."

Adam said, "There was one letter to Aunt Serena, my usual chatty stuff, in which I told her I hoped to continue Adam II's work. I meant in marine biology, but Nausinio thought I meant CIA stuff." He laughed, but it wasn't funny.

Cook continued, "So Adam's mail was checked at Port Stanley, and in the pouch that carries mail to the stations, and your warning letter to Adam about the messages in your school locker was confiscated."

"You never got it?" I asked Adam.

"No."

Cook looked at me. "Vicky, has it occurred to you who might have written those warnings?"

I had feared it was Cook. But suddenly it clicked. "Suzy's Spanish teacher?"

"Right. He's ardently Vespugian, sees Adam as an enemy, and assumes anyone connected with him is also trying to hold Vespugia back. He faxed his suspicions to Guedder, so both of you were listed as potential dangers to the Vespugian state."

"That's crazy."

Papageno nodded. "Of course. Much of history is."

Sam had come all the way into the cabin and was perched

300

on a high stool. "Esteban was well indoctrinated into believing that whatever he was asked to do was for the good of Vespugia, but when Captain Nausinio pushed you on the pyramid, Esteban was torn, deeply torn."

"But why did Captain Nausinio push me?"

My voice had risen, and Dick warned, "Vicky. Calmly."

Papageno said, "Nausinio is quite a stupid man, and he assumed you were a danger to the Vespugian plans in Antarctica. And men like Nausinio enjoy killing."

"Esteban was a musician." Siri's voice was deep with pain. "With a passion for his country that had nothing to do with understanding politics or economics." She shook her head as though to clear it. "Such a waste . . ."

Benjy put his arm about Siri.

She leaned against it. "Vacillation is deadly. When Esteban decided he could not condone what Jorge was doing, he should have held to his resolve. I'm sorry, Vicky, I'm not making it any easier for you."

My voice was heavy. "I don't think it was ever supposed to be easy."

"No. But I don't want to add to the pain. I'm sorry. I do tend to treat you as a contemporary."

"Thanks."

Sam said, "Esteban was truly smitten with you, Vicky, and he didn't want to hurt you. He was just beginning to see that other people's patriotism was not as pure and simple as his own."

Siri looked at Cook. Blinked back tears. "Cookie, you'll pray for him?"

301

Cook nodded.

"Otto—" I asked.

"He is on the bridge with the captain," Sam said. "There is a considerable amount to explain. He is very shaken by what has happened, but he will be all right."

There was a moment of silence. Then Cook's voice came, utterly quiet. "Otto did what he had to do to save you and Adam."

"But he—"

"Yes, Vicky, he was caught in Jorge Maldonado's net, but he managed to get out of the net, and Esteban did not."

I shuddered. Felt the bile of horror rise in my throat. Swallowed. Finally managed to speak. "The net—what was the net?"

Papageno said, "The net was money and power. Zlatovica needs money. Vespugia needs power."

"Jack—what did Jack have to do with all this?" Until Jack dumped me into the Zodiac, he had not fitted in with any of my suspicions.

"The triangle," Benjy said, "is that Jack Nessinger is a drug trafficker feeding major syndicates in the United States." He looked at Papageno, who continued:

"Jorge represents the most powerful drug cartel—a government monopoly—in Vespugia, controlled by Guedder. Jorge therefore had the money to buy for Vespugia what he needed from Zlatovica, and thus Otto had the hard currency to bring back to his people."

I made a sound halfway between a grunt and a groan. "I had this crazy idea about Otto dumping nuclear waste."

Benjy's arm was still comfortingly around Siri. "Your crazy idea was not that crazy. Part of the bargain was that Vespugia would help get rid of some of Zlatovica's weapons, including the Chernobyl-type reactor, which Otto knew was a danger to his country."

I said, "Otto wanted everyone to sit under his own vine and fig tree."

Cook said, "Special lubricants are needed for jet turbines, so both Otto and Jorge were buying jojoba bean oil from Jack, and as far as Otto knew, that was Jack's only involvement."

That rang a bell. Something in one of Todd's lectures. Yes. Jojoba bean to replace whale oil instead of—I didn't remember what.

Papageno continued, "Jorge needed not only to sell drugs to Jack but to buy the oil of the jojoba bean from him."

Benjy smiled at me. "Back to your theory, Vicky: Jorge did indeed plan to dump the residue of the Zlatovican warheads in Antarctica. But they hadn't gone that far in their plans."

"What, then?"

Papageno rubbed his hand over the bald spot on top of his head in exactly the same way that Cook did. But he did not look like a monk. "There are cities in what was the former Soviet Union which are not on any maps. Although the U.S. knew about them, they were not included in U.S. maps, either. They remained secret."

"Zlatovica had one of these cities?"

"Yes. When the Soviets pulled out of their Eastern European satellites, they did not take with them all their resources, including top-secret research, because everything was happening

303

so swiftly they could not. For instance, they left papers behind in Zlatovica with instructions on how to build a fan blade made from a single crystal of metal."

I looked blank, and Papageno continued, "I'll try to simplify this for you. In the workings of nuclear fission and fusion, whether for peaceful or for military purposes, there are turbines which require fan blades. The higher the temperature at which you can burn fuel, the more effective the turbine, and these blades will take unbelievable temperatures."

"So that's where the jojoba bean oil fits in."

"Right. It's used for many other purposes, such as cosmetics and soap, so Jorge's interest in it did not strike Otto as suspicious."

"Yes. I can see that."

"Also important to Jorge," Papageno went on, "are instructions from the Zlatovican secret city on how to make helicopter blades that will rotate at twice the speed of sound, because of tiny jet engines at their tip."

"So the helicopters can go faster?"

"Incredibly faster."

"Okay."

"Such new copters would require less fuel and have more speed as well. So such fan blades would be, as the old saying goes, worth their weight in gold. Actually, much more."

Benjy added, "It was this kind of sensitive information that Otto had in his cases, camouflaged with useless material."

"But the case he threw overboard—"

"Otto is a pacifist," Papageno said. "When he realized that

Jorge was not opposed to war, that his interest in Jack's jojoba bean oil was military, Otto's first act of rebellion, of separating himself from what was going on, was getting rid of the material Jorge wanted. He had copies of everything salient back in Zlatovica."

Benjy said, "Unfortunately, Jorge kept a watch during the entire trip. You were seen. Otto was seen."

There was a long silence, during which I tried to absorb all this.

Dick patted my shoulder. "Vicky, love, we know there's more you have to have cleared up, but let's wait till Otto has finished talking with the captain. Meanwhile, you've been through a horrendous experience, and you need rest."

Cook's voice was gentle. "So rest, Vicky. Dick's pumped you full of antibiotics, and we got to you just in time to prevent frostbite. Thank God the temperature was mild."

Mild! I thought. But probably it was, for Antarctica.

I felt like a small child as Cook tucked the blanket carefully around my shoulders. He put the back of his hand against my forehead. "I thought you'd be safe on the *Argosy*. I knew something ugly was going on in Vespugia, but I believed the *Argosy* was a safe place. I should have known better."

"Hush," Papageno reprimanded. "Vicky knows that you would give your life for her if need be." He came over to me, bent down, and kissed me gently. "Angels watch over you," and I heard the echo of Aunt Serena, of Owain, of Cook, who had had no way of knowing the *Argosy* was a place of danger for me.

·   ·   ·

305

I was hardly aware of the cabin emptying as I slid into sleep. When I woke up I saw Adam sitting across from me on the other couch. He had pushed up the cushions to prop his arm.

"Hi!" His face lit up.

I looked at his shoulder. "Nausinio shot you."

"You'd have been next," Adam said, "after he'd finished me off. He couldn't have left us alive."

"Esteban—"

"—is dead, Vicky. We have to let him go."

I shuddered. "Aunt Serena said some judgments are best left to God."

"She's right. Can you abide by that?"

"I can try."

He shifted position. "We both owe our lives to this Otto guy."

"The Prince of Zlatovica," I said flatly.

Adam's face was dark. "Both he and Esteban were trained from childhood. Programmed. They both tried to escape. Otto managed."

"I'm sad."

"Yeah," Adam said. "I know. I know." He eased himself off the bunk as though to go.

"Adam." My voice was urgent.

He sat down again, at the foot of my bunk.

"Your letters—"

"Didn't you understand?"

"No."

"Vicky!"

I looked at him, questioning, waiting.

He said, "My mail was gone over. The long letter I wrote to Aunt Serena never even got mailed. I'd even written her about Adam II, and his murder. I called it that. Murder. And I mentioned I'd written to you, too, so that put you in the spotlight."

"I already was," I said. "I thought it was I who was putting you in the spotlight."

He laughed, grimly. "What fools we mortals be." He put his hand against his shoulder as though to push back pain. "It was lousy when I realized Esteban was—was not the friend he pretended to be."

"Maybe wanted to be," I put in. He nodded. "Adam, that awful letter where you said, 'cool it'——"

"You took it seriously?"

"Well, Adam, yes."

"Oh, Vicky, Vicky—you couldn't have——"

"I did."

"But——I assumed you'd realize the letter was a warning."

I said flatly, "It seemed very real. Logical. Awful."

Adam groaned. "Vicky, I'm sorry, I should have realized——"

"And then there was the science-gibberish one with the code——"

He hunched over. "By the time I wrote that, I'd figured maybe the *Argosy* wasn't safe for you, after all, and I wanted to warn you, but I wasn't even sure just what I was warning you about."

I looked down at the little bulge my toes made in the blanket. "I'm sorry I didn't understand what you were getting at in your letters."

"I knew there was a faint likelihood you wouldn't, but I had to risk it. All I wanted to do was get you out of the loop before something happened. I didn't know you were already in it. Forgive?"

"Sure."

"Dick told me I wasn't to stay long. You're supposed to rest. You've made some good friends on this ship."

"I know. They're terrific."

"Dick says you're not up to coming to the dining room. Angelique will bring you a tray. Sleep now, sweetie." I hated it when Jack called me sweetie. I loved it when Adam did. He bent down and kissed me.

I heard the door click behind him. And I slept.

When I woke up, I was slept out. The cabin was empty. I felt too weak to get up and make my way down to my own cabin. My backpack was on the round copper table, so I reached for it and pulled out my notebook. I didn't want to write in my journal. Not yet. What could I say but, "Esteban is dead. Otto shot him." That was too heavy, required too much explanation. I held my pen over a blank page. Scribbled. Crossed out. Scribbled.

> *Nobody promised a happy end.*
> *Nobody said the story is told.*
> *Till the last page is turned,*
> *Nobody knows*
> *If it's good or it's bad,*
> *If it's new, if it's old.*
> *It's all happened before,*

Betrayal and sorrow,
Redemption and grief,
And a hope for tomorrow.

I put my pen down. I wasn't sure what to hope for. I tore out the page, held my pen over a fresh one. I sighed and wrote a lament, a lament for Esteban and his music. And then I wrote some silliness, because I wanted something for Siri to sing that would cheer us up. Esteban's music had really meant something to her, and it was the death of his music as much as the death of his self that was grieving her, though I knew the two could not be separated.

There was a knock on the door and Angelique came in, bearing a tray. She put it down on the copper table, then sat beside me on the couch and took me into her arms and rocked me, and suddenly, surrounded by her strong and loving arms, I began to cry. I cried and cried and she rocked and soothed and murmured and I cried until there were no tears left.

Then she reached for the tray. She had brought me a cold meal of salads, sliced meats, cheeses, so the wait didn't matter. I discovered that I was hungry. Famished. She sat with me while I ate. Then she put the tray on the other bunk.

"Thank you, Angelique."

She asked, "Will you speak to Otto?"

I looked at her.

"Otto is devastated. He came on the *Argosy* blithe as a bird, with no idea of the mess he was already in. When he found out, he discovered that it was almost impossible to get out. And the price was high: Esteban's death."

I closed my eyes, "Otto . . ."

"Esteban and Nausinio had orders to kill Otto."

"Did Otto know—"

"Not then. He does now. But he's torn to shreds. Will you speak to him?"

"Well, sure. Of course. But I don't know what to say."

"When you see him, you'll know." Angelique smiled at me. "Had enough to eat?"

"Plenty."

"Dick will check on you again before bedtime. There are a couple of small frostbites that need watching. Your body is marvelously resilient after that terrible experience. Dick and I are especially fond of you, Vicky."

Tears came back to my eyes. "I'm especially fond of you, too."

Before she left, I tore some pages out of my notebook. "Will you give these to Siri?"

"Of course."

I didn't see Otto till the next morning. Dick came in early to check me over, and then Leilia brought me breakfast. She said, "I'm sorry about Esteban, Vicky."

I looked at her questioningly as she placed the tray on my knees. She had remembered that I like oatmeal. She'd also brought sticky buns and a dish of orange and grapefruit sections as well as coffee and hot milk.

She said, "What we have been told is that there was an accident and Esteban was killed. You were stranded alone for a while and nearly froze, and your friend Adam found you. Jorge and Jack have returned to Vespugia to take care of things, and then I suppose Jack will go back to Texas. Everybody's delighted to see Cookie again. I gather Papageno was here briefly to bring Cookie and has gone back to the Falklands. I'm not sure I believe all of Quim's pleasant little story, but I'm willing to live with it and not ask questions. That's something I've learned in a long life."

"Thanks, Leilia."

"Oh, yes, and I forgot Greta. Poor Greta, she is unfortunately forgettable. Whatever Quim's reason for her absence, it was acceptable." She poured coffee for me, and laughed her nice, normal laugh.

Greta. Greta had been Jorge's stooge all along, willing to lie, to tell us that Sam had fallen, to do anything Jorge told her to do. I hoped that Leilia was right and that she would be forgettable.

Leilia smiled at me. "I gather Dick told you you could get up for lunch."

"Yes. I'm fine, really."

"No rush. We'll be at sea most of today. You look a little washed out, but not bad." She stayed with me while I ate, chatting about the veritable city of icebergs we were moving through, the penguins we'd seen, the hope that we might see more whales. Then she left me. She knew when not to ask questions. That's a rare virtue.

There was a knock on my door and Otto came in. He stood by my bunk. "Vicky, can you forgive me?"

"I'm not sure what I'm supposed to forgive you for."

"I used you," Otto said. "I played with you. I was serious and I wasn't serious."

311

I laughed. "Otto, I never expected to be the Princess of Zlatovica."

"Vicky, about Esteban——"

"I know you had to," I said. "I know that."

"I know it, too, though it was Nausinio I was aiming for, not Esteban. In my country there has been too much killing. I wanted hard currency to help make peace, to stop killing, to unite warring factions. To be a pacifist and to be naïve is a dangerous combination. There was much I did not understand."

I sighed. "Me, too."

"But you are not a prince, responsible for the lives of many people."

"Being responsible for myself is more than enough."

"Vicky, are we friends?"

I looked at him, his amber eyes, his golden skin and hair, his expensive clothes. I was no longer dazzled. But without Otto I would not be alive. "Yes."

"Sometime——I would like to invite you to my country."

"That would be terrific, Otto. Sometime."

After Otto, Adam came.

"You're okay." Adam sighed with relief.

"I'm fine." Then I asked, "Esteban was going to be killed, no matter what, wasn't he?"

Adam's voice was somber. "Yes. They could not risk his defection."

I closed my eyes. "I don't understand killing people because they disagree with you."

312

Adam said, "Let's hope you never understand." Then he grinned. "Did you ever figure out what Jorge had in those camera cases?"

I looked at him questioningly.

"Cameras."

I laughed with him.

Adam said, "When you begin to suspect somebody, you tend to suspect everything."

"Yeah." Then I asked, which I hadn't thought to do the day before, "Did Dick have to take the bullet out?"

"No, it went right on through and buried itself in the ice. It's probably not the first bullet to lodge in Antarctic ice, but I don't like the idea."

"Neither do I."

"Your Otto and I had a good talk last night."

"He's not my Otto."

"Would he be, if he weren't a prince?"

I shook my head. "He's"——I couldn't think of any other word—"dazzling, sort of."

"Looks every inch a prince."

"But I'm not looking for a prince."

"A friend, maybe?"

"That's a much better idea."

Then Adam kissed me.

That was a really good idea.

I got up and dressed for lunch, not difficult, since dressing meant warm jeans, turtlenecks, sweaters. I brushed my hair thoroughly, put on a little lipstick, just enough to keep my lips from looking pale. Cook and Adam came to walk me up the stairs and into the lounge, and I was grateful for their strong arms because I felt amazingly wobbly. Almost everybody was there before us, and I was warmly greeted as though people were really glad to see me.

Benjy beckoned us to a table where he was sitting with Siri and Sam, Dick and Angelique. Otto came in, and Benjy called to him to come join us. I sat down and Benjy surprised me by kissing me, with a loud smack, on my cheek.

I laughed, said, "Thank you!" and then I noticed a piece of red string tied around the fourth finger of Siri's left hand.

Benjy took her hand and held it in his. "There's no place in Antarctica where I can buy Siri a real ring. This will have to do till we get home."

There was applause, and appreciative laughter. Somebody said, "Big surprise."

Siri glowed. "It was a surprise to me." She smiled at all of us around the table. "I swore I'd never love or marry again. Your poem helped, Vicky."

Quim came in then, beaming at everybody. "Siri's going to sing for us. Two songs, music by Siri, words by Vicky. One rather sad, because we're all grieved at Esteban's death. And after that, something else you'll really enjoy."

Benjy handed Siri her harp. She played a series of slow, somber chords. "This is called 'Lament for a Young Musician.'" She paused, then played and sang:

The music is stilled. No sound
Of melody fills the fearsome air.

314

> *No chord, no harmony is found.*
> *The sky is high and fair*
>
> *Taunting our hearts. The price*
> *Of death is high. Tears chilled*
> *By grief are like primordial ice.*
> *The melody is stilled, is stilled.*

Otto spoke to me in a low voice. "Can you write a lament for the killer?"

"You're not a killer. You did what you had to do. Adam would be dead. I would be dead. And if you hadn't killed Esteban then, Nausinio would have, later."

"I know," Otto said. "But I killed him."

Siri switched to major chords. Without introduction she sang:

> *If it has feathers I give you my word*
> *It won't be a dolphin, it won't be a whale.*
> *It may be an angel, it may be a bird;*
> *Whatever it is, it can tell us a tale.*
>
> *It may be a penguin, it won't be a seal,*
> *It may point to a place where a song is dwelling.*
> *If it's an angel I'm sure it's real*
> *And will give us a story worth the telling.*
>
> *It gives us no answers, it promises naught,*
> *Except that we all have a say in the words.*

If it has feathers, we've all been taught,
It may be the most unexpected of birds!

When she was through, the mood had switched for most of the passengers. Only a few of us knew what had happened on the ice floe, or indeed that there had been anybody on an ice floe. Siri's melody was as light as my words. There was lots of clapping and cheering. The assembled group was unusually full of laughter and warm feeling.

Angelique said in a low voice, "Bless you, Vicky. Siri, too."

Leilia, sitting at the table next to ours, smiled at me warmly. "Good work."

Cook touched my hand gently. "Vicky is not a penguin. She understands how to be vulnerable, and how to be a friend."

"Encore! Encore!" Several people were shouting.

Adam twined his fingers through mine.

"Siri, play it again!" Sam called.

Siri picked up her harp. I was glad we'd had the lament first, because I knew that something light was needed now. Benjy and Siri sat together. Then Adam put his arm around me and I leaned back and listened.

The L'Engle Cast

THE AUSTIN FAMILY

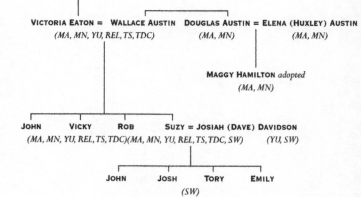

GRANDFATHER EATON = CARO EATON
(MA, MN, REL)

VICTORIA EATON = **WALLACE AUSTIN** **DOUGLAS AUSTIN = ELENA (HUXLEY) AUSTIN**
(MA, MN, YU, REL, TS, TDC) *(MA, MN)* *(MA, MN)*

MAGGY HAMILTON *adopted*
(MA, MN)

JOHN **VICKY** **ROB** **SUZY = JOSIAH (DAVE) DAVIDSON**
(MA, MN, YU, REL, TS, TDC)(MA, MN, YU, REL, TS, TDC, SW) *(YU, SW)*

JOHN **JOSH** **TORY** **EMILY**
(SW)

BOOKS FEATURING THE AUSTINS:

Meet the Austins (MA)   Troubling a Star (TS)
The Moon by Night (MN)   The Twenty-four Days
The Young Unicorns (YU)   Before Christmas (TDC)
A Ring of Endless Light (REL)   A Severed Wasp (SW)

# of Characters

THE MURRY-O'KEEFE FAMILY

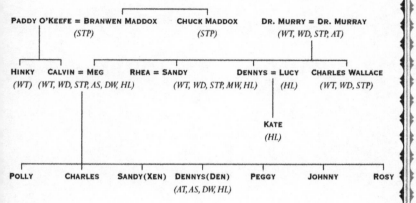

PADDY O'KEEFE = BRANWEN MADDOX   CHUCK MADDOX   DR. MURRY = DR. MURRAY
(STP)   *(STP)*   *(WT, WD, STP, AT)*

HINKY   CALVIN = MEG   RHEA = SANDY   DENNYS = LUCY   CHARLES WALLACE
(WT)   *(WT, WD, STP, AS, DW, HL)*   *(WT, WD, STP, MW, HL)*   *(HL)*   *(WT, WD, STP)*

KATE
(HL)

POLLY   CHARLES   SANDY(XEN)   DENNYS(DEN)   PEGGY   JOHNNY   ROSY
(AT, AS, DW, HL)

BOOKS FEATURING THE MURRY-O'KEEFES:

A Wrinkle in Time (WT)   *An Acceptable Time (AT)*
A Wind in the Door (WD)   *The Arm of the Starfish (AS)*
A Swiftly Tilting Planet (STP)   *Dragons in the Waters (DW)*
Many Waters (MW)   *A House Like Lotus (HL)*

CHARACTERS WHO APPEAR IN BOTH SERIES:

CANON TALLIS *(AS, YU, DW)*   MR. THEOTOCOPOULOUS *(YU, DW)*
ADAM EDDINGTON *(AS, REL, TS)*   EMILY GREGORY *(YU, DW, SW)*
ZACHARY GREY *(MN, REL, AT, HL)*

GOFISH

MADELEINE L'ENGLE

What did you want to be when you grew up?
A writer.

When did you realize you wanted to be a writer?
Right away. As soon as I was able to articulate, I knew I wanted to be a writer. And I read. I adored *Emily of New Moon* and some of the other L. M. Montgomery books and they impelled me because I loved them.

When did you start to write?
When I was five, I wrote a story about a little "gurl."

What was the first writing you had published?
When I was a child, a poem in *CHILD LIFE*. It was all about a lonely house and was very sentimental.

Where do you write your books?
Anywhere. I write in longhand first, and then type it. My first typewriter was my father's pre–World War I machine. It was the one he took with him to the war. It had certainly been around the world.

What is the best advice you have ever received about writing?
To just write.

What's your first childhood memory?
One early memory I have is going down to Florida for a couple of weeks in the summertime to visit my grandmother. The house was in the middle of a swamp, surrounded by alligators. I don't like alligators, but there they were, and I was afraid of them.

What is your favorite childhood memory?
Being in my room.

As a young person, whom did you look up to most?
My mother. She was a storyteller and I loved her stories. And she loved music and records. We played duets together on the piano.

What was your worst subject in school?
Math and Latin. I didn't like the Latin teacher.

What was your best subject in school?
English.

What activities did you participate in at school?
I was president of the student government in boarding school and editor of a literary magazine, and also belonged to the drama club.

Are you a morning person or a night owl?
Night owl.

What was your first job?
Working for the actress Eva Le Gallienne, right after college.

What is your idea of the best meal ever?
Cream of Wheat. I eat it with a spoon. I love it with butter and brown sugar.

Which do you like better: cats or dogs?
I like them both. I once had a wonderful dog named Touche. She was a silver medium-sized poodle, and quite beautiful. I wasn't allowed to take her on the subway, and I couldn't afford to get a taxi, so I put her around my neck, like a stole. And she pretended she was a stole. She was an actor.

What do you value most in your friends?
Love.

What is your favorite song?
"Drink to Me Only with Thine Eyes."

What time of the year do you like best?
I suppose autumn. I love the changing of the leaves.
I love the autumn goldenrod, the Queen Anne's lace.

Which of your characters is most like you?
None of them. They're all wiser than I am.

Austin Family Chronicles

MEET THE AUSTINS

For a family with four kids, two dogs, assorted cats, and a constant stream of family and friends dropping by, life in the Austin family home has always been remarkably steady and contented. When a family friend suddenly dies, the Austins open their home to an orphaned girl, Maggy Hamilton. The Austin children—Vicky, John, Suzy, and Rob—do their best to be generous and welcoming to Maggy. Vicky knows she should feel sorry for Maggy, but having sympathy for Maggy is no easy thing. Maggy is moody and spoiled; she breaks toys, wakes people in the middle of the night screaming, discourages homework, and generally causes chaos in the Austin household. How can one small child disrupt a family of six? Will life ever return to normal?

978-0-312-37931-5, $6.99 US/$7.99 Can.

THE MOON BY NIGHT

As if simply being fourteen-years-old weren't bad enough—what with the usual teenage angst and uncertainty—Vicky Austin's always comforting and reliable home life is changing completely. Her brother John is going off to college in the fall. Maggy has gone to live with her legal guardian. And the rest of Vicky's family is moving from their quiet house in the country to the heart of New York City. But before the big move, the entire Austin family is taking a meandering trip across the country in their station wagon, stopping to camp along the way, with no set schedule and not a single night of camping experience among them. Wild animal attacks. Life-threatening natural disasters. Cute boys on the prowl. Anything can happen in the great outdoors.

978-0-312-37932-2, $6.99 US/$7.99 Can.

THE YOUNG UNICORNS

The Austins are trying to settle into their new life in New York City, but their once close-knit family is pulling away from each other. Their father spends long hours working alone in his study. John is away at college. Rob is making friends with people in the neighborhood: newspaper vendors, dog walkers, even the local rabbi. Suzy is blossoming into a vivacious young woman. And Vicky has become closer to Emily Gregory, a blind and brilliant young musician, than to her sister Suzy. With the Austins going in different directions, they don't notice that something sinister is going on in their neighborhood—and it's centered around them. A mysterious genie appears before Rob and Emily. A stranger approaches Vicky in the park and calls her by name. Members of a local gang are following their father. The entire Austin family is in danger. If they don't start telling each other what's going on, someone just might get killed.

978-0-312-37933-9, $6.99 US/$7.99 Can.

A RING OF ENDLESS LIGHT

After a tumultuous year in New York City, the Austins are spending the summer on the small island where their grandfather lives. He's very sick, and watching his condition deteriorate as the summer passes is almost more than Vicky can bear. To complicate matters, she finds herself as the center of attention for three very different boys. Zachary Grey, the troubled and reckless boy Vicky met last summer, wants her all to himself as he grieves the loss of his mother. Leo Rodney has been just a friend for years, but the tragic loss of his father causes him to turn to Vicky for comfort—and romance. And then there's Adam Eddington. Adam is only asking Vicky to help with his research on dolphins. But Adam—and the dolphins—may just be what Vicky needs to get through this heartbreaking summer.

978-0-312-37935-3, $6.99 US/$7.99 Can.

TROUBLING A STAR

The Austins have settled back into their beloved home in the country after more than a year away. Though they had all missed the predictability and security of life in Thornhill, Vicky Austin is discovering that slipping back into her old life isn't easy. She's been changed by life in New York City and her travels around the country while her old friends seem to have stayed the same. So Vicky finds herself spending time with a new friend, Serena Eddington—the great-aunt of a boy Vicky met over the summer. Aunt Serena gives Vicky an incredible birthday gift—a month-long trip to Antarctica. It's the opportunity of a lifetime. But Vicky is nervous. She's never been away from her family before. Once she sets off though, she finds that's the least of her worries. She receives threatening letters. She's surrounded by suspicious characters. Vicky no longer knows who to trust. And she may not make it home alive.

978-0-312-37934-6, $6.99 US/$7.99 Can.

ALSO AVAILABLE:

A Wrinkle in Time, 978-0-312-36754-1
A Wind in the Door, 978-0-312-36854-8
A Swiftly Tilting Planet, 978-0-312-36856-2
Many Waters, 978-0-312-36857-9
An Acceptable Time, 978-0-312-36858-6

SQUARE
FISH

Available at your local bookstore, or visit
www.squarefishbooks.com.